Russell Th
1885-1

My father, Russell Thorndike, was born in 1885 in Rochester, where his father was the vicar of St. Margaret's; from an early age he wanted to write and to act; his first study was a chicken shed at the vicarage, where, as a young boy, he wrote religious dramas. After being a leading chorister at St George's Chapel, Windsor and schooling at Rochester, he and his sister Sybil entered the Ben Greet Acting Academy and later joined his Shakespeare company playing all over America. It was while touring there that he divulged his idea for the plot of Doctor Syn (see Sybil's preface)

The book was eventually written in his Dymchurch study, a boat house on the sea-wall, near his mother's cottage, and published while he was serving in the Gallipoli campaign in 1915; he was invalided out after being badly wounded, but as soon as he could walk, he resumed his acting with his sister Sybil at the Old Vic in the early Shakespeare seasons under Lilian Baylis. Thereafter he had a long and distinguished career as an actor and his writings included the seven Doctor Syn stories and nine other novels and some general books. He died in November 1972.

Daniel Thorndike

DOCTOR SYN

✻

Doctor Syn is in sequence the seventh of the
Doctor Syn Saga.

When this story opens there were two things of
paramount interest in Dymchurch. One was
Romney Marsh—visited, so the villagers whispered, by flaming Demon Riders and Jack
O'Lanterns. The other was Doctor Syn, their
genial, kindly, well-loved vicar. To be sure it was
a little incongruous at times to hear this godly
man break out into the most ungodly refrain:

Here's to the feet that have walked the plank,
Yo-ho for the dead man's throttle!

For that was the favourite song of the redoubtable Clegg. But Clegg had been hanged as a
pirate—so it was said—full ten years before.

How Syn's real identity was finally revealed
when the King's men came to Dymchurch, and
the strange part he played in the mystery of
Romney Marsh, make this a decidedly unusual
and thrilling story.

DOCTOR SYN

by

Russell Thorndike

ROMNEY PUBLISHING

First Published in 1915

This Edition published
under Licence from Rhona Thorndike
by Romney Publishing 2010

ISBN 978-0-9533726-1-4

Cover Illustration by Charles Newington 2010

Line drawings by Emily Goddard 1998

Contents

CONTENTS

Foreword

BY DANIEL THORNDIKE

The books about Doctor Syn have long been out of print. The first edition was in 1915 (with father's name spelt incorrectly with a 'y', which makes it a rarity) and the last reprint was in 1972, the year of my father's death. He would have welcomed this reprint of his first novel called simply "Doctor Syn"

This book was initially meant to be a single volume and unfortunately father killed off the character at the end of the story. However, such was the response of the public to the smuggler-parson, the nightriders and their mysterious leader "the Scarecrow", that father had to make up tales of Syn's earlier life and adventures. These followed Syn's career from shortly after being created Doctor of Divinity at Oxford in about 1754 until the year 1793, with the original "Doctor Syn" being tacked on at the end of the series at the turn of the century—so the first book became the last book but can so easily stand, as it did originally, as a single volume.

The Saga was completed in 1944 but was not confined to the books. A stage play with Russell in the lead role was put on at the Strand Theatre in 1923. In 1936 a film was produced by London Films Ltd. starring George Arliss and Margaret Lockwood. Two further films followed in the mid-sixties, one by Walt Disney starring Patrick McGoohan and one by Hammer Films starring Peter Cushing.

The renewed interest in Doctor Syn caused by the films coincided with Dymchurch's own tribute, a pageant and a fete. Such was the success of this event that a bi-annual "Day of Syn" is held on August Bank Holiday Monday. On that day many of the villagers don 18th century costumes and re-enact scenes from the

Syn Saga through the village in the morning, followed by a procession along the High Street, culminating with a fete on the recreation ground in the afternoon. Dr Syn is usually played by the current Rector of Dymchurch.

On the Sunday before the Bank Holiday an 18th century evensong service is held in the parish church of St. Peter and St. Paul and is well attended by the people participating in the "Day of Syn". The service is open to all who wish to come and worship in this beautiful old church, and so Doctor Syn, alias the Scarecrow, still lives on in the hearts of those with a sense of romance and adventure and the dreaded song of Clegg the pirate is still heard in Dymchurch-under-the-Wall.

How proud father would have been that this fete is still continued and that his permission to use the stories has brought contributions to local charities, also that the royalties from the sale of this latest reprint of Doctor Syn are being given to the Church of St Peter and St Paul, where his memorial plaque records the creation of the fictional Syn and my father's connection with the village.

David Thorndike

Romney Marsh
July 1998

Preface

BY SYBIL THORNDIKE

Dear Russell,

Do you remember a long journey to Spattanburg, South Carolina—I, rigid with fear and thrill, openmouthed—you, unfolding horror upon horror—the day 'Dr. Syn' was born?

Do you remember how on arriving at the hotel, some kindly fate playing up to us so nobly, arranged for a perfectly good murder to take place on the front steps right under our window—and how the corpse lay there all night, and we being too frightened to go to bed so sitting up most of the night, I making countless pots of tea, while you with bulging eyes gloated over the double-dyings and doings of that splendid criminal, 'Dr. Syn'?

It was a far cry from South Carolina to the Romney Marsh, but I think it was some longing for home and the Kent lands that made you develop his story with that background instead of the more obviously thrilling country in which we were travelling.

What a pal the old parson-smuggler became to us! I know for me he joined the merry band—the Men of Kent—the Dickens Men of Kent who made the white roads famous.

I envy those who are to make his acquaintance for the first time. I remember with thrill the feeling I had when you first showed him to me. Here was another of those creatures of the family of Daniel Quilp (Our first great love, wasn't he?). Creatures that are above the ordinary standard of right and wrong—tho, even if they murdered their favourite aunt would have been forgiven—they being so much larger and more lovable than aforesaid Aunt.

Was Syn a play or a novel first? I forget—He walks in Romance and it matters not at all to me if I meet him again in prose or verse or in actuality—poking his head out of a dyke in our dear beloved Marsh. I shall say Good Luck to him in whatever form he may appear—the souls like us who love a thrill will be jollier for the meeting.

SYBIL

1

Dymchurch-under-the-Wall

To those who have small knowledge of Kent, be it known that the fishing village of Dymchurch-under-the-Wall lies on the south coast midway between two of the ancient Cinque Ports, Romney and Hythe. In the days of George III with Trafalgar still unfought, our coast watchmen swept with keen glasses this broad bend of the Channel; watched, not for smugglers (for there was little in Dymchurch to attract the smuggler, with its flat coast-line open all the way from Dover cliffs around Dungeness to Beachy Head), but for the French men-o'-war.

Dymchurch was a happy little village in those days—ay, and prosperous too, for the Squire, Sir Antony Cobtree, though in his younger days a reckless adventurer, a gambler, and a duellist, had of late years resolved himself into a pattern Kentish squire, generous to all, and vastly popular. Equally popular was Dr. Syn, the Vicar—a pious and broad-minded man, with as great a taste for good Virginian tobacco and a glass of something hot as for the penning of long sermons which sent every one to sleep on Sundays. Still, it was his duty to deliver these sermons, for, as I have said, he was a pious man, and although his congregation for the most part went to sleep, they were at great pains not to snore, because to offend the Doctor would have been a lasting shame.

The little church was old and homely, within easy cry and it was pleasant on Sunday evenings, during the Doctor's lengthy prayers, to hear the swish and the lapping and endless grinding of the waves upon the sand.

The heavy drag of the long sermon and never-ending prayers was lifted when the hymns began. There was something about the Dymchurch hymns that made them worth singing. True, there was no organ to lead them; but that didn't matter; for Mr. Rash, the schoolmaster—a sallow, lantern-jawed young man, with a leaning towards music—would play over the tune on a fiddle. Then, led by the Doctor's sonorous voice, and seconded by the soul-splitting notes of Mipps the sexton, the choir, recruited entirely from seamen, whose voices had been cracked these many years at the tiller, would roll out some sturdy old tune, shaking the very church with its fury, and sounding more like a rum-backed capstan song than a God-fearing hymn. They felt it was worth while kneeling through those long, long prayers to have a chance at the hymns. The Doctor never chose solemn ones, or, if he did, it made no odds, for just the same were they bellowed like a chanty, and it was a long-drawn note of regret that the choir drawled out the final amen.

Very often, when a hymn had gone with more spirit than usual, the Doctor would thump on the desk of the three-decker and address the choir with a hearty 'Now, boys, that last verse once again.' Then he would turn to the congregation and would add, 'Brethren, for the glory of God, and for our own salvation, we will sing the—er—the last two verses again.' Whereat Mr. Rash would scrape anew upon the fiddle, Doctor Syn would pound out the rhythm with a first banging on the pulpit side, and after him would thunder the sea salts from the choir with an enthusiasm that bade fair to frighten the devil himself.

When they had hardly a note left in their bodies, the service would be rounded off by the Doctor, and the congregation would gather in little groups outside the church to bid him good-night. Doctor Syn would take some minutes changing his black gown for his cloth surcoat; besides, there was the collection to be counted and entered into the book, and a few words of parochial business with the sexton. But at last it was all finished) and he would come forth to receive the homage of the parish. He would be accompanied by Sir Antony, who was warden and a regular church-goer, as the well-thumbed pages of a large Prayer Book in the family pew could prove. Bestowing a cheery word here and a kindly nod there, the gentlemen would pass on to the Court House, where, after a hearty supper, Doctor Syn would, metaphorically, lay aside his robes of righteousness, and over a long pipe of his favourite tobacco and a smoking bowl of bishop, with many an anecdote of land and sea, make the jolly Squire laugh till his sides ached.

While the Vicar entertained his patron at the Court House, Mr. Mipps in a like manner held court behind the closed doors of the old Ship Inn. Here, with his broken clay pipe asmoke like a burning chimney, and with eminent peril of singeing the tip of his nose, he would recount many a tale of horror and adventure, thoroughly encouraged by Mrs. Waggetts, the landlady, who had perceived the sexton's presence to be good for trade. Thus it was that, by working his imagination to good effect, Doctor Syn's parochial factotum was plied with many a free drink at the expense of the 'Ship.' The little sexton was further encouraged in yarning because it gratified his vanity to see that they all believed in him. It was exhilarating to know that he really made their flesh creep. He felt a power and chuckled in his heart when he saw his audience swallowing his emotions for gospel as easily as he himself could swallow rum—for Mipps liked rum, having served for a great part of his life as a ship's carpenter. As a seasoned traveller they respected him, for what he hadn't seen of horrors in the far-off land— well, the whole village would have readily staked their wigs—was not worth seeing.

The Coming of the King's Frigate

Now Doctor Syn was fond of the sea, and he was never far away from it. Even in wintertime he would walk upon the sea-wall with a formidable telescope under his arm, his hands thrust deep into the pockets of a long sea-coat, and his old black, three-cornered parson's hat cocked well forward and pulled down over his eyes. And although the simple old fellow would be mentally working out his dry-as-dust sermons, he would be striding along at a most furious speed, presenting to those who did not know him an although alarming appearance, for in tune to his brisk step he would be humming the first verse of a sea chanty that he had picked up from some ruffianly sea-dog of a parishioner. As he strode along, with his weather eye ever on the look-out for big ships coming up the Channel, the rough words would roll from his gentle lips with the most perfect incongruity,—

'Oh, here's to the feet that have walked the plank—
   Yo-ho! for the dead man's throttle;
And here's to the corpses afloat in the tank,
   And the dead man's teeth in the bottle.'

He was as proud of this song as if he had written it himself, and it was a continual source of amusement to the fishermen to hear him sing it. He frequently did this of an evening in the parlour of the old Ship Inn, when he went there for a chat and a friendly pipe; for Doctor Syn was, as I have said, broad-minded, and held views that would certainly have been beyond the diocesan dignitaries. The very sight of a parson drinking with the men in a public inn had a good effect, he declared, upon the parish, for a good parson, like a good sailor, should know when he has had enough. The Squire would back him up, and there they would both sit every evening, laughing and talking with the fishermen. But on Sunday nights they dined at the Court House, leaving the field open for the redoubtable Mipps, who, as I have hinted, took full advantage of it.

Now, the ungainly little sexton had a great admirer in the person of Mrs. Waggetts, the landlady of the 'Ship.' Her husband had been dead for a number of years, and she was ever on the look-out for another. She saw in the person of Mipps her true lord and master. He was enterprising, he had also money of his own, for he was parish undertaker as well as sexton, and ran, from his small coffin shop in the village, every trade imaginable. You could buy anything, from a bottle of pickles to a marline-spike, in that dirty little store, and get a horrible anecdote thrown in with your bargain from the ready lips of the old rascal.

But the passion that smouldered in the breast of the 'Ship' landlady was in no way shared by the little sexton.

'Mrs. Waggetts,' he would say, 'folk in the death trade should keep single. They gets their fair share of misery, Lord above knows, in these parts with the deaths so uncommon few.'

'Well,' Mrs. Waggetts would sigh, 'I often wish as how it had been me that had been took instead of Waggetts. I fair envy him lying up there all so peaceful like, just a-rotting slowly along of his coffin.'

But the sexton would immediately fly into a rage with a 'Waggetts' coffin rottin', did you say, Waggetts? Not mine. I undertook Waggetts, I'd have you remember; and I don't undertake to rot. I loses money on my coffins, Mrs. Waggetts. I undertakes, ma'am—undertakes to provide a suitable affair wot'll keep out damp and water and cheat worm, grub, slug, and slush.'

'Nobody could deny, Mr. Mipps,' the landlady would answer in a conciliatory tone, 'as how you're a good undertaker. Any one with half an eye could see as how you knocks 'em up solid.'

But Mipps didn't encourage Mrs. Waggetts when she was pleased to flatter, so he would take himself off in high dudgeon to avoid her further attentions.

This very conversation took place one November afternoon, and the sexton, after slamming the inn door to give vent to his irritation, hurried along the sea-wall towards his shop, comforting himself that he could sit snug inside a coffin and cheer himself up with hammering it.

On the way he met Dr. Syn, who was standing silhouetted against the skyline, with his telescope focussed upon some large vessel that was standing in off Dungeness.

'Ah, Mr. Mipps' said the cleric, handing his telescope to the sexton, 'tell me what you make of that.'

Mipps adjusted the lens and looked. 'The devil!' he ejaculated.

'I beg your pardon,' said the Doctor; 'what did you say?' One of the King's Preventive men had come out of his cottage and was approaching them.

'I don't make head nor tail of it,' replied the sexton. 'Perhaps you do, sir.'

'Well, it looks to me,' continued the parson—'it—looks to—me—uncommonly like a King's frigate. Can't you make out her guns on the port side?'

'Yes,' cried the sexton. 'I'll be hanged if you're not right, sir; it's a damned King's ship as ever was.'

'Mr. Mipps,' corrected the parson, 'again I must ask you to repeat your remark.'

'I said, sir,' replied the sexton, meekly handing back the glass, 'that you're quite right. It's a King's ship, a nice King's ship!'

'And she's standing in, too,' went on the parson. 'I can make her out plainly now, and, good gracious, she's lowering a long-boat!'

'Oh! said Mr. Mipps; 'I wonder wot that's for?'

'A revenue search,' volunteered the Preventer.

Mipps started; he hadn't seen the Preventer.

'Hello!' he said, turning round; 'didn't know you was there, Sir Francis Drake. What do you make of that there ship?'

'A King's frigate,' replied the Preventive man. 'She's sending a boat's crew ashore.'

'What for?' asked the sexton.

'I told you—a revenue search; to look for smugglers.'

'Smugglers!' laughed the parson; 'here in Dymchurch?'

'Ay, sir, so they say. Smugglers here in Dymchurch.'

'God bless my soul!' exclaimed the parson incredulously.

'How silly,' said the sexton.

'That remains to be seen mister,' retorted the Preventer.

'What do you say?' said the sexton.

'I say, mister, it remains to be seen.'

' 'Course it does,' went on the sexton. 'Let's have another blink at her. Well,' he said at length, closing the telescope with a snap and returning it, 'King's ship or no, they looks to me more like a set of mahogany pirates, and I'm a-goin' to lock up the church. King's men's one thing, but havin' the plate took's another, and one thing that I don't fancy, being held responsible. So good-afternoon, sir!'—touching his hat to the Vicar—'and good-afternoon to you, Christopher Columbus!' and with this little pleasantry, which struck him as being the height of humour, the grotesque little man hopped off at high speed in the direction of the inn.

'Odd little man that, sir,' said the Preventer.

'Very odd little man,' said the Vicar.

3

The Coming of the King's Men

Meantime the little sexton had arrived, breathless and panting, at the inn. Here he was accosted with a breezy 'Hello, Mr. Mipps! Where's the Doctor?' The speaker was Denis Cobtree, the only son of the Squire.

This young gentleman of some eighteen summers was being prepared in the paths of learning by the Vicar, with a view to his entering the university; but Denis, like his father before him, cared very little for books, and the moment the Doctor's back was turned, off he would slip to talk to some weather-beaten sea-man, or to attempt a flirtation with Imogene, the dark-haired girl who assisted the landlady at the inn.

'Just been talkin' to the Vicar on the sea-wall,' said Mipps, hurrying past into the parlour and calling loudly for Mrs. Waggetts.

'What do you want?' said that good lady, issuing from the kitchen with a teapot in her hand. Tea was a luxury she indulged in.

'A word,' answered the sexton, pushing her back into the kitchen and shutting the door behind him.

'Whatever is it?' asked the landlady, in some alarm.

'What's the time?' demanded the sexton.

'A quarter to four,' replied Mrs. Waggetts, turning pale.

'Good, said the sexton. 'School will be closing in a minute or two, so send Imogene round there to ask Mr. Rash to step across lively as soon as he's locked up. But no,' he added thoughtfully—'I forgot : Rash is a bit struck on that girl, and they'll linger on the way. Send young Jerk, the potboy.'

'Jerk's at school hisself,' said Mrs. Waggett.

'Then you go,' retorted the sexton.

'No,' faltered the landlady. 'It's all right; I'll send the girl, for she can't abide Rash, so I'll be bound she won't linger. And while she's gone I'll brew you a nice cup of tea.'

'Throw your tea to the devil,' snarled the sexton. 'One 'ud think you was a diamond duchess, the way you consumes good tea. When shall I knock it into your skull that tea's a luxury—a drink wot's only meant for swells? Perhaps you don't know what a power of money tea costs!'

'Come now,' giggled the landlady, 'not to us, Mister Mipps. Not the way we gets it.'

'I don't know what you means,' snapped the wary sexton. 'But I do wish as how you'd practise a-keeping your mouth shut, for if you opens it much more that wagging tongue of yours'll get us all the rope.'

'Whatever is the matter?' whimpered the landlady.

'Will you do as I tell you?' shrieked the sexton.

'O Lord!' cried Mrs. Waggetts, dropping the precious teapot in her agitation and running out of the back door towards the school.

Mipps picked up the teapot and put it on the table; then, lighting his short clay pipe, he waited by the window.

In the bar sat Denis Cobtree, making little progress with a Latin book that was spread open on his knee. From the other side of the counter Imogene was watching him.

She was a tall, slim, wild creature this Imogene, dressed as a fisher, with a rough brown skirt and a black fish blouse, and she wore neither shoes nor stockings. Her hair was long and her eyes bright and dark. She had no parents living, for her father—none other than the notorious pirate Clegg—had been hanged at Rye—hanged publicly by the redcoats for murder; and the mother—well, no one knew exactly who the mother was, Clegg having lived a wild, roving life; but it was evident that she must have been a Southerner, from the complexion and supple carriage of this girl. Imogene was a great favourite with all the men on account of her good looks and her dauntless courage when on the boats at sea; for she loved the sea, and was wonderful upon it, her dark eyes flashing, her hair blowing wild, and her young bosom heaving with the thrill of fighting the waves.

Imogene liked Denis because he was nice to her; and, besides, he made her laugh—his ways were so funny, his high manners were so very funny; but his shyness attracted her most.

He was shy now because they were alone, and the boy knew that she was watching him, so he made a feint of studying his book; but Imogene could see that his mind was not on his reading.

'You don't get on very fast, Mr. Denis,' she said.

Denis looked up from the book and laughed. 'No,' he said, 'not very, I'm afraid. I'm not very fond of books.'

'What are you fond of?' said the girl, leaning across the bar on her bare elbow.

'Oh, what a chance to say "You"!' thought the young man; but somehow the words wouldn't come, so he stammered instead, 'Oh, nothing much. I like horses rather; yes, I like riding.'

'Is that all?' said the girl.

'About all,' said the boy.

'Mr. Rash the schoolmaster tells me that he likes riding;' went on the girl mischievously. 'He also likes books; he reads very fast—much faster than you do.'

'Not Latin books, I'll be bound,' said young Denis, starting up scarlet with rage, for he hated the schoolmaster, in whom he saw a possible rival in the girl's affection. 'And as for riding,' he cried, 'a pretty fellow that to talk of riding, when he doesn't know the difference 'tween a filly and a colt. He sits on an old white scrag-bones, jogs along the road at the rate of dyke water, and calls it riding. Put the fool on a horse, and he'd be skull under the hoofs before he'd dug his heels in. The man's a coward, too. I've heard tales of the way he only uses the birch on the little boys. Why, if they'd any sense they'd all mutiny, and kick him round the schoolhouse.'

'You're very hard on the schoolmaster, Mr Denis,' said the girl.

'You don't like him, do you?' asked the boy seriously. You can't!'

But the girl only laughed, for into the bar-parlour had come Mrs. Waggetts, accompanied by the gentleman under discussion, and followed by young Jerk, the potboy.

Jerry Jerk, though only a lad of a dozen years, possessed two excellent qualifications—pluck and a head like a bullet. He had got through his schooling so far without a taste of the birch. Not that he hadn't deserved it, but the truth was that Mr. Rash was afraid of him. Once he had rapped the little urchin very severely on the head with his knuckles—so hard, indeed, that the blood had flowed freely, but not from Master Jerk's head—oh no!—from the pedant's knuckles; upon which young Jerry had burst into a peal of merriment, stoutly declaring before the whole class that when he grew up he intended to be a hangman, just for the pleasure of pulling the bolt for the schoolmaster; So ever after Jerry went by the name of 'Hangman Jerk,' and whenever the pale, washy eye of the sandy-haired Mr. Rash fell on him, the schoolmaster pictured himself upon a ten-foot gallows, with that fiend of a youngster adjusting the running noose around his scraggy neck.

This young ruffian, entering on the heels of the schoolmaster, and treading on them hard at every step, took over the bar from the girl, Mr. Rash remarking with a show of sarcasm that 'he hoped he didn't interrupt a pleasant conversation, and that if he did he was more sorry than he could say to Mr. Denis Cobtree.'

Denis replied that he shared the schoolmaster's sorrow himself with a full heart; but, the door being open, he—the schoolmaster—could easily go out as quickly as he had come in. At this young Jerk let out a loud guffaw and doubled himself up behind the bar. But the conversation was rudely interrupted by the head of Mr. Mipps appearing round the kitchen door, inquiring whether it was their intention to keep him waiting all night.

'Quite right, Mr. Mipps, quite right,' said the school-master. And then, turning to Imogene, he said, 'Mr. Mipps wants us at once.'

Denis was about to make an angry retort, but Imogene passed him and went into the kitchen, followed by Mrs. Waggetts and the sandy-haired Rash, the latter carefully shutting the door behind him.

Denis now found himself alone with young Jerk. The would-be hangman was helping himself to a thimble of rum, and polite-ly asked the Squire's son to join him; but Denis refused with a curt 'No he didn't take spirits.'

'No?' replied the lad of twelve years. 'Oh, you should. When I feels regular out and out, and gets fits of the morbids, you know, the sort of time when you feels you may grow up to be hanged man and not the hangman. I always takes to myself a thimble of neat rum. Rum's the drink for Britons, Mr. Cobtree. Rum's wot's made all the best sailors and hangmen in the realm.'

'If you go on drinking it at this rate,' replied Denis, 'you'll never live to hang that schoolmaster.'

'Oh,' answered Jerry thoughtfully—'Oh, Mr. Denis, if I thought there was any truth in that, I'd give it up. Yes,' he went on with great emphasis, as if he were contemplating a most heroic sacrifice—'yes, I'd give up even rum to hang that school-master, and it's hanging is what'll get him, and not old Mipps the coffin knocker.'

Denis laughed at his notion, and crossed to the kitchen door, listening. 'What can they be discussing in there so solemnly?' he said, more to himself than to his companion. But Jerry Jerk tossed off the pannikin of rum, clambered on the high stool behind the bar, and leant across the counter, fixing Denis with a glance full of meaning.

'Mr. Cobtree,' he whispered fearfully, 'you are older than I am, but I feel somehow as if I can give you a point or two, because you've got sense. I'm a man of Kent, I am, and I'm going to be a hangman sooner or later; but above all I belongs to the Marsh and understands her; and them as understands the Marsh—well, the Marsh understands them, and this is what she says to them as understands her: "Hide yourself under the green, until you feels you're ready to be real mud." I takes her advice, I do: I'm "under the green," I am; but I can be patient, because I knows as how some day I'll be real dirt. You can't be real dirt all at once, so keep green till you can, and if I has to keep green for years and years I'll get to mud one day, and that'll be the day to hang that Rash, and cheat old Mipps of his body.' And to encourage himself in this resolve Jerry Jerk took another thimbleful of rum.

'I'm afraid I can't follow you,' said Denis.

'Don't try to,' replied the younger, 'don't try to. You'll get it in time. The Marsh'll show you. She takes her own time, but she'll get you out of the green some day, and ooze you up through the sluices, and then you'll be a man o' Kent, and no mistaking you.'

Denis, not able to make head or tail of this rigmarole, laughed again, which brought Jerry Jerk with a bound over the bar.

'See here, Mister Cobtree,' he hissed, coming close to him, 'I likes you; you're the only one in the village I does like. Oh, I'm not wanting anything from you; I'm just speaking the truth. You're the only one in the village I hanged in my mind, and, what's more to the point—you won't blab if I tell you—you're the only one in the village I COULDN'T GET HANGED!'

'What on earth do you mean?' said the Squire's son.

'What I've said,' replied the urchin, 'just what I've said, and not another word do you get from me but this. Listen! Do you hear that sexton in there a-mumbling? Well, what's he mumbling about? Ah, you don't know, and I don't know (leastways, not exactly); but there's one who does. Come over here,' and he led Denis to the back window and pointed out over Romney Marsh. 'She knows, that there Marsh. She knows everything about this place, and every place upon her. Why, I'd give up everything I've got or shall get in this world, everything except that school-master's neck—to know all she knows, 'cos she knows everything, Mister Cobtree, everything, she does. In every house there's murmurings and mumblings a-going on, and in every dyke out there there's the same ones, the very same ones a-going. You can hear 'em yourself, Mister Cobtree, if you stands amongst 'em. You try. But oh, Mister Denis'—and he grabbed his arm imploringly—'don't try to understand them dykes at night. She don't talk then, she don't; she does, she just does then. She does all wot the mumbles and murmurs have whispered to do; and it's DEATH on the Marsh at night. I found that out,' he added proudly. 'Do you know how?'

'How?' queried Denis.

'By going out on her in the light, and gradually getting used to wot she says. That's how, and that's the only way.'

Just then a most infernal noise arose from the front of the inn, and before Denis had disengaged himself from the earnest clutches of his guardian angel, and before the murmurs of Mr. Mipps had ceased in the kitchen, the bar was swarming with sailors—rough, mahogany men, with pigtails and brass rings, smelling of tar and—much to the admiration of Jerk—reeking of rum, filling the room with their jostling, spitting, and laughing, and their calls on the potboy to serve them with drink. Their entrance was so sudden, their appearance so startling, and their behaviour so alarming, that the young hangman was for the moment off his guard, for there he stood, open-mouthed and awe-struck, watching the giants helping themselves freely from the great barrels. To Denis they had come with no less surprise. He had seen Preventive men before; he had many friends amongst the fishermen; but these were real sailors, men who had lived through a hundred sea-fights, and seen hell-fire on the high seas. Yes, the King's men had come to Dymchurch.

4

The Captain

Just as suddenly as the pandemonium had begun, just so suddenly did it cease, for there strode through the door a short, thick-set man, with a bull neck and a red face, a regular rough fighting dog, whom, by his dress and the extraordinary effect he produced upon the men, Denis and Jerk at once knew to be an officer.

'Bos'n,' he said in a thick voice, addressing one of the sailors, in a quarter of an hour pipe the men outside the inn, and we'll see to the billeting. Meantime make 'em pay for their drinks, and no chalking. Hi, youngster!' he cried, catching hold of young Jerk by the ear, 'if you're the pot boy, tumble round behind and look after your job.'

Jerk, mentally consigning him to the gibbet, did as he was ordered, for his ear was hurting horribly.

'And now, sir,' went on the officer, addressing himself to Denis, 'is there any in this law-forsaken hole who can answer questions in King's English?'

'Certainly, sir,' said Denis proudly, 'if they are asked with a civil tongue. I am Denis Cobtree, and my father, the Squire, is the best-known man on the Marsh.'

'Then,' ordered the sea-dog curtly, 'fetch him along here quick.'

'Really, sir,' retorted Denis hotly, 'I do not think you would afford him sufficient interest. He has not the honour of your acquaintance, and I am bound to think that he'll have no great zeal to make it.'

'Nor I neither,' said Mr. Mipps, who had been looking round the kitchen door; 'I don't like his looks.'

The infuriated officer was inside the kitchen like a hurricane, glaring at the little sexton with all the condensed fury of the British Navy.

'What's this?' he said, addressing himself again to Denis, who had followed him into the kitchen to be quit of the crowd of seamen. 'I suppose you'll tell me that this shrivel-led-up little monkey is a squire's son too, eh?'

'A squire's son!' repeated the sexton. 'Oh, well, if I is, I ain't come into my title yet.'

'Don't you play the fool with me, sir,' thundered the King's man.

'And don't you try the swagger with me, sir,' volleyed back the sexton.

'The swagger with you, sir?' exploded the officer.

'Right, sir,' exclaimed the sexton; 'that's what I said, sir—the swagger, sir.'

But the other swallowed his wrath and answered coldly, 'I am Captain Collyer—Captain Howard Collyer, Coast Agent and Commissioner—come ashore to lay a few of you by the heels, I've no doubt.'

'Oh, is that all?' replied the sexton, with a sigh of relief. 'Well, there, I have been mistook. I'd quite made up my mind that you was the Grand Turk, or at least the Lord Rear-Admiral of the Scilly Isles.'

Ignoring the sexton, the Captain turned to Denis and said, 'Who is this fellow?'

But Mipps was not so easily crushed, and he cried, 'A man to be looked up to in these parts. I undertakes for the district. The only one wot does it for miles round. They all comes to me, rich and poor alike, I tells you, for they know that Mipps knocks 'em up solid.'

'Knocks what up solid?' demanded the Captain furiously. 'Coffins up solid,' replied the sexton promptly.

'Coffins!' repeated the Captain. 'Oh, you're a coffin-maker, are you? Yes, you look it. Thought you might be the landlord of this run-amuck old inn here. That's the man I want. Where can I find him?'

Mipps pointed out of the window towards the church. 'Up in the churchyard,' he said.

'What's he doing in the churchyard?' demanded the Captain.

Mipps came right up to him and whispered in his ear the significant word, 'Worrumps!'

'What?' shouted the Captain, who didn't understand.

'Sh!' said Mipps, pointing across at Mrs. Waggetts, who had begun to weep into her apron. 'He's a-keepin' 'em out.'

'Keeping who out?' snapped the Captain.

'I keep telling you,' replied the sexton—'worrumps!'

'Hanged if I can make out what you say.' The Captain's patience was well-nigh exhausted. 'Go and fetch the landlord,' he ordered.

'Oh, would that he could!' sobbed Mrs. Waggetts. 'Oh dear, oh dear!'

The Captain turned on her with an oath. 'What's the matter with you, my good woman?' he said.

'That good woman is the landlord,' volunteered Mr. Mipps.

'You exasperating little liar!' shouted the Captain, seizing the enigmatical sexton and shaking him violently. 'You said the landlord was in the churchyard a minute ago.'

A minute ago!' cried the breathless undertaker. 'Why, he's been there a year and a half, and there he'll stop wot time as they gets him. Though I must say I gave him the best pine, and knocked him up solid with my own hands—

> Released from Mrs. Waggetts,
> I left him to the Maggots.

And there's Waggetts, and she's the landlord.'

'Well, ma'am,' said the Captain, coming to the point at once, 'you must really blame yourself if your scores are not settled. A little pot-boy who has to stand on tiptoe to look over the bar is not the sort of person to prevent people helping themselves, and that's what my seamen are doing now—helping themselves.'

Mrs. Waggetts with a scream rushed from the kitchen, followed by Imogene, the sexton and the schoolmaster being glad enough to follow their example and so escape from the Captain, who was now left alone with Denis.

'Now then, Mr. Squire's Son, listen to me,' he said.

'My name is Denis Cobtree,' returned the young man. 'The name Cobtree is well enough known upon the Marsh to be remembered by a sea captain.'

'Look here, young fellow,' said the officer warningly, 'I am here representing the law, as commissioned by King George.'

'I have heard that the King's taste may he called in question,' Denis replied.

'I can prove to you otherwise,' returned the Captain, 'for it so happens that Captain Collyer tops the score for stringing up smugglers. I have sent more from the coast to the sessions than any of His Majesty's agents. And damme, sir, I believe I have landed on a perfect hornets' nest here. Now tell me,' he went on, with that tone of authority that Denis found so aggressive, 'what do you know of the smuggling business in these parts? I have small doubt but that your father finds it a pretty valuable asset to his land revenues, eh? I warrant me half goes to your own pockets, and the rest to the Jacobites.'

Denis took great pains to hold his temper in check. 'Let me tell you, sir,' he said, 'my father is no Jacobite—no, nor yet his father before him. Although he has withdrawn from political strife, he is still a sound Whig; and on that score he and I have but little sympathy together, for I stoutly affirm that the Dutchman had no right whatever in England, and I never lose an opportunity of drinking to our King over the water, and praying for a speedy restoration.'

'You just bear in mind, young man,' said the Captain, 'that the year '45 was not so very long ago. I am here to look for smugglers, not rebels; but there's still a price on their heads, so you should keep whatever opinions you may hold to yourself.'

'If you are really here to look for smugglers,' said Denis, 'you must first take pains to curry favour with my father, for he is the head of our jurisdiction. The Marsh has its own laws, sir, and you will find, to your inconvenience, I fear, that the "Leveller of the Marsh Scotts"* is a big power.'

'I hold my commission from the King's Admiralty, and that's enough for me,' laughed the Captain, 'and for Marsh men too, as you'll find.'

'Possibly, sir, you have not heard the old saying that "the world is divided into five parts—Europe, Asia, Africa, America, and Romney Marsh." We are independent on the Marsh.'

'The Act of Parliament,' retorted the Captain largely, 'brought in by the late King William against all smugglers will cook that goose, young sir.'

'Ah, well,' said Denis finally, 'it's no odds to me; but let me tell you this: your King George may rule at Whitehall, but my father rules on Romney Marsh.' And, humming an old Royalist tune— much to the annoyance of the Captain—the young man sauntered out of the inn.

* The old title of head magistrate on the Marsh.

5

A Bottle of Alsace

Left to himself, the Captain rapidly examined the kitchen; then, going to the door that led to the bar-parlour, he called out, 'Bos'n, come in here, and bring that mulatto with you.'

The bos'n answered with alacrity, pushing before him into the kitchen an altogether horrible apparition—a thin mulatto in the dress of a navy cook. His skin was cracked like parchment, and drawn tightly over the prominent cheek-bones. His black eyes shone brightly, and the lids turned up at the corners like those of a Chinaman. The unusual brilliance of his eyes may have been accounted for by the scrags of pure white hair that grew from the skull.

These were bound at the back into a thin pigtail, leaving the sides of the head bare; and it must have been this that gave him that curiously revolting look for the foreigner had no ears. Another terrible thing about him was that he could not speak, for his tongue had been cut out by the roots. He had evidently suffered much, this cook.

'Job Mallett,' said the Captain, when the door was shut, 'we have now got this room to ourselves, and as there is no time like the present, turn that white-haired old spider of yours on to the floor and walls. This panelling seems likely.'

The bos'n approached the mulatto and jabbed some weird lingo into his ear-hole, which immediately made the uncouth figure hop about the room, spreading his lean arms along the panels, which he kept tapping with his fingers, at the same time executing a curious tattoo with his bare feet upon the floor. In this fashion he encircled the room twice, apparently without achieving any result. In the corner of the room was fixed a wooden table with a heavy flap which reached nearly to the ground. Upon this table was a large assortment of cooking utensils, whilst underneath, almost entirely hidden by the flap, there reposed a like collection of buckets, pails, and old saucepans.

The mulatto, after his double journey round the room, turned his attention to this table. He stuck the flap up, and, pushing aside the pots and pans, uttered a strange, excited gurgle.

'Ha, ha!' said the Captain to the bos'n, 'your spider has caught a fly, eh?'

Job Mallett looked under the table, and saw the mulatto pulling desperately at a brass ring that was fixed to the floor. Pushing him aside, the bos'n had pulled up a trap and was descending a flight of steps before the Captain had even locked both the doors.

'What is it?' he whispered, for the bos'n had entirely disappeared.

'Here you are, sir,' said the sailor, reappearing with a bottle in his hand. 'There's a wine cellar down there the size of an admiral's cabin.'

'Oh!' replied the Captain. 'Well, like enough it's the regular cellar.'

'Then why should they be at such pains to hide the entrance, sir?' returned the bos'n.

'There's nothing in that,' replied the Captain. 'It's natural that they don't want every Tom, Dick, and Harry going into the wine cellar.'

'I suppose it is, sir,' agreed the bos'n; 'but it looks a costly bottle, thought it could do with a bit of a shine-o,' he added, spitting on it and giving it a vigorous rub with his sleeve.

'Let's look at the label,' said the Captain. '"Alsace, White, Rare 500." What on earth does "500" mean?'

'The date, sir,' ejaculated the bos'n—it's the date. My eye! that's enough to give a man a bad head. It's over a thousand years old.'

'Nonsense, my man, said the Captain, laughing. 'it means that this bottle is one of a cargo of five hundred.'

'Of course,' said the bos'n, slapping his knee. 'What a thundering old idiot I am, to be sure. You're right, sir, as you always are, for I see the other four hundred and ninety-nine down below there. But,' he added ruefully, 'we've got no proof that they're smuggled.'

'We'll soon get that,' said the Captain, thrusting the bottle into the capacious skirt pocket of his sea-coat. 'Put these things back, and summon the landlady.'

Then the Captain unlocked the door quietly and opened it. Coming up quickly from a stooping position near the keyhole was Mr. Mipps, the sexton.

'You're a fine fellow,' he said, not at all put out of countenance by the Captain having found him eavesdropping—'a very fine fellow to come looking for smuggling, with a gang of blasphemous scoundrels wot kick up more to-do than the Tower of Babel. Look here, sir; are you coming in to keep order or not? I only want a word, Yes or No, for I shall go straight round to the Court House and report you to the Squire. And then perhaps he won't put you and your crew into the cells there; perhaps he won't—only *perhaps*, 'cos I'm dead sure he will.'

'What are my boys doing?' laughed the Captain.

'What are the little dears not doing!' answered the sexton, thoroughly angry. 'Oh, nothing, I assure you! Only upsettin' the barrels, throwin' about the tankards, stealin' the drinks, and making fun of Mrs. Waggetts.'

'Oh, that's all right,' said the Captain. 'Tell Mrs. Waggetts to come here.'

'You tell worse men than yourself to do your dirty work,' replied the sexton. 'Do you think I'm a powder-monkey that I should fetch and carry Mrs. Waggetts for you? Fetch her yourself, or send old Fat-sides there,' he added, jerking his thumb at the bos'n, 'or that dear old white-haired admiral wot's lost his yellow ear-flaps. As for me, I'm a-going to the Court House, and if you don't know what for, you'll soon learn—you and old Fat-sides.'

The bos'n made a grab at him, but Mipps slipped through the crowded bar, and was running up the highroad.

The Captain stepped into the bar. Order was at once restored. 'Now, ma'am,' he said to Mrs. Waggetts, 'while the bos'n is seeing that your score is paid, give me a bottle of wine.

'Port or claret, sir?' said the landlady.

'Neither,' said the Captain. 'I have a fancy to try a bottle of Alsatian. Yes, a white wine from Alsace.'

But before the Captain had time to smack his lips Mrs. Waggetts replied, 'Oh, we don't keep that, sir.'

'No?' queried the Captain.

'No indeed, sir,' said the landlady. 'You see, there's no call for it in these parts. And then the customs are so high we couldn't afford to stock it for the few-and-far-betweens as might ask for it. Why, for my own part, sir, though I've been in the business these—well—many years now—I've never even heard of it.'

'Really!' said the Captain. 'Well, it's a good wine, ma'am. Now, bos'n, pipe the men outside.'

'Won't you try a bottle of claret, sir?' said the landlady with persuasion.

'No, said the Captain. 'Later on, perhaps; I'll see. By the way, is there any old barn about where I could quarter my men? I'm loath to billet them on the village.'

'No, I don't know anywhere,' returned the landlady. 'Do you, Mr. Rash? Perhaps you'd loan the schoolhouse to the Captain?'

'Yes, and give us a holiday for once in a way,' murmured the pot-boy.

'It's not to be thought of,' said the schoolmaster, walking out of the inn.

'No one uses the church on weekdays, I suppose,' said the Captain. 'I dare say there's room for them there, in the vestry or the tower, perhaps, or even in the crypt.'

'Them drunken ruffians in the church!' cried out young Jerk, pulling a horrified face and indicating the rough sailors, who were now outside the inn. 'You'd better watch out what you're up to, or you'll have the Vicar on your track.'

'I'll tell you where you'll end, my lad,' said the Captain, turning on him sharply.

'Where, sir?' said young Jerk, looking really interested.

'If not upon the scaffold, uncommon near it, I'll be bound,' the Captain replied.

'I hope so indeed,' thought Hangman Jerk; 'and I hopes it'll be a-fixing the noose round your bull neck.' But he kept his thought to himself, for he suddenly remembered that the Captain could be rather too playful for his liking; so he watched the sailors shouldering their bundles, falling into line, and eventually swinging out of the old 'Ship' yard, followed by the Captain.

6

Doctor Syn Takes Cold

You can imagine that the coming of the King's men caused some stir in Dymchurch, for after leaving the Ship Inn they were marched round the village and drawn up in front of the Court House. Here they waited while the Captain knocked upon the front door and asked for the Squire.

'Sir Antony Cobtree has gone riding,' said the butler.

But at that instant a clattering of hoofs was heard upon the highroad, and the Squire himself came along at an easy trot and drew rein before the house. 'My faith!' he cried, looking from the butler to the Captain, and then at the line of naked cutlass, 'have the French landed at last?'

'Captain Howard Collyer, of the King's Admiralty, sir,' said the Captain, saluting; 'and if you are the Squire, very much at your service.'

The jolly Squire returned the salute, touching his hat with his riding whip. 'Indeed, Captain?' he said, dismounting. 'And I would prefer to be your friend rather than your foe so long as you have these sturdy fellows at your back. Is it the renewed activity of the French Navy that we have to thank for your presence here, or the coast defence?'

'I should like a word with you alone,' said the Captain.

'Certainly,' returned the Squire, throwing the reins to a groom and leading the way to the house.

They crossed the large hall, and the Squire, opening a door at the far end, invited the Captain to enter the library.

There, in the recess of the old mullioned window, sat Doctor Syn, deep in a dusty tome that he had taken from the bookcase.

'Ah, Doctor,' said the Squire, 'they didn't tell me you were here. No further need to fear the French fleet. The King's Admiralty have had the kind grace to furnish us with an officer's complement. Captain Collyer—Doctor Syn, our Vicar.'

'Not the Collyer who sank the *Lion d'Or* at the mouth of the St. Lawrence River, I suppose?' he said, shaking hands.

'The same,' returned the Captain, highly delighted that the achievement of his life had been heard of by the parson. 'Captain Howard Collyer, then commanding the *Resistance*, a brigantine of twenty-two guns. Indeed, sir, the French Government kicked up such a devil of a row over that little affair that I lost my command. So now, instead of sinking battleships, the Admiralty keep me busy nosing out smugglers. A poor enough game for a man who has done big things at sea, but it has its excitements.'

'So I should imagine,' said the parson.

'And what have you come here for?' asked the Squire.

'To hang every smuggler on Romney Marsh,' said the Captain

'Do you believe in ghosts?' said the Squire.

'What do you mean?' retorted the Captain.

'What I say,' returned the Squire. 'Do you believe in ghosts?'

"Well, I can't say I do,' laughed the Captain, 'for I have never yet met one.'

'No more have I,' returned the Squire. 'But they say the Marsh is haunted at night. They've said so so long that people believe it. Whenever a traveller loses his way on the Marsh and disappears, folk say that the Marsh witches have taken him. When the harvest are bad, when the wool is poor, when the cattle are sickly—oh, it's always the Marsh witches that are blamed. They set fire to haystacks. They kill the chickens. They blast the trees. They curdle the milk. They hold up travellers and rob them of their purses. In fact, all the vices of the Marsh, really performed by Master Fox, or Master Careless, or Master Footpad, are all put down to the poor Marsh witches, who don't exist except in the minds of the people. I know the Marsh as well as any man ever will, and I've never seen a witch; and it's the very same with smugglers—the whole thing's a fancy. I've never caught 'em at it; and I keep a stern enough eye on my farms, I can tell you. Why, I'm a positive king, sir. Do you know that if a man working in the neighbourhood doesn't please me, I can shut every door of the Marsh against him? Why, these farmers are all scared stiff of me, sir. I'd like to see the man who went against the laws of Romney Marsh. I can tell you, sir, that I'd soon settle his business.'

'You are perhaps too confident, sir,' suggested the Captain.

'Not a bit of it, sir,' exclaimed the Squire. 'Mind you, I don't trust 'em—O Lord, no! I just know 'em to be honest, because I don't give 'em the chance to be otherwise. They never know when or where I'll be turning up. Why, I have a groom in my stables awake all night in case I want to surprise a farm ten miles away. Smuggler—pooh—rubbish!'

'Then you consider that I am here on a wildgoose chase?' said the Captain.

'Not even that,' said the Squire, 'for you will find no wild geese to chase. However, you need not regret having been sent here, for we can give you good entertainment; and I'll bet my head that, after you have stayed with us a week or so, you'll he sending in your papers to the Admiralty, and settling down on the Marsh as a good Kentish farmer.'

'I'm afraid not, sir,' laughed the Captain.

'Oh yes, you will,' went on the Squire. 'And I'll be bound that we'll have you bothering Doctor Syn to put the banns up for you and some country beauty. What do you say, Doctor?'

'Well,' chuckled the parson, 'if a man wants to marry and settle down, and live happily ever after, as the saying goes, why, then, Kent's the place for him. It's a great country, sir—especially south and east of the Medway—famous for everything that goes to make life worth living.'

'Yes, take him on the whole,' said the Squire, 'the King can boast of no greater jewel in the crown of England than the average man of Kent.'

'Well,' agreed the Captain, 'I've heard say that Kent has fine clover fields, and it's evident to me that I'm a lucky devil and have fallen into one. But I must see to the billeting of my men. Perhaps you can advise me?'

But the Squire would not hear of business until the Captain had cracked a bottle of wine with them and promised to lodge himself at the Court House, Doctor Syn readily placing the large brick-built vicarage barn at the disposal of the men.

So, having settled all amicably, and promising to return within the hour for supper, the Captain, piloted by Doctor Syn, and followed by the seamen, proceeded to inspect the barn; and it was not long before the sailors had converted it into as jolly a lodging as one could wish to see, with a great log-fire ablaze in the stone grate, and a pot of steaming victuals swinging from a hook above the flames.

'Are you all here?' said the Captain to the bos'n, before rejoining the Doctor outside the door.

'All except Bill Spiker and the mulatto, sir,' returned Job Mallett. 'I sent 'em for rum. Here they are, if I mistake not.' And, indeed, up to the barn came two seamen carrying a barrel.

'Now,' said the Captain to Doctor Syn, 'I am ready to return to the Court House.'

But the parson's eyes were fixed on the men carrying the barrel, who were passing him. 'Who's that man?' he said to the Captain, shivering violently, for a cold fog had risen with the night.

'That's Bill Spiker, the gunner,' said the Captain. 'Do you know him?'

'No, the other—the other!' exclaimed the Doctor, still watching the retreating figures, who were now being received with shouts of welcome from the barn.

'Oh, that fellow's a mulatto,' returned the Captain; 'useful for investigation work. An ugly enough looking rascal, isn't he?'

'A very ugly rascal,' muttered the Doctor, walking rapidly from the barn in the direction of the Court House.

'You look cold,' remarked the Captain as they stood outside the Court House door.

'Yes, it's a very cold night,' returned the Doctor. 'Why, I declare my teeth are chattering.'

7

Clegg, the Buccaneer

There was one man who knew Romney Marsh as well as the Squire. This was Sennacherib Pepper; and, what's more, he knew the Marsh by night as well as by day, for he was the visiting physician to the Marsh farms, and his work often called him to patients at night. He had seen curious things upon the Marsh, from his own account, hinting darkly about the witches and devils that rode on fiery steeds through the mists. The villagers, of course, believed his yarns, but the Squire pooh-poohed them; and as it was well known that Sennacherib Pepper was a hard drinker, some people put his stories down to that. But although he gave no credence to his tales, Sir Antony rather enjoyed the physician, and he was a frequent visitor to the Court House. He had prevailed upon him to stay to supper this very night, introducing him to the Captain as his dear friend Sennacherib Pepper, the worst master of physics and the most atrocious liar on Romney Marsh; for although Sennacherib was a very touchy old customer, and was ever on the brink of losing his temper, Sir Antony could never resist a joke at his expense.

'Zounds, sir,' he retorted, 'if I were presenting you to Sir Antony, I should most certainly style him the worst man of business upon the Marsh.'

'How do you make that out?' cried the Squire.

'My dear sir,' went on Sennacherib to the Captain, 'his tenants rob him at every turn. Everybody but himself knows that half the wool from his farms finds its way over to Calais.'

'My dear Captain,' said Doctor Syn, who was warming himself at the fire-place, 'our good friend Pepper is repeatedly coming into contact with the Old Gentleman himself upon the Marsh. Why, only last year he informed us that he met at least a score of his bodyguard riding in perfect style and most approved manner across from Ivychurch, on fire-snorting steeds.—And how many witches is it now that you have seen? A good round dozen, I'll be sworn; and they were riding straddle-legs—a thing that we could hardly credit.'

'Well, let us hope,' said the physician, 'that the presence of the King's men will frighten the devils away. I've seen 'em, and I've no wish to see 'em again.'

'You can set your mind quite at rest, sir,' returned the Captain, 'for if, as you say, their horses breathe fire, they will afford excellent targets on the flat Marsh; we'll hail the ship and see what ninety good guns can do for the devils.'

All through supper was this vein of banter kept up, until the meal was finished and pipes were alight, and Denis had retired to his room with a glum face, to steer, most surely against his will, upon a course of literature. Then the conversation gradually drifted into the Southern Seas, and the Captain began telling stirring tales of Clegg, the pirate, who had been hanged at Rye.

'I should like to have been at that hanging,' he cried, finishing a tale of horror, 'for the fellow, as you have just heard, was a bloodthirsty scoundrel.'

'So it is always said,' replied Doctor Syn; 'but don't you think that some of his exploits may have been exaggerated?'

'Not a bit of it,' exclaimed the Captain. 'I believe everything I heard about that man—except that last blunder that put his neck into the noose at Rye.'

'That is his only exploit about which there is any certainty,' said the physician.

'It was a mistake murdering the Revenue man,' agreed Doctor Syn; 'but Clegg was drunk, and threw all caution to the devil.'

'Clegg had been drunk enough before,' said the Captain, 'and yet he had never made a mistake. No, he was too clever to be caught in the meshes of a tavern brawl. Besides, from all we know of his former life he would surely have put up a better defence at his trial. You don't tell me that a man who could terrorize the high seas all that time was going to let himself swing for a vulgar murder in a Rye tavern!'

'But it is a noticeable thing,' put in the parson, 'that all great criminals have made one stupid blunder that has caused their downfall.'

'Which generally means,' went on the Captain, 'that up to that moment it was luck and not genius that kept them safe. But we know that Clegg was a genius. I've had it first hand from high Admiralty men—from men who have lived in the plantations, and traded in Clegg's seas. The more I hear about that rascally pirate the more it makes me wonder; and some day I mean to give the time to clearing up the mystery.'

'What mystery?' said the parson.

'The mystery of how Clegg could persuade another man to commit wilful murder in order to take his name upon the scaffold,' said the Captain. 'It takes some power of persuasion to accomplish that, you'll agree.'

'What on earth do you mean?' said the parson.

'Simply this,' shouted the Captain, beating the table with his fist—'that Clegg was 'never hanged at Rye.'

There was a pause, and the gentlemen looked at him with grave faces. Presently the Squire laughed. 'Upon my soul Captain,' he said, 'you run our friend Sennacherib here uncommon close with staggering statements. I wonder which of you will tell us first that Queen Anne is not dead.'

'Queen Anne is dead,' exclaimed the Captain, 'because she was not fortunate enough to persuade somebody else to die for her. Now I maintain that this is exactly what Clegg did do.'

'Can you let us have the reasons that led you to this theory?' said the parson, interested.

'I don't see why not,' replied the Captain. 'In the first place, the man hanged at Rye was a short, thick-set man, tattooed from head to foot, wearing enormous brass earrings, and his black hair cropped short as a Roundhead's.'

'That's an exact description of him,' said Doctor Syn, 'for, as everybody knows, I visited the poor wretch in his prison at Rye, and at his desire wrote out his final and horrible confession.'

'Is that so?' said the Captain. 'Oh yes, I remember hearing of how he was visited by a parson. I thought it a bit incongruous at the time.'

'And so it was,' agreed the parson, 'for I have never seen a more unrepentant man go to meet his Maker.'

'Well, now,' went on the Captain, his eyes glistening with excitement, 'I have it on very good authority that the real Clegg in no way answered this description. He was a weird-looking fellow, thin face, thin legs, long arms, and, what's more to the point, never tattooed in his life save one by some unskilled artist, who had tried to portray a man walking the plank, with a shark waiting below. This picture was executed so poorly that the pirate would never let any one try again. Then I also have it on the very best evidence that Clegg's hair was grey, and had been grey since quite a young man; so that does away with your black, close-cropped hair. And again, I have it that Clegg would never permit his ears to be pierced for brass ring; affirming that they were useless lumber for a seaman to carry.'

'Don't you think,' said the Squire, 'that all this was a clever dodge to avoid discovery?'

'A disguise?' queried the Captain. Yes, I confess that the same thing occurred to me.'

'And might I ask how you managed to obtain your real description of Clegg?' asked the Vicar.

'At first,' said the Captain, 'from second or third sources; but the other day I got first-hand evidence from a man who had served aboard Clegg's ship, the *Imogene*—that ugly-looking rascal who was helping Bill Spiker carry the rum barrel. The bos'n questioned him for upwards of three hours in his queer lingo, and managed to arrive, by the nodding and shaking of the man's head, at an exact description of him.'

'He was one of Clegg's men?' said the Vicar, amazed. 'Then pray, sir, what is he doing in the Royal Navy?'

'I use him as a tracker,' replied the Captain. 'You know, some of these half-caste mongrels, mixtures of all the bad blood in the Southern Seas, have remarkable gifts of tracking. He's invaluable to me on these smuggling trips. It's positively uncanny the way this rascal can smell out a trap door or a hiding-place. I suppose you've nothing of the sort in this house?'

'There's a staircase leading to a priest's hole in this very chimney corner, though you would never guess it,' returned the Squire. 'And, what's more, I bet a guinea that nobody would discover it.'

'I'll lay you ten to one that the mulatto will—ay, and within a quarter of an hour.'

'Done!' cried the Squire. 'This will be sport; we'll have him round,' and he summoned the butler.

There's one condition I should have made,' said the Captain, when the butler opened the door. 'The rascal is dumb, and cannot speak a word of English; but my bos'n can speak his lingo, and will make him understand what we require of him.'

'Fetch 'em both round,' cried the Squire. 'Gadzooks, it's a new sport, this!'

The butler was accordingly dispatched with the Captain's orders to the bos'n that he should step round at once to the Court House with the mulatto. Meantime Denis was summoned from the paths of learning, and the terms of the wager having been explained to him, he awaited in high excitement the coming of the seamen.

'How is it that the fellow's dumb?' asked the physician.

'Tongue cut out at the roots, sir,' replied the Captain. 'He might well be deaf too, for his ears have also gone—probably along with his tongue. But he's not deaf: he understands the bos'n all right.'

'Did you ever find out how he lost them?' asked the Squire.

'It was Clegg,' replied the Captain; 'and after having been tortured in this pleasant fashion he was marooned upon a coral reef.'

'Good God!' said the Vicar, going pale with the thought of it.

'How did he get off?' asked the Squire.

'God alone knows,' returned the Captain.

'Can't you get it out of him in some way?' said the Squire.

'Job Mallett, the bos'n, can't make him understand some things,' said the Captain, 'but he located the reef upon which he'd been marooned in the Admiralty chart, and it's as God-forsaken a piece of rock as you could wish. No vegetation; far from the beat of ships; not even registered upon the mercantile maps. As well be the man in the moon as a man on that reef, for all the chance you'd have to get off.'

'But he got off,' said the Squire. 'How?'

'That's just it,' said the Captain—'how? If you can find that out you're smarter than Job Mallett, who seems the only man who can get things out of him.'

'By Gad, I'm eager to look at the poor devil!' cried the Squire.

'So am I,' agreed the physician.

'And I'd give a lot to know how he got off that reef" said Doctor Syn.

But at that instant the butler opened the door, and Job Mallett shuffled into the room, looking troubled.

'Where's the mulatto?' said the Captain sharply for the bos'n was alone.

'I don't know, sir,' answered the bos'n sheepishly. 'He's gone.'

'Gone! Where to?' said the Captain.

'Don't know, sir,' answered the bos'n. 'I see him curled up in the barn along of the others just afore I stepped outside to stand watch, and when I went to wake him to bring him along of me, why, blest if he hadn't disappeared.'

'Did you look for him?' said the Captain.

'Well, sir, I was a-looking for him as far as down to the end of the field where one of them ditches run,' said the bos'n, 'when I see something wot fair beat anything I ever see'd afore. It was a regiment of horse, some twenty of 'em, maybe, but if them riders weren't devils, well, I ain't a seaman!'

What were they like?' screamed Sennacherib.

'Wild-looking fellows on horses wot seemed to snort out fire, and the faces of the riders and horses were all moonlight sort of colour; but before I'd shouted "Belay there!" they'd all disappeared in the mist.'

'How far away were these riders?' said the Captain.

'Why, right on top of me, as it seemed,' stammered the bos'n.

'Job Mallett,' said the Captain, shaking his large finger at him, 'I'll tell you what it is, my man—you've been drinking.'

'Well, sir,' admitted the seaman, 'the rum did seem extra good tonight, and perhaps I did take more than I could manage; though, come to think of it, sir, I've often drunk more than I've swallowed to-night and not seen a thing, sir.'

'You get back to the barn and go to sleep,' said the Captain, 'and lock the door from the inside. There's no need to stand watches to-night, and it won't do that foreign rascal any harm to find himself on the wrong side of the door for once.'

Job Mallett saluted and left the room.

'You see what it comes to, Sennacherib,' laughed the Squire. 'Drink too much, and you're bound to see devils!'

'I don't believe that fellow has drunk too much,' said the physician, getting up. 'But I'm walking home, and it's late. Time I made a start.'

'Mind the devils!' laughed the Vicar, as he shook hands. 'They'll mind me, sir,' said Sennacherib, as he grasped his thick stick.

And so the supper party broke up, the Squire lighting the Captain to his room, Doctor Syn returning to the vicarage, and Sennacherib Pepper setting out for his lonely walk across the devil-ridden Marsh.

The window of the Captain's room looked out upon the courtyard; he could see nothing of the sea—nothing of the Marsh. Now as these were the two things that he intended to see—ay, and on that very night—he waited patiently till the house was still; for he considered that there was more truth in Sennacherib Pepper's stories than the Squire allowed. Indeed, it was more than likely that the Squire disallowed them for reasons of his own. This he determined to find out. So half an hour after the Squire had bade him good-night he softly crossed the room to open the door.

But the door was locked on the outside!

8

Dogging the Schoolmaster

Now Jerry lived with his grand-parents, and they went always early to bed. Indeed, by ten o'clock they were both snoring loudly, whilst Jerry would be tucked up in the little attic dreaming of the gallows, and hanging Mr. Rash. Jerry was troubled a good deal by dreams; but upon this particular night they were more than usually violent, whether owing to the great excitement caused by the coming of the King's men, or due to the extra doses of rum that the younger had indulged in, who can say? He dreamt that he was out on the Marsh chasing the schoolmaster; that was all very well, quite a pleasant dream to young Jerk, and not at all a nightmare. But, unfortunately, there were things chasing Jerry as well, and the nearer he seemed to get to the flying schoolmaster the nearer got the things behind him. There was no doubt at all in the dreamer's mind as to what they were: they were the Marsh devils, that he had heard about from infancy, the very demon riders that old Sennacherib Pepper was credited with having seen. He glanced over his shoulders, and saw them pounding after him, grim riders on the most ghastly steeds. The noise of the hoofs got nearer and nearer, and run as he would, he felt that he would never reach the schoolmaster before he himself was caught by the demons. Then in the dream the schoolmaster turned round, and Jerk with a scream saw that what he had been chasing was no longer the school-master but the devil himself! So there he was, between the demon riders and the very Old Gentleman that Doctor Syn preached about on Sundays. Now, although Jerry was no coward, he was not quite proof against such a shock as this, so he just uttered the most appalling scream, and fell into a ditch that had suddenly appeared before him. The fall into the ditch was very hard—so hard, indeed, that the sleeper awoke to find that he was sitting on the floor with the bedclothes on top of him. But he was still uncertain whether or not he was awake, for although he rubbed his eyes exceedingly hard, he could still hear the pounding hoofs of the demon horses, and they were coming nearer. He rubbed his eyes again, twisted his fingers into his ears, and listened. Yes—there was really no mistaking it; there were horses coming along the road before the house, and he was certain in his mind that they were the phantoms of his dream. So he went to the casement and looked out. Prepared for a surprise he certainly was, but not such a terrible one as he got.

Along the road at a gallop went a score or so of horsemen. That they were not of this world was very easy to see, for there was moonlight shining from their faces and from the faces of the horses as well. The riders were fantastically dressed in black, and wore queer tail hats, the like of which Jerry had only seen in ghost books. They were fine riders, too, for they seemed to the terrified boy actually to grow out of their horses. Jerry noticed, too, that there were long streamers of black flying from the harness. The curious light that shone upon the riders made it possible for Jerry to see their faces, which were entirely diabolical, for one and all were laughing as they rode. They were going at a good pace, so that as they appeared, just so sudden did they go. Jerk opened the casement and hung out of the window, but the mist had entirely swallowed the riders up, although he could still hear the distant noise of their horses. It sounded as if one of them was coming back—yes, he was sure of it! So he very quickly shut the window again. The clatter of hoofs got louder, and presently Jerk, through the pane, caught sight of a rider trotting out of the mist. Now there seemed something familiar about

this figure and the peculiar jogging of the steed; but the rider was
well under the window before Jerk discovered that this was no
demon, but the hated schoolmaster. What was he doing riding
out at this hour? thought the boy. Was he in league with the
spirits of the Marsh, and so could pass through them without
being scared? for there was no other turning along the road,
and the schoolmaster, although very repulsive to behold, was
not looking in any way concerned. So Jerry came to the rapid
conclusion that his deadly enemy was in some way or other con-
nected with that mysterious band of horse. 'So,' he thought, if
he's up to mischief, I must find out what that mischief is, and if
it's a hanging business, all the better.' quickly and silently Jerk
pulled on his breeches and coat, and with his boots in his hand
crept out upon the stairs.

Everything was very still, and the creaks and cracks of the
old oak were horrible; and then his grandfather did snore so
very loud, and just as he was entering the kitchen he heard his
grandmother cry out, 'Jerry, come here.' That nearly made him
jump out of his skin, but he heard immediately afterwards her
wheezing snore mingled with those of her better half, so he con-
cluded that she had only cried out in her sleep. In the kitchen he
put on his boots, and just as he was opening the back door he
heard the tall clock in the front room striking eleven. He left
the door on the latch, and, climbing through a hedge, struck
out across the Marsh. He knew well enough that by running he
could pick up the road again so as to be ahead of the rider; but
it was difficult going at night, and by the time he had scrambled
through the hedge again he saw the schoolmaster passing round
at the back of Mipps's shop. There was still a light burning in the
front window, and after tying up his bony horse, the schoolmaster entered the shop. 'What's he wanting at a coffin shop at
this hour?' thought Jerk. 'I wish he was ordering his own, I do!'
With this uncharitable thought he crept along the road and
approached the house. A coffin shop isn't a pleasant thing to
behold at night. Rows of coffin planks leaned up against the
provision shelves, for Mipps supplied the village with bread and
small eatables .A half-finished coffin reposed on trestles in the

centre of the floor, and around the room hung every conceivable article that had to do with coffins. The atmosphere of coffins spread over everything in the store, and whether young Jerk looked at the bottles of preserves on this shelf or the loaves of dark bread on that, to him they meant but one thing—death; and he was quite satisfied that any one bold enough to eat of the food in that grizzly shop well deserved to be knocked up solid in one of Mipps's boxes.

The sexton himself was examining with great care a mixture that he was stirring inside a small cauldron. Mr Rash approached him, and asked if there was enough.

'Of course there is,' answered the sexton. 'Ain't the others all had theirs? And there's only you left; last again, as usual. Hang the pot on to your saddle and come along.'

Jerk fell to wondering what on earth could be inside that pot. He could smell it through the broken casement, and a right nasty smell it was. Mipps led the way through the back of the shop, and Jerk, by changing his position, could see the sexton fixing the pot to the saddle, as he had suggested. Then, springing on to the horse's back with marvellous agility for so ancient a man, he went off through the village, with the schoolmaster trotting at the side, and the wary Jerk following in the shadows,

They led him right through the village to the vicarage, and tied the horse behind a tree at the back. Then Mipps, producing a key, opened the front door, and a minute later Jerk, from a point of vantage behind the low churchyard wall, saw the sexton throw a log on to the low smouldering fire in the old grate of the old front room that was the Doctor's study. Mipps also lighted a candle that stood upon the chimney-board. Jerry could see into the room quite distinctly now; he could see the old sexton curled up in the oak settle by the fire-place, and the schoolmaster's shadow flickering upon the wall. He also had a good view of the Court House, where there were still candles burning in the library, and the hearty voice of the Squire would keep sounding out loud and clear. Presently the door opened and a figure came out, going off in the direction of the vicarage barn, and Jerk had no difficulty in recognizing the bos'n of the King's men.

As soon as he had disappeared Jerk got another surprise, for there came across the churchyard, dodging in and out of the tombstones, a truly terrible thing. Its face seemed to the boy like the face of a dead man, for it looked quite yellow, and its white hair gave it a further corpse-like expression. Jerk was terrified that the thing would see him, but it didn't, for the shining black eyes, unlike anything he had ever seen before, were directed entirely upon the lighted window of the vicarage. Up to it the figure crawled, and peeped into the room. The schoolmaster was standing with his back to the window, but he presently turned and went to the door. The weird figure crouched in the flower-bed under the sill, while Mr. Rash opened the front door and went round to the back of the house to the tree where he had tied the horse.

As soon as he had gone the yellow-faced man entered the house. Now Jerry fell to wondering what this was all about, and what the little sexton would do if he caught sight of the apparition.

But the sexton's eyes were closed and his mouth wide open, and Jerry could hear him beginning to snore, when the door of the room was opened, and the figure cautiously crossed towards the fire. The sexton didn't move; he was asleep.

Now above the chimney-piece hung a harpoon. It belonged to Dr. Syn, who was a collector of nautical curiosities, and this harpoon had once been Clegg's. It was of a curious shape, and it was supposed that only one man in the Southern Seas besides the pirate had ever succeeded in throwing it.

The figure was now between Mipps and the firelight, and it began examining the curios upon the mantel-board. Suddenly it perceived the harpoon, and with a cry unhooked it from its nail. The sexton opened his eyes, and the figure swung the dangerous weapon above his head, and Jerk thought that the sexton's last moment had come. But Mipps, uttering a piercing cry, kicked out most lustily against the chimney-piece, and backwards he went along with the settle.

Perhaps it was the horrible cry that frightened the thing, because it came running out of the front door with the harpoon still in its hand, and, leaping the churchyard wall, disappeared amongst the tombstones in the direction of the Marsh.

Mipps got up and ran to the door, crying out for Rash, and at the same time the door of the Court House opened, and Doctor Syn came striding towards the vicarage.

'No more parochial work, I trust, to-night, Mr. Sexton?' he said cheerily; but then, noticing Mipp's terrified demeanour, he added, 'What's the matter, Mr. Mipps? You look as grave as a tombstone.'

'So would you, sir, if you'd seen wot I see'd. It was standin' over me lookin' straight down at me, as yellow as a guinea.

'What was?' said the parson.

'A thing!' said the sexton.

'Come, come, what sort of thing?' demanded the vicar. 'The likes of a man,' replied the sexton, thinking, 'but not a livin' man—a sort of shape—a dead 'un; and yet I can't help fancyin' I've see'd it somewheres before. By thunder!' he cried suddenly, 'I know. That's why it took Clegg's harpoon. For God's sake, come inside, sir.' And in they went hurriedly, followed by Rash, who had just arrived back on the scene. Inside the room, Mr. Mipps again narrated in a horrified whisper what he had just seen, pointing now out of the window in the direction taken by the thing, and now at the empty nail where Clegg's harpoon had hung.

Doctor Syn went to the window to close the shutters, and saw Sennacherib Pepper crossing the far side of the churchyard.

'Good-night, Sennacherib,' he cried out, and shut the shutters.

A minute later out came the schoolmaster; but instead of going round for his horse as Jerry expected, he walked quickly after Sennacherib Pepper. 'How long is this going on for, I wonder?' thought young Jerk, as he picked himself up and set off after the schoolmaster.

9

The End of Sennacherib Pepper

For half a mile out of the village Mr. Rash kept well in the rear of Sennacherib Pepper, and Jerk kept well behind the schoolmaster. It was a weird night. Everything was vivid—either very dark or very light. Such grass as they came to was black grass; such roadways as they crossed were white roads; the sky was brightly starlit, but the mountainous clouds were black; the edges of the great dyke sluices were pitch black, but the water and thin mud were silver steel, reflecting the light of the sky. Sennacherib Pepper was a black shadow ahead; the schoolmaster was a blacker one; and Jerk—well, he couldn't see himself; he rather wished he could, for company.

Although Mr. Rash was a very black-looking figure, there was something small and ugly that kept catching the silver steel reflected in the dyke water. What was it? Jerry couldn't make it out. It was something in Mr. Rash's hand, and he kept bringing it out and thrusting it back into one of his overcoat pockets. But the young adventurer had enough to do keeping himself from being discovered, else he might have understood, and so saved Sennacherib's life.

When they got about a mile from the village Mr. Rash quickened his pace. Jerry quickened his accordingly; but Sennacherib Pepper, who had no object in doing so, did not quicken his. Once the schoolmaster stopped dead, and the young hangman only just pulled up in time, so near was he; and once again the silver steel thing came out of the pocket, but this time Mr. Rash looked at it before thrusting it back again. Then he began to run.

'Is that you, Dr. Pepper?' he called out.

'Now this is strange,' thought Jerk, 'for the schoolmaster must surely have known what man he was following, and why hadn't he cried out before?'

Sennacherib stopped. Jerk drew himself down amongst the rushes in the dyke, and crept as near to the two men as he dared; he was within easy earshot, anyhow.

'Who is it?' asked Pepper; and then, recognizing the young man, he added, 'Why, it's the schoolmaster!'

'Yes, Doctor Pepper,' replied Rash; 'and it's been a hard job I've had to recover you, for it's an uncanny way over the Marsh.'

Just then there was the sound of horses galloping in the distance; Jerk could hear it distinctly.

'What do you want me for?' asked the physician.

'It was the Vicar sent me for you, sir,' replied the schoolmaster. 'He wants you to come at once; there's somebody dying in the parish.'

'Do you know who it is?' said the physician.

'I believe it's old Mrs. Tapsole in the bakehouse, but I'm none too sure.' Indeed, it seemed to Jerk that uncertainty was the whole attitude of the schoolmaster. He seemed to be listening to the distant noise of galloping, and answering old Sennacherib at random. Perhaps the physician also noticed something in his manner, for he looked at him pretty straight and said, 'I don't think it's Mrs. Tapsole either, for I saw her to-day, and she was as merry as a cricket.'

'She's had a fit, sir; that's about what she's had, replied the schoolmaster vaguely.

'Then,' said the physician, 'you do know something about it, do you?'

'I know just what I was asked to say,' returned the schoolmaster irritably. 'It's not my business to tell you what's the matter with your patients. If you don't know, I'm sure I don't. You're a doctor, ain't you?'

No doubt old Pepper would have pulled the schoolmaster up with a good round curse for his boorishness had he not at that

instant caught the sound of the galloping horses. 'Look there!'
he cried.

At full gallop across the Marsh were going 'a score or so of
horsemen, lit by a light that shone from their faces and from
the heads of their mad horses. Jerk could see Rush shaking as if
with the ague, but for some reason he pretended not to see the
hideous sight.

'What are you looking at?' he said; 'for I see nothing.'

'There, there!' screamed old Pepper; 'you must see something
there!'

'Nothing but dyke, marsh, and the high-read,' faltered the
schoolmaster.

'No? There—look—riders—men on horses, Marsh fiends!'
yelled the terrified physician.

'What, in hell's name, are you trying to scare me for?' cursed
the trembling Rash. 'Don't I tell you I see nothing? Ain't that
enough for you?'

'Then God forgive me!' cried poor Sennacherib, 'for I can see
'em and you can't; there's something wrong with my soul.'

'Then may God have mercy on it!' The words came somehow through the schoolmaster's set teeth; the silver steel leapt
from the pocket of his overcoat, and Sennacherib was savagely
struck twice under the arm as he pointed at the riders. He gave
one great cry and fell forwards; whilst the schoolmaster, entirely gone to pieces, with quaking limbs and chattering teeth
stooped down and cleaned the knife by stabbing it swiftly up to
the hilt in a clump of short grass that grew in the soil by the
roadside.

The sudden horror of the thing was too much even for the callous Jerk; for his senses failed him, and he slid back into the
dyke amongst the rushes, and when he came to himself the first
streaks of dawn were rising over Romney Marsh.

10

Doctor Syn Gives Some Advice

That he was still dreaming was Jerry's first thought, but he was so bitterly cold—for his clothes were wet with mud and dyke water—that he quickly realized his mistake. However, it took him a power of time and energy, and not a little courage, before he dared creep forth from his hiding-place. When he did the Marsh looked empty. The sheets of mist had rolled away, and it looked as innocent a piece of land as God had ever made. There was no sound save the ticking bubbles that rose from their mud-bed to burst amidst the rushes, no one in sight but the old gentleman lying outstretched upon the road. Jerry crept up to him and looked. He was lying face downwards, just as he had fallen, and the white road was stained with a dark bloody smudge.

'Well,' he said to himself, 'here's another job for old Mipps and a trip to the ropemarker's;' and shivering with cold and horror, he set off as fast as he could go towards the village.

Now, when he was within sight of his house, he began to consider what it was his duty to do. He had his own eyesight to prove the schoolmaster's guilt; but would he be believed? Could the schoolmaster somehow turn the tables upon him? If he breathed a word to his grandparents, he would at once be hauled before that brutal Captain; and the Captain, he felt sure, would not believe him. The Squire might, but the Captain would, of course, take the side of authority, and back up the schoolmaster. Denis Cobtree was not old enough to give him counsel, and besides that the Captain was staying at the Court House.

No; Doctor Syn was the man to go to. He was kindly and patient, and would anyhow give one leave to speak without interruption. So, crossing the fields, in order to avoid his grand-parents' windows, he struck out for the vicarage.

Just as he was skirting the churchyard he heard the tramp of feet, and the Captain passed along the road followed by the King's men. Two of them were bearing a shutter. Then the murder was known already. They were going to get Sennacherib's body. Yes, that was it most certainly, for there was affixed to the church door a new notice. Jerry approached, and read the large glaring letters.

'A hundred guineas will be paid to any person or persons who shall directly cause the arrest of a mulatto, a seaman. White hair; yellow face; dumb; no ears; six feet high; when last seen, wearing Royal Navy cook's uniform. Necklace of sharks' teeth around neck; tattoo marks of a gibbet on right forearm; a cockatoo on left wrist; and a brig in full sail executed in two dyes of tattoo work upon his chest. This man wanted by the Crown for the murder of Sennacherib Pepper, Doctor of Physics, of Romney Marsh.'

(Signed)   'ANTONY COBTREE,
'Leveller of the Marsh Scotts,
Court House, Dymchurch;
and
'HOWARD COLLYER,
'Captain of His Majesty's Navy, and
Coast Agent and Commissioner,
Court House, Dymchurch.'

The writing on this notice was executed in most scholarly Style, and Jerk knew the familiar lettering to be the handiwork of the murderous schoolmaster himself. This colossal audacity was terrifying to him. It looked as if it had been written in the blood of the victim, for the ink was still wet.

As he gazed the church door opened, and Doctor Syn came out. He looked pale and worried, as well he might, for indeed this shocking affair had already caused a most terrible sensation in the village.

'This is a bad business, boy,' he said to Jerk, who was still gazing at the notice.

'You may well say that, sir,' replied the boy.

'Poor old Sennacherib!' sighed the cleric. 'To think that you went from my friend's house to meet your death Well,' he added hotly, shaking his fist across the Marsh, 'let's hope they catch the rascal, for we will give him short shrift for you, Sennacherib.'

'Ay, 'deed, sir,' replied young Jerk, 'and let's hope as how it'll he the right un when they does.'

'The right what?' asked Doctor Syn.

'The right rascal,' said young Jerk, 'for that ain't him'

'What do you know about it, my lad?' said the Doctor.

'The whole thing,' replied Jerk, 'for I see'd the whole of the ugly business. I see'd the man with the yellow face last night; I see'd him a-coming out of your front door with a weapon in his hand.'

'You saw that?' cried the cleric, his eyes shining with excitement. 'You could swear that in the Court House?'

'I could do it anywheres,' replied Jerk, 'let alone the Court House; and what's more, I could swear that he never killed Doctor Pepper.'

'How can you possibly say such a thing?' said Doctor Syn.

'Because I see'd the whole thing done, as I keep telling you,' answered Jerk, 'and it wasn't him as did it.'

'How do you know?' asked the Doctor hastily. 'Where were you?'

'Out on the Marsh,' said Jerk, 'all night.'

'What!' ejaculated the Vicar, looking at the boy doubtfully. 'Are you speaking the truth, my lad?'

'The solemn truth,' replied young Jerk.

'You were out on the Marsh all night?' repeated the astonished parson. 'And, pray, what were you doing there?'

'Dogging that schoolmaster,' replied Jerk, with conviction.

'Come into the vicarage,' said Doctor Syn, 'and tell me all about it.' And he led the boy into the house.

When he had finished his tale, Doctor Syn took him into the kitchen, and lit the fire, bidding him dry his wet clothes, for

Jerk was still shivering with the cold of the dyke water. Then he boiled some milk in a saucepan, and set it before him with a cold game pie and a loaf of bread. Jerk made a hearty meal, and felt better, his opinion of clergymen going up at a bound when he discovered that a strong dose of excellent ship's rum had been mixed with the milk. 'Rum's good stuff, my lad, on occasions,' he said cheerily, 'and I've a notion that it'll drive the cold out of you.' And Jerry thought it a very sensible notion too.

'And now look here, my lad,' the Doctor went on when Jerry could eat no more: 'what you've seen may be true enough, though I tell you I can hardly credit it. It's a good deal for a thinking man to swallow, you'll allow, what with the devil riders and all that; besides which, I can see no earthly reason for the schoolmaster committing the crime. As yet I really don't know what to say, my boy. I'm beat, I confess it. I must think things over for an hour or so. In the meantime, I must strongly urge you to keep this adventure to yourself. It is very dangerous to make accusations that you have no means of proving, and certainly you can prove nothing, for there is nothing to go on but what you thought you saw. Well, a nightmare has upset better men than you before now, Jerry, and it is possible that your rich imagination may have supplied the whole thing. Go back, then, to your house, and get a couple of hours' sleep, and then go to school as if nothing had happened. Then I'll tell you what we'll do, my lad: you come round here and we'll have a bit of dinner together, and talk of this again.'

'Thank you, sir" said Jerk, very flattered at being asked to dine with the Vicar. 'I consider that you've behaved very sensible over this horrible affair, though where you get wrong, sir, is over my "rich imagination." That part ain't true, sir. I knows what I see'd, and I see'd Rash stick Pepper twice under the arm with his pencil sharpener.'

But Doctor Syn dismissed him with further adjurations to hold his tongue, adding that the whole thing seemed most odd.

On the way back from the vicarage Jerk met the sailors returning to the Court House, bearing the remains of Sennacherib Pepper upon the shutter. After his conversation with Doctor Syn, he thought it best to keep out of sight, as he was not desirous of being questioned by the Captain; and so, when they had passed, he slipped home and managed to get into bed before his grandparents were astir. After his goodly feast at the vicarage he found it difficult to eat his usual hearty breakfast, but he did his best, saying that the sound of this horrible murder, and the thought of the man with the yellow face who was wanted by the King's men, must have put him off his feed. And so his night's adventure passed unheeded, for everybody was too busy discussing the murder and setting forth their individual opinions upon it to trouble themselves about any suspicious behaviour of 'Hangman Jerk.'

11

The Court House Inquiry

Jerry Jerk made it a golden rule to be always late for school, but on this particular morning he intended to be there before the schoolmaster, for he wanted to watch him, and, if he saw an opening, make him nervous, without in any way betraying his secret. In the comfort of daylight he had lost all those terrors that had oppressed his spirit; indeed, ever since he had unburdened his mind to Doctor Syn, he had entirely recovered his usual confidence. So with jaunty assurance he approached the schoolhouse, determining to be there before the murderer. But this same determination had evidently occurred to the schoolmaster, for when Jerry arrived at the schoolhouse he could see Mr. Rash already bending over his desk. Jerry, imagining that he had miscalculated the time, felt highly annoyed, fearing that he might have missed something worth seeing; but on entering the schoolroom he found that not one of his school-fellows had arrived, and consequently his entrance was the more marked. As a master of fact, Jerk's young colleagues were hanging about outside the Court House until the last possible moment, for there was much going forward—sailors on guard outside the door, people going in and coming out, and the gossips of the village discussing the foul murder of the unfortunate Pepper. Jerk went to his desk, sat down, and waited, narrowly watching the schoolmaster, who was writing, keeping his face low to the desk. The boy thought that he never would look up, but after some ten minutes he did, and Jerk stared the murderer straight in the face.

The schoolmaster bravely tried to return the stare, but failed; and then Jerk knew that he had in a measure failed also—failed in his trust to Doctor Syn—for in that glance Jerry had unconsciously told the malefactor what he knew. Presently Rash spoke without looking up. 'Where have those other rascals got to?'

Promptly Jerk answered, 'If you're addressing yourself to a rascal, you ain't addressing yourself to me, and I scorn to reply; but if I'm mistook—well, I think you knows where they are as well as I do, who ain't no rascal, but a respectable pot-boy and no scholard, thank God!'

'I don't know where they are,' replied the schoolmaster, looking up. 'Be so good as to tell me, Jerk, and I'll take this birch' (and his voice rose high) 'and beat 'em all up to the schoolhouse like a herd of pigs, I will!' Then, conquering his emotion, he added, 'Please, Jerk, where are they?'

But Jerk was in no way softened, so, placing his forefinger to the side of his nose, and solemnly winking one eye, he said, 'I don't know no more than you do, mister; but if you does want me to guess, I don't mind putting six and six together, and saying as how you'll find 'em hanging about to get a glimpse at old Pepper's grisly corpse, wot was brought from the Marsh on a shutter.'

'I'll teach them!' shrieked the schoolmaster, flourishing the birch and flying out of the door.

'That's it,' added Jerk, 'you do; and I'll teach you, too, my fine fellow, who rapped my head once. I'll teach you and teach you till I teaches your head to wriggle snug inside a good rope's noose.' And Jerk followed the schoolmaster to see the fun.

The crowd outside the Court House was quite large for Dymchurch. Everybody was there, and right in front, enjoying the excitement, gaped and peered the scholars of the school. But Rash elbowed his way through the throng, and fell upon them like a sudden squall, using the terrible birch upon the youngsters' shoulders, quite regardless of the cries of 'Shame!' and 'Stop him!' from the villagers. But the onslaught of Rash came to a sudden conclusion, for the heavy hand of the Captain's bos'n fell upon him and ordered him immediately inside the Court House. Jerk saw Rash turn the colour of a jelly-fish, asserting wildly that there must be some mistake, and that, having his duty to perform at the school, he must beg to be excused.

'It's my opinion,' replied the bos'n in a hard voice, 'that them lads will get a holiday to-day. The inquiry is going forward about this murder and I have orders to see that you attend.' So, keeping his rough hand upon the pedant's shoulder, he led him, still protesting vehemently, inside the Court House, with the jeers and jibes of the scholars ringing in his ears.

Jerk had by now worked his way to the front of the crowd, and there he stood, looking with wonder at the two great seamen who, with drawn cutlasses, were guarding the open door. Dymchurch was having the excitement of its life, and no mistake: a holiday for the school—even the tragedy of Sennacherib Pepper's death was forgotten in the glory of that moment—and the hated schoolmaster publicly stopped thrashing the boys and himself ordered into the Court House.

'I wonder what for!' thought young Jerk; 'I wonder!' He would have given a lot to see inside that upper room, where the inquiry was now about to proceed. Presently the Captain himself came out of the hall, and stood for a moment on the gravel outside, looking at the crowd. Now there were sailors keeping the crowd back—never had there been such formal times in Dymchurch. The Captain glanced at the little knot of schoolboys with their satchels, and suddenly catching sight of Jerk, called out, 'Hi, you! you're the pot-boy of the Ship Inn, ain't 'you? Well, I want you. Step this way.' So his wish was granted, and, followed by the wonder and admiration of the crowd, Jerry Jerk, pot-boy of the 'Ship,' strutted after the King's Captain into the Court House.

12

The Captain Objects

Up the old stairway to the court room Jerk followed the Captain, wondering why he had been called, what the Captain knew about last night, and whatever Doctor Syn would advise him to say if he were questioned. These were nutty problems for Jerry's young teeth to crack; but although somewhat nervous of his difficult position, he was, on the whole, highly delighted at seeing the fun.

The procedure of the inquiry was evidently biling the Captain's presence, for as soon as he had taken his seat at the high table, the Squire rose and in a few words announced the inquiry to be set and open. The Captain seemed to have forgotten the presence of Jerk, who was left standing in the doorway surveying the august company. There were an attorney-at-law and a doctor of medicine from Hythe, an attorney from Romney and a doctor from Romney. At the high table these four gentlemen sat facing the Squire, who was in the centre, with Doctor Syn upon his right. On his left was the chair just occupied by the Captain, and on fixed oak benches round the room sat the leading lights of Dymchurch: the head Preventive officer, three or four well-to-do farmers, two owners of fishing luggers, Denis Gobtree, Mrs. Waggetts, and the schoolmaster, besides two or three leading villagers. Nobody took much notice of Jerk when he came in, for all eyes were on the Captain, but Doctor Syn not only took notice, but the trouble to point out an empty space on one of the benches.

'Are all those summoned for this inquiry present?' asked the Captain, looking round at the assemblage.

'All but Mr. Mipps,' said the Squire, referring to a list of names before him. 'While we were waiting for you he took the opportunity of viewing the body next door.'

The Captain signed to one of the two sailors who were guarding the door of the adjoining room, and he accordingly summoned the undertaker, who, with an eye to business, was measuring the corpse. Jerk caught a glimpse of this as the door opened, and of the form of Sennacherib Pepper lying on a table. The undertaker, with a footrule in his hands, took his place on one of the benches. Mipps's entrance seemed to revive the tragedy of the whole business, for there was a pause after the Squire's opening words. But the Captain was the first to speak. He arose and, to the astonishment of everybody, took up and lit a pipe which had been lying upon the table in front of him.

'Sir Antony Cobtree and gentlemen,' he said in his great, husky, sea voice, as he drew the smoke deliberately through the long clay stem and volleyed it back from his set mouth in blue battle clouds across the table, 'we have met here to discuss, as Sir Antony Cobtree has already said better than I ever could, the sad and sudden death of Doctor Sennacherib Pepper, killed violently last night on Romney Marsh. The form of this inquiry I leave to the lawyers, whose business it is, but before they get busy I've got a few things bottled up that I must and will say. I don't possess the knack of a crafty tongue myself, and I've the reputation amongst my colleagues of being the most tactless man in the service; but I've also a reputation as a fighter, and when I do fight, it's a hard fight—a straightforward, open fight. So what I've got to say will, like enough, cause offence to every man in this room, from Sir Antony Cobtree downwards. I'm no good at strategy. As I say, I fight open, and when I think things—well, I can't bottle them up: I say 'em out bluntly at the risk of offence So here it is. I don't like this business—this Doctor Pepper business!'

The Captain here paused to roll a large volume of smoke across the room. The Squire took advantage of the pause, and said, 'If that's all, Captain, come now, which of us do?'

The Captain thought a moment and added, 'If the party or parties who committed the crime didn't like it, why in thunder's name did they do it?

'You should know that better than we do,' returned the Squire hotly, 'for that the murderer was under your employment is fairly obvious.'

'You are referring to the mulatto seaman,' said the Captain. 'In the first place, I consider that you should have asked my permission before you issued that public notice affixed to the church door. Until the mulatto is found and can be examined, I deny your right or any man's right to brand him as a murderer.'

'You remarked just now, sir,' cried the Squire, that you preferred to leave the business of lawyers to the lawyers. Please do so, and remember that whilst I am head of this jurisdiction on Romney Marsh, I'll brook no dictation from Admiralty men— no, sir, not from the First Lord downwards.'

'Come, come, gentlemen!' said Doctor Syn, drumming with his fingers on the table; 'I think that this is an ill-fitting time and place for wrangling. The Captain has got a bee in his bonnet somehow, and the sooner we get it out for him the better. Let us please hear, sir, what he has to say.'

The Squire nodded his head roughly and sat silent, whilst the rest of the company waited for the Captain to continue, which he presently did, still pulling vigorously at his long clay pipe.

'The next thing I don't like,' he went on, 'is Dymchurch itself. I don't like the Marsh behind it; and I don't like the flat, open coastline, it looks a deal too innocent for me on the surface, and not being a strategist I don't like it.'

The Squire was on edge with irritation.

'I am sure, sir,' he said sarcastically, 'that had the Almighty been notified of your objection during the process of the creation. He would have extended Dover Cliffs round Dungeness.'

The Captain didn't seem to notice the interruption.

'Next, I don't like the people here. Leaving Doctor Syn out of it—for he's a parson, and I never could make head or tail of parsons—I say that from the Squire down you're none of you swimming the surface. Sir Antony Cobtree went to great pains

to entertain me lavishly yesterday, in order that he might polite-
ly imprison me last night. I enjoy good entertainment and the
conversation of clever men, but not at the price of a locked
door.'

'I don't know what you are talking about!' said the Squire,
livid with rage.

'Don't you, sir?' retorted the Captain. 'Well, I do, as I had to
risk breaking my neck when I climbed down the ivy from your
top window.'

'You had only to tell me of your eccentric habits,' said the
Squire, 'and I would have set a ladder against your window in
case the door stuck.'

'The door was locked, and well you know it, sir,' cried the
Captain, suddenly turning on the Squire. 'For half an hour after
I had climbed back through the window—to be exact, at half-
past four—I heard stealthy feet come along the passage and
unlock it; by which I know that for a period of the night you
wanted to make sure of me inside my room. When, on inquiring from your servants, I discover that I am the first guest who
has ever slept in that particular room, and that the furniture
was put into it for the occasion from one of the spare rooms, I
begin to see your wisdom, for that room contained no view of
the high-road, no view of the Marsh or sea.'

'Gad, sir, you are the first man who has dared to question
my hospitality. Perhaps you expected me to give up my room for
your accommodation!'

'Nothing of the kind!' answered the Captain; 'but I expected
to be dealt with straight. And this brings me to the end of my
complaints, and let me tell you this: I saw enough last night on
the Marsh to keep Jack Ketch busy for an hour or so.
Gentlemen, I am warning you. You'll not be the first I've sent
from the coast to the sessions, nor will you be the last. I warn
you, one and all, that I'm going to strike soon. I'm not afraid of
your tales of Marsh devils and demon riders. 'I'll rout 'em out
and see how they look by daylight. I've men behind me that I can
trust, and they're pretty handy fighters. If your demon riders
are not of this world, then they'll do our good steel no harm; but

if they are just men playing hanky-panky tricks to frighten fools from the Marsh, well, all I've got to say to them is, if they relish British cutlasses in their bowels—well, let them continue with such pranks as they played upon poor Pepper, and they'll get Pepper back and be damned to them, for it's Jack Ketch or the cold steel, and nothing else.' Having thus hurled his challenge at the assembly, the Captain put his pipe upon the table and sat down.

You can imagine that a speech of so staggering a nature had a strange effect upon the company. So sudden was it, so ferocious, so uncalled for, that nearly a minute elapsed before any one moved. At last the Squire rose, speaking quietly, but in that clear voice that everybody in Dymchurch knew so well and respected.

'Gentlemen, Doctor Syn spoke very wisely, as it is ever his wont to do, when he rebuked us for wrangling, for, as he said, both time and place are ill fitting. This is the first time that I have been insulted during my long sojourn in Romney Marsh, and I am glad that it has been in the presence of my friends and tenants of Dymchurch, who know me well and will do me right in their own minds, never allowing themselves to be warped for an instant by the unjust remarks of a stranger, upon whom I have, to the best of my ability, bestowed hospitality and every mark of friendship. On the other hand, I must honestly affirm that Captain Howard Collyer has insulted me in a straightforward way. In his defence I must say that the Admiralty have chosen a bad man to do their spying for them; when I say "bad" I mean, of course, the *wrong* man. I know the Captain to be a brave and a good sailor. The splendid drubbing that he gave to the French man-o'-war *Golden Lion* in the mouth of the St. Lawrence River shows exactly the sort of character he carries; and if the Admiralty had left him in command of the *Resistance*, we should have been at war with the odious French long ago. I now give the Admiralty credit for being weather-wise seamen and diplomatists, and think them shrewd in depriving him of a command. Having now, as it were, given the devil his due, I say to him in the presence of you all that his words here this morn-

ing have been altogether preposterous. It is not in accordance
with either my private or public dignity that I should answer
the hinted accusation of this Captain. As I said before, I am
judge here, and whilst I hold the most honourable position of
"Leveller of Marsh Scotts," I decline to entertain any imputa-
tions; for should I ever consider myself to be in the position of
being reasonably accused of any crime, I should, for the honour
of my office and the welfare of Romney Marsh, promptly resign.
This I have no intention of doing, for it is clearly now my bound-
en duty to see my poor friend Sennacherib Pepper righted and
avenged; and for that duty I sweep aside Captain Collyer's statements as impertinent. You gentlemen in this Court House are all
good Marsh men, and one and all know me as well as I know
myself. When you consider me unfit to be your judge I will retire,
but not till then.'

A storm of applause greeted the Squire as he sat down, but it
was checked by Doctor Syn, who again reminded the assemblage of the event that had brought them to the Court House,
and begged them, out of respect for the dead gentleman in the
next room, to abstain from further acclamation.

13

The End of the Inquiry

The lawyers now asserted themselves, and for some three hours questioned and cross-questioned everybody. The Squire left things in their hands, seeming to take small interest in the proceedings; whilst the Captain, with his chin resting on his great hand, obviously took none at all. Doctor Syn, however was at great pains to follow through the whole business, making notes of anything he deemed important upon a scrap of paper.

But with all their cleverness the lawyers were greatly at sea, for they only ended up where they began—namely, that Sennacherib Pepper was dead, and by violent means; that a foreign sailor was missing, and that this same sailor had stolen at a short period before the murder a certain harpoon from the house of Doctor Syn; and that from the nature and size of the wound upon the body sudden death was most certainly caused by this same weapon. To this false, though obvious conclusion, Doctor Syn, to Jerk's intense surprise, unhesitatingly agreed. Jerk couldn't understand this at all. Why had he been called to the trial if the Vicar had not believed his story?—for he found on being summoned to the witness box that all he was required to state was, whether or not he had seen the mulatto enter the vicarage on the previous night, and leave it a few minutes later with the harpoon in question in his hand. Having sworn to this, he was on the point of taking matters into his own hands and exposing the schoolmaster, when he was peremptorily ordered to stand down. Returning to his place, he plainly noted the relief on the face of the schoolmaster. A warmer time of it had Mr. Mipps. There was something about Mipps that would always be called in question. If a great crime had been committed within a fifty-mile radius of Mipps, he would most assuredly have been detained upon suspicion. His quizzical appearance of injured innocence was quite enough to label him a likely culprit. On this occasion he acted upon the attorneys like a red rag to a bull.

'If I'm to be kept standing through this examination,' he remarked on his way to the witness box, 'I must beg of you to be more brisk and businesslike than you have shown yourselves already. Perhaps in your profession you are paid for wastin' your time, but in mine you ain't, so please remember it. As our worthy Vicar knows, I has a lot of work to get through, so the sooner you get on with this here dismal business the better temper you'll keep me in; see?'

'You keep your mouth shut, my man, till you're questioned,' sang out one of the attorneys sharply.

'I'll keep my mouth shut for nobody but Squire and Doctor Syn,' retorted the sexton. 'And in your future remarks don't "my man" me, please. I ain't your man, and it's mighty pleased I am I ain't.'

When ordered to give an account of what had happened on the previous night, he obstinately refused to open his mouth until they had removed to the other side of the room the two sailors who were guarding the witness box. 'For,' said he, 'I can't abide the look or the smell of 'em; they fair turns me up.

This caused much laughter among the villagers; and, indeed, the little sexton was so ready with his scathing remarks at the expense of the lawyers, that in order to preserve their dignity they were obliged to give him up.

'Have I now your permission to go back to my measuring?' said Mipps, producing his footrule; 'or will any more advice from me be required?'

The lawyers tartly observed that he had been little or no use, and turned to the next witness.

After the schoolmaster had been called upon to bear out certain points of evidence, the three hours' useless palaver came to a conclusion, the attorneys agreeing with Doctor Syn that

Sennacherib Pepper had been murdered by the mulatto, and that as soon as he was taken he would get swift trial and short shrift. Meantime 'any one found sheltering, feeding, or in any way abetting the said mulatto would be prosecuted.'

As it was now approaching dinner-time, further matters were left over until such time as the mulatto should be caught.

This, Dr. Syn vehemently urged, was of grave import to the Marsh folk; for so long as that maniac starved upon the Marsh with a good weapon in his hand, they were open to the same fate as that which had befallen the inoffensive Pepper.

The Captain rose first, left the Court House, and set off for the Ship Inn without a word to the Squire; the latter, accompanied by the attorneys and medical men, repairing to the dining hall below. Doctor Syn, however, went from group to group, impressing the necessity for 'posses' of men to scour the Marsh for the missing seaman.

This gave Mr. Rash an opportunity of approaching Jerk, who, being due to dine at the vicarage, was awaiting the parson's pleasure.

'Well, and what do you think of Court House inquiries, Mister Jerk?' he said affably. 'Impressive, ain't they?'

'Not to me,' replied Jerry. 'I don't think nothing at all of 'em. After all the messing of them lawyers, I shouldn't be surprised if they hadn't got hold of the wrong end of the stick; should you?'

'What do you mean—the wrong end?'

'What I say. The wrong end ain't the right 'un, I believes.'

'Then you don't think the mulatto committed the murder?'

'From what that there sea-captain said, I should say you than got no right to put thoughts into my head any more than words into my mouth.'

'Come Jerk,' said the schoolmaster suavely, 'no offence.'

'Never said there was,' replied Jerry.

'Then come and have a bite with me at my house, as there's no school to-day. I should be honoured—indeed I should.' And the schoolmaster beamed upon him.

'Would you, though! I wonders,' mused the boy. 'Sorry to disappoint you,' he added airily, 'but I'm a-dinin' at the vicarage.'

'Oh, with the Vicar?'

'No, with the Shah of Persia.' Then, in a tone of supreme condescension, he added, 'I believes vicars lives in vicarages!'

'Ah! so-so! quite right,' returned the schoolmaster. 'Doctor Syn, then, has asked you to dine?'

'Well, I don't see anything so very remarkable in that; do you?'

'Oh, not at all; all very right, proper, and pleasant.'

'Well, it's *right* enough, you can lay to that, 'cos I tells you it is; and as to its being *proper*, well I don't see as how it's *improper*, so I suppose it is; and as to its being *pleasant*, And if you'll excuse me I'll be off now, 'cos I believe Doctor Syn is waiting for me.'

Indeed, at that moment Doctor Syn approached, and, putting his hand affectionately on Jerk's shoulder, with a friendly nod to the schoolmaster, he led the hoy from the room of inquiry, out of the Court House and so to the vicarage, where a cold meal was already prepared.

14

At the Vicarage

Now, although it was comparatively early in the afternoon, Doctor Syn did a rather curious thing—or so it seemed to Jerry: he had the wooden shutters of the dining-room fastened, and they dined by the light of candles. This had quite an uncanny effect—to dine by candles in broad daylight; but Jerk thought perhaps this was always done when gentry entertained company.

Doctor Syn was gloomy through the meal, and although he kept pressing Jerry to 'take more' and to 'help himself,' he made no effort at keeping up conversation; in fact, had not the food been good and plenteous, Jerry very much doubted whether he would have enjoyed himself at all, for Doctor Syn's manner was peculiar. He seemed strained and excited, and not once or twice but many times during the repast he would get up and stride about the room, and once he broke out into the old sea song that Jerry had so often heard at the Ship Inn

> 'Here's to the feet wot have walked the plank—
>   Yo-ho! for the dead man's throttle;
> And here's to the corpses afloat in the tank,
>   And the dead man's teeth in the bottle!'

Now to make Conversation, Jerry was bold enough to interrupt this song by inquiring what exactly was meant by the 'dead man's throttle.' Doctor Syn stopped in his walk and looked at him. Filling two tots of rum, one of which he handed to Jerk, he tossed off the other himself and said:

'Ah, you may well ask that, sonny. I don't know exactly myself, but I suppose if poor Pepper was to come in here now and throttle us, man and boy—him being stone dead, as we both well know—well, we should be having the "dead man's throttle" served on us.'

'Oh, I see,' replied Jerk with interest. 'Then I take it that the rest of the song has some sort of meaning too? What's the "tank" that the corpses float round in, sir?'

'The sea,' replied the Doctor, 'the sea; that's the great tank, my lad, and that there are corpses enough floating round in it I don't think you and I could doubt.'

'That's plain and true,' said Jerk; 'but I don't see no sense about the "dead man's teeth in the bottle." '

'That's plain too,' cried the Doctor, taking a stiff swig from the black bottle itself. 'It was in England's day that I wrote that. He cut a nigger's head off with a cutlass because the rascal was drinking his best rum on the sly, and the shock as he died made the black brute bite through the glass neck of the bottle.'

'Did you see it, sir?' asked Jerk, carried away by the tale.

'Who said I saw it?' demanded the parson sharply.

'Well, you said you wrote the song, sir, and at the time it happened.'

'Nothing of the kind—I said nothing of the kind. The song's an old one—an ancient thing. God knows what rascal invented it; but you can depend upon it a rascal he was. I don't know why I should hum it; I don't know what it means—can't make head or tail of the jargon.'

'You explains it very sensible, I thinks,' replied Jerry.

'I don't—I don't. I give you my word it's Greek to me.'

'But Greek's easy to parsons, ain't it?'

'Yes, yes—well, Chinese, Fiji—what you will, what you will. Have some rum?'

The Doctor's manner was really very strange indeed. Add to this the shuttered room, the candle light, and the strong spirit in his head, and it was small wonder that Jerry felt none too comfortable, especially as at the conclusion of the meal the door opened and Mr. Rash entered the room.

'Well, my lad,' said the Vicar, 'now you know where I feed, drop in again. Parochial matters to attend to with the school-master. Must choose the hymns, you know, for Sunday, or the choir will have nothing to sing.' And with this he led the boy out into the hall. He then dropped his voice to a whisper. 'You were wrong about the schoolmaster last night, sonny. I'll explain things to you some day. Meanwhile here's a crown piece. You're a smart lad, ain't you? Well, keep a weather eye open for that mulatto rascal; there's more in this ugly business than we imag-ine. I'll tell you all about it when I know more myself. But you made a mistake last night, and I begin to see how you made it; but I can't tell you just yet, because I'm not quite sure of my ground. It's dangerous ground we're treading, Jerry, you and I. Now here's another crown. That's one for keeping your eye open; do you know what the other's for?'

'What?'

'Keeping your mouth shut. Don't you remember anything about last night till I tell you; you wouldn't understand if I were to explain. You're very young, you know, Jerry lad, but smart's the word that describes you. You're smart and bright—as bright as the buttons on that sea-captain's coat, as bright as a thousand new guinea bits just served from the Mint; that's what you are, and no mistake!'

'I hope so,' replied Jerk, stepping out. 'I thinks I am.'

'God bless you!' said the Doctor, shutting the door and return-ing to Rash, who was waiting in the shuttered room by the light of the guttering candles.

15

A Landed Proprietor
Sets Up a Gallows Tree

Back to the 'Ship' and to duty went Hangman Jerk, with much to think over in his bullet head, and much to digest in his tight little stomach. To make head or tail of the Doctor's remarkable manner was beyond him, so he dismissed it from his mind, and instead fell to contemplating the two silver crowns: one, payment for keeping his weather eye open—easily earned; the other, the schoolmaster's safety—directly against his highest hopes. Yes, a crown was poor payment for that, especially as it was now possible for him to be the direct means of hanging his enemy.

Approaching the bar door, he paused, for he heard voices within—voices that he knew released him from work—the voices of Mrs. Waggetts and the pride of her life, the sexton Mipps.

Jerk knew exactly how the land lay with Mrs. Waggetts, and he was always wondering whenever (and if ever) she would succeed in folding that queer little man within the safe bonds of matrimony. Now, whatever Jerk's failings may have been, he was loyal to his friends; and Mrs. Waggetts was not only his friend, but his employer, and had done him many good turns. For one thing, she had given him a money-box in which to save a portion of his weekly wage. That doesn't sound a great deal on the surface, it is true; but her kindness had not ended there, as you shall see. Jerk's teeth were not sweet, like those of most boys of his age. He never bought sweetmeats—barley sugar and such child's trash. No; when he wanted a pick-me-up it was a grown man's pick-me-up that he liked—a pannikin of rum, a whiff of tobacco, and a long shot at the china spittoon that stood in the front of the bar. These indulgences had no effect on his purse, for the cravings of the first two were easily satisfied from the bar store when nobody was. looking, and the third he was at liberty to practise whenever he felt so disposed. And thus it was that, although but approaching thirteen years of age, he had, through the good offices of the landlady, and a systematic use of her money-box, already become a landed proprietor. When the landlady heard that Jerk wanted to spend his savings on such a very strange thing as land, she had exclaimed in some surprise:

'Lord bless the boy! Land! What can a boy of that age want with a plot of land?'

'The money's good enough, ain't it, ma'am? Very well, then, I want land—a nice little bit of snug mud-bank, where I can hide and learn about the Marsh. If I've a bit of mud wot's all mine on Romney Marsh, well, I'll he a Marsh man, and it's a Marsh man proper I wants to be.'

So Mrs. Waggetts consented, and bought a plot for him, situated about a mile and a half from the village, and a rough half-mile from the sea. As land it was of no use in the commercial sense; in fact the farmer had thought the landlady clean crazed to buy it, though the price was small enough, as prices go on the Marsh. It was more mud than land, surrounded by two broad dykes that slowly oozed round to meet in a sluice channel. This was Jerk's estate—measuring twelve yards by ten all told, and only solid in one spot near the centre, a patch of about ten square feet which formed a nobbly mound surrounded by great bulrushes. But the mound was not such a small affair, for it rose high enough to top the loftiest rush, and that is quite a noticeable height on the flat of Romney Marsh. This mound was given by its owner the dignified name of 'Lookout Mountain'—a name well deserved, for by sitting on the top of it upon the great stone which he had dragged from the sea-wall and carried a mile across the Marsh for the purpose, he could view from Dover cliffs to Dungeness, and in the other direction the long line of hills which bound the Marsh inland, with old Lympne Castle frowning from the top. Jerk wouldn't have changed his stronghold for any other, Lympne Castle included. It suited him admirably. From it he studied the Marsh and the creatures therein: the great brown water-rat that came out in the evening to hunt in the rushes; the swift-winged dragon-fly that could stand in mid-air stock still, as it seemed, to look at you; the myriad mosquitoes with their fantastic air dance, hunting in tribes along the sluggish water; the tadpole, who looped about in the water below; and more especially the flap of the night-prowling bat, who hung all day head downwards from a decayed old tree trunk that was rotting on the opposite bank to Jerk's estate. Now this same tree trunk had put ideas into young Jerk's head. It was obviously no good to anyone, and yet Jerk found himself regretting that it had not lived and died upon his land, for it was shaped uncommonly like a gallows tree, and if he could only erect a gallows upon the summit of Look-out Mountain, he would be more than ever living up to his reputable name of Hangman Jerk. He half thought at one time of digging it up and replanting it on his own property; but when he caught hold of the branch one day, and it had crumbled away in his hand, he considered that, although very nice and weird to behold, it wasn't much use as a genuine gibbet, and a genuine gibbet he then and there resolved to possess. Now the silver crowns of Doctor Syn would buy the most glorious scaffold, a regular professional affair, fixed snug and firm in the ground, and capable of supporting the weight of a culprit. Mipps was the first man to undertake the job, for he was a first-rate carpenter, and there was wood and to spare in the yard behind the coffin shop. Yes, if any man could supply him with a gibbet, Mipps could; and there he was talking in the bar ready to hand, and here were the silver crowns in Jerk's pocket. But to buy the gibbet and then to have to keep his mouth shut about the schoolmaster was no good. Mipps would never do the job for one crown, but for two Jerk thought he might. Well, he would see about that, and if he were unsuccessful he must find a way of raising the money; and then as soon as the apparatus was ready he would get Rash condemned, and offer the authorities the loan of a brand-new gibbet. Oh, to watch the murderer swinging from the top of Look-out Mountain right away on the lonely, wind-swept Marsh! That, indeed, was a glorious thought. Yes, he must come to terms with the undertaker at once; an undertaker now with a vengeance—Rash's undertaker. But the little gentleman in question was talking to Mrs. Waggetts, so Jerry had to wait in honour bound, for he was staunch to his benefactress and would not have interrupted for the world. The conversation going forward in the bar was carried on in earnest tones but low. Jerk began to think that Mrs. Waggetts was at last drawing the sexton into a proposal of marriage, and his interest in this one-sided love affair made him crouch by the bar door in hopes of gathering up some scraps of the honeyed words. But the few disjointed phrases he did catch were more akin to anger than to love.

'Alsace! One bottle gone! Damn that Captain's soul!'

Yes, there was passion but no love. 'We know how to use the mist; they don't.'

'It's safe enough; lots of it to-night——'

No, there was no vestige of love in that. And presently the conversation was terminated with the most uncomplimentary remark from the sexton.

'You can lay your old top-knot, and throw in your face, that there'll be a good haul out to-night and a good haul in here.' Saying which, with a knowing slap at his pocket, he came hurriedly out of the bar door and fell all asprawl over the crouching body of young Jerks.

'Why, in the name of all wot rots, couldn't you tell me where you was?' cursed the sexton.

''Cos I prefers to tell you what I wants,' replied Jerk.

'A thrashin'?'

'A gallows!'

'Ay, that you do, if any one did.'

'Will you make it for me, then?' said the boy.

'What do you mean?'

'What I says. Will you make me one?'

'At a price.'

'And that is?'

'Depends on the size. Wot do you want a gallows for now?'

'That don't concern you,' returned Jerk. 'You'll have all you can do making it, without askin' questions.'

'And you'll have all you can do when 'tis made a-preventin' me a-stringin' you up on it, if I has any more o' your impertinence.'

But Jerry was in no way put out, and replied, 'If you don't want to build my gallows, say so, and I'll soon find some other cove wot does. Come, wot's your price?'

'And wot's your game?'

'My business, not yourn,' said the boy. 'But you'll find as how yourn won't improve by annoyin' your employers.'

'employers? And who might they be now?' said the sexton.

'Well, I'm a-trying to be one,' said Jerk, jingling the coins about in his pockets, to lend weight to his words. 'What price for a gallows, eh?'

The jingle of coins also made the sexton think. 'Wot size?' said he.

'Big enough and strong enough to hang a man on, of course, and allowin' for a good foot or two of timber in the earth.'

The sexton scratched his head. 'Well, I'm cursed,' said he.

'That's naught to me,' replied Jerry. 'Come on. Your price?'

'Well, say two crowns for makin' and one for fixin'.'

'One for makin' and one for fixin'.' said Jerk, holding them out.

'No,' said the sexton, eyeing the coins.

'Then hang the fixin',' cried the boy, 'for I'll fix it myself. So it's one for makin and the wood, ain't it, Mister Sexton?'

'No; it's two for makin', and I lose on that.' Very well,' agreed Jerk, desperately handing over the money; 'and please, Mister Sexton, make it now, 'cos I wants it quick.'

So the bargain was struck there and then, and off they both set to the coffin shop to carry it out. The gallows was made by nightfall, and set up upon Jerk's property, the sexton carrying it there himself, digging the hole, and fixing it up; a regular professional affair with a jangly rusty chain aswing through the hook, and all this for the nominal price of two silver crowns, only one of which belonged to the purchaser.

'Ah!' cried Jerk, as they viewed the completed erection from the other side of the dyke; 'ain't it fustrate?'

'Slap up,' agreed the sexton.'

'Quite strong, ain't it?' inquired the owner anxiously.

To which the sexton replied imperiously:

'It were Mipps as knocked it up, as you see'd yourself; and when Mipps knocks up, you can lay it's solid wot's knocked.' And he turned and strode off towards the village, followed by Jerk.

When they had gone about half a mile Jerk looked back and called to the sexton to do the same. Darkness was already creeping over the Marsh, but sharp and black against the skyline—no toy, but real, weird, and convincing—-stood Jerk's gibbet.

'What do you think of Look-out Mountain now?' sung out the boy.

'That you can better the name of it Hangman Jerk. Why not call it Gallows Tree Hill?'

'Why, so I will!' cried the singular youngster. 'It's a good name, and so I will; and let's hope as how the tree'll bear fruit?'

'As how it won't," muttered the sexton.

'But it will, you can lay to that.' For he could already picture the schoolmaster hanging there.

As they neared the village, with sudden fear Jerk said to the sexton, 'I suppose the smugglers won't take my gibbet as a personal offence and knock it down?'

But the wary Mipps disarmed his fears with, 'There ain't no smugglers, for one thing; 'sides if there was, how could they knock down wot's knocked up so solid?'

'Well, dig it up, perhaps,' suggested Jerk; ' 'cos, Mister Sexton, it do catch the eye somewot, don't it? Look, you can see it even from here, and it don't look exactly pleasant, do it?'

'Pleasant ain't the word, I agrees, but you needn't worry your-self on that score. If them damned King's men had put it up now, I don't say as how it mightn't get mobbed and knocked about a bit, 'cos them King's men ain't wot you might term pop-ular favourites in the village; but as it weren't, don't you worry, for I'll soon pass the word, young Jerry, as how it's you wot owns it.'

'Thank you,' said Jerry. 'They wouldn't knock it over if you asked 'em not to, I'll be bound.'

'Asked who not to?' demanded the sexton quickly. 'Why, any of 'em,' replied Jerk innocently. 'Marshmen, smugglers, Jack-o'-lanterns, demon riders, wot you will; for I'll lay they're all a-scared of Sexton Mipps, ain't they?'

But Sexton Mipps was not to be caught by such dangerous flattery, and he replied, 'There ain't no such things as smugglers hereabouts, as I thinks I've already remarked; and as for demon riders—why, uncanny they be, and I holds no truck with 'em, thank the Lord. Folks wot- has dealin' with them has sold their souls for the bargain, and I ain't a-goin' to do that.'

'Bein' such a very good and respectable Christian? Oh, no!' said Jerk, winking.

'Why, certainly,' answered the sexton. 'And might I ask wot you're a-winkin' about?'

'Nothing. I was only thinkin'.'

'Wot about?'

'A dream—a nightmare I had last night, that's all.'

'Wot about?' asked the sexton again.

'Nothing particular,' returned the boy casually.

They had now reached the coffin shop, so thanking the sex-ton for his assistance, Jerk bade him good night.

'Where are you bound for now?' Mr. Mipps called after him.

'The vicarage.'

'Wot for?'

'To tell the Vicar as how I've borrowed a crown off of him, that's all.'

'Wot's that?' cried the sexton, making as if to follow; but the boy waved him back with a fierce gesture.

' 'Tain't nothin' to do with you. You're paid, ain't you? And it didn't get stole from the poorbox either, so don't you start a-worritin'.'

And thrusting his hands deep into his breeches pocket, Jerk set off for the vicarage to tell Doctor Syn that, although he couldn't accept the silver crown for holding his tongue, he had taken the liberty of borrowing it from him.

And in this way was the gibbet set up on Look-out Mountain, and the name changed to Gallows Tree Hill.

16

The Schoolmaster's Suit

It was now dark, as Jerk passed through the cluster of quaint little houses that make up the one street of Dymchurch-under-the-wall, and so on to the vicarage. Just at the corner where the Court House stands amidst the great trees he heard singing, and recognized the voice and figure of Imogene. She was carrying a basket from the direction of the 'Ship,' and was probably bound, like himself, for the vicarage. As she passed the Court House she paused, and, to Jerk's astonishment, felt amongst the ivy that grew around the old front door. There, in a certain branch, was a piece of paper, which she took from its hiding-place as if she expected to find it. The message it contained she read by the light of the lantern that hung above the door, and then, thrusting it into the bosom of her rough dress, she went on towards the vicarage gate. But out from the shadows of the trees stepped a man, whom Jerk perceived to be the schoolmaster. Imogene hesitated when she saw him, for he was standing directly in her path; but when she tried to rush past, Rash stopped her and spoke.

'So, mistress, now that you have got your lover's written promise from the ivy there, you think you can afford to pass by such a humble one as the schoolmaster. But you're mistaken, and I'll trouble you to show me that letter.'

The girl's hand went involuntarily to her bosom, where the note was securely tucked away, and she answered back clear and straight, 'No, Mr. Rash, you've no right.'

'Right is might, mistress, as you'll find, and I think we shall be able to come to terms now. I want you to come along with me to the vicarage. Doctor Syn is there, and I've something to say before you both.'

'Let us go, then,' said Imogene, trying to pass.

'All in good time,' returned the schoolmaster, stopping her. 'There's no immediate hurry, I think, for the Doctor won't come out of that shuttered room of his till morning, so we can afford to keep him waiting, and I've something to say to you first—alone.'

The girl tossed her head impatiently, as if she knew what was coming, but Rash continued.

'A few weeks back I asked you to marry me I, the esteemed schoolmaster, asked you, the daughter of a criminal. You, whose father was a proved murderer, a dirty pirate, hanged publicly at Rye for a filthy tavern crime. You, who were born in a Raratonga drinking-hell, some half-caste native girl's brat—Ecod, it's laughable! I offered to make you respectable and put your banns up in the church, and you refused. Now I know why. You think because that young fool Cobtree is pleased to admire you, that you will catch him in your toils, do you? You're a clever one, ain't you? I dare swear that, sooner or later, you'd succeed in getting hold of him. Let the young idiot ruin you, eh? Then make a virtuous song about it to the Squire, and a settlement to keep your mouth shut, perhaps.'

'Beast!' cried the girl, and she struck him sideways across the mouth with her clenched hand.

'Hello! thought Jerk, crouching in the bushes, 'here's another one having a go at him. Well, the more the merrier, so long as I'm the last.'

The schoolmaster recoiled, trying to look as if the stinging blow had not hurt; but the blood was flowing from his lip, and from the hand of the girl as well.

'So that's it, is it?' he sniggered. 'A real love-match, perhaps? The Squire's consent, the wedding hells, and live happily ever after, eh? Ecod, my lady, I think not. Rash is your man, see ?—and lucky you are to get him; you whose father's gibbet chains are still swinging in Rye.'

'And yours are swinging a bit nearer than that,' said Jerry Jerk to himself.

'You leave my father out of it,' went on the girl, 'for, from all I've heard of him, he was a better man than you, and he was fond of me, too; so it's lucky for you he's not here to hear you speaking bad of his child.'

'You know nothing about him; he was a drunken rascal.'

'Doctor Syn knew him well, and he's told me things. A rough man he was certain, and none rougher; reckless, too, and brave, a law-breaker on land as well as sea, pitiless to his enemies, staunch to his friends. But a cur he never was, and so, Mr. Rash, you can afford to respect him; and I say again that I wish he were here to make you'

'Shouldn't care if he was,' replied the schoolmaster, 'for there's always the law to look after a man.'

'So there is,' chuckled Jerk, 'and that you'll find.'

'Bah! what's the good of haggling and squabbling?' said Mr. Rash. 'You're mine, or you'll have to bear the consequence.'

'And that is?' asked the girl defiantly.

'The rope for your friends, when I turn "King's evidence."'

'You wouldn't dare, you coward, for you'd be hanging yourself as well.'

'King's evidence will cover me all square.'

'So you're determined to turn it, are you?'

'I am, unless you change your mind.'

The girl didn't reply to that, so Mr. Rash, thinking that he was making progress, continued, 'Think, Imogene. This Cobtree fellow will be packed off to London in a month or so, and from there on to Oxford; and after a college career of drinking, gambling, and loose living, with precious little learning, he'll settle down to the gentleman's life, marry some lady of quality, and you—eh? What of you then?'

'I earn my living now, don't I?' replied the girl. 'Well, what's to prevent me going on the same?'

'Don't you want to marry?' went on the schoolmaster's suit. 'Don't you want a house of your own? Don't you want to be the envy of all the girls in the village?'

'Not at the price of my happiness; and, besides, I'm not so sure that I do want all those things so desperate. I'm afraid the wife of Mr. Rash would be too genteel a job for me.'

'Oh, I'd soon educate you up to that,' returned the schoolmaster graciously.

'It would be a great nuisance to both of us, wouldn't it?'

'I shouldn't mind—it would be a pleasant business making a respectable woman of you, Imogene. You see, you're not common like these village girls, and that's what attracts me. Otherwise it might have been better for me to have fixed my choice on one of them; one that hasn't a bad mark against her, so to speak. But I don't mind what folk say. I suppose they'll talk a bit and laugh behind my back. Well, let 'em, say I. I don't care, because I want you.'

'Then it's a pity that I'm not the same way of thinking.'

'What do you mean?'

'That I wouldn't marry you—no, not though you got the whole village the rope!'

'You ungrateful wretch! Not after all they've done for you!'

'You're not the sort of party to talk to others about being ungrateful, are you now?'

'I wasn't born of jail folk.'

'No; and you can hope your children, if you're ever cursed with any, will be able to say the same, for I doubt it very greatly, Mister Schoolmaster. And as to your threats—I set no store on them, for from my heart I despise you. I despise you because you are willing to betray your fellows; but I despise you more because I know you are too great a coward to do it.'

'We shall see,' cried the schoolmaster; 'for who's to stop me?'

'Parson Syn,' answered the girl. 'Parsons can keep all manner of secrets and not betray them. That's their business, and Doctor Syn's a good man, so I'll tell him everything.'

'That shows how little you know about things, Mistress Ignoramus; for it's that very same good man, Doctor Syn, who is going to read out your banns on this next Sabbath as ever is, and it's Rash who is going to make him; and if you won't come along with me to church—well, I'll threaten other parties in this

little place who'll help me to make you. Folk are none too anxious to be exposed these days, with King's men in the village, and
so you'll see——' The schoolmaster stopped talking suddenly.

17

The Doctor Sings a Song

Now, although Jerry had employed all his faculties for the over-hearing of this conversation, he had unconsciously listened to something else—a slight noise that now and again came from the direction of the vicarage, a small,. whirring noise, the kind of noise that he had heard in Mipp's coffin shop when a saw was working its way through a piece of wood: yes, a whirring noise, with an occasional squeak to it.

He hadn't bothered to ask himself what it was, he had just gone on hearing it. But now another noise arose in the night, that not only claimed his immediate attention, but made him feel cold all over. It had the same effect upon Mr. Rash, for he stopped talking suddenly, and gripped the post of the gate with one hand and with the other pulled Imogene roughly into the denser black of the bushes. Then the noise grew louder and louder; what at first could only be described as a gibbering moan, rose into shriek after shriek of mortal terror. It was a man's voice—a man scared out of all knowledge; and then over the gate leaped a dark form, agile and quick, that went bounding away through the ghostly churchyard. There was something familiar in that figure to Jerk. He had seen it almost from the same spot the night before. It was the man with the yellow face. The schoolmaster came out from the bushes, followed by Imogene. Quickly they went through the gate and towards the vicarage, and silently Jerk followed, with his heart thumping loud against his ribs; for although only the echoes of those drum-cracking shrieks vibrated in his ears, the gibbering moans still continued.

To the back of the house went the girl and the schoolmaster, and to the front went Jerk. It was all dark—indeed, no lights were showing from any of the rooms but one, and that was the Doctor's sitting-room, with the shutters still close fastened. But a jagged little hole in the corner of one of the shutters sent a shaft of yellow candle-light straight out into the blackness. Yes, the moaning, the gibbering moaning, was coming from the Doctor's room. Jerk crossed a bed of flowers and gravel path and applied his eye to the jagged hole in the shutter. This little hole accounted for the whirring and squeaking that he had just heard for it was newly cut, and Jerk put his hand upon several little pieces of split wood that had fallen upon the outer sill. It was plain, then, that the awful apparition he had just seen had been looking into the room. He had evidently made the hole for the purpose, and made it with that awful weapon he carried, that same harpoon over which there had been so much talk at the Court House inquiry. Now the shutter, being an outside shutter, backed right against the lead-rimmed glass casement, and thus it was that he had to wait for a few seconds before seeing plainly anything in the room, for the candle-light flickered and danced upon the glass.

The very second he had put his eye to the hole the moans within the room steadily rose, and Jerk's thumping heart increased its already unnatural pace, for he expected the loud shrieks to follow. But soon his eye got accustomed to the light, and one thing became visible—the form of Doctor Syn. He was sitting in a high-backed chair in the centre of the room, gripping the oaken arms with his long white fingers, and upon his face was a look of indescribable horror. His neck was stretched up alert and straight, his eyes dilated, glazed and terrible; his hair unkempt, and his thin legs pressed hard against the floor.

But his mouth was neither set nor rigid, like the rest of his members—his mouth was loose and hanging open, like the mouth of a madman; and from it was coming that inarticulate gibber, that gibbering moan that had arrested the hearing of Jerry Jerk. Straight at the shutter stared the demented Doctor; straight into Jerk's eye at the jagged hole. Suddenly his hand

shot out over the table. He picked up the great plated cande-
labra, and hurled it—lighted candles and all—full at the window.

Jerk started back at the rattle of glass, and at the same time
a heavy hand fell upon his shoulder, and another was passed
over his mouth, while a familiar voice whispered in his ear, 'For
God's sake, be quiet!' It was the Captain, and he stood holding
the boy tightly, keeping his eye on the jagged hole with something approaching terror upon his strong face. It was dark now,
of course, for there was no light in the house; but presently Jerk
and the Captain heard low, frightened voices, and a light suddenly showed through the hole. The Captain stooped and put his
eye to it. Yes, the door of the Doctor's sitting-room was opening,
and Imogene and the schoolmaster entered. Imogene came first,
with a lighted candle held high above her head.

The Doctor was now kneeling on the floor. He had a black
bottle in his hand; the same rum bottle from which he had treated Jerk that very day. He seemed to recognise Imogene, for he
smiled as she entered—smiled as he slowly raised the bottle, and
tilted the contents, neat and raw, down his throat. And then he
saw the schoolmaster. His upper lip twitched, curled, and rose,
disclosing his white upper teeth; his under lip stretched down
and showed his lower teeth—shining white teeth, that shone
and glistened underneath the bottle's neck. There was a snap,
and a quick, crunching sound. The Captain gasped for breath,
for Doctor Syn had bitten through the glass neck, and seized
the bottle by the broken end. Slowly he dragged one leg from its
kneeling position, and pushed it out before him, with the blood
still trickling from his cut lip; and motionless stood the wild
girl, Imogene, with the candle held above her head. Syn was
about to spring, Rash was waiting to be seized, and nothing
moved in the room but the slow oozing blood on the parson's
lip. Nothing else moved at all, except perhaps the light itself,
shed by the flickering candle, which cast shadows of the two
men upon the whitewashed wall. Then, with a hissing sound,
Syn leapt, swinging the bottle as he came, and brought it down
with a sickening crash at the white face before him. Over went

Rash, senseless, blinded with blood and the shivered glass. Then
Syn laughed, and sang at the top of his voice:

> 'Here's to the feet wot have walked the plank—
> Yo-ho for the dead man's throttle!
> And here's to the corpses afloat in the tank
> And the dead man's teeth in the bottle.'

And as he sang he danced, and stamped the senseless face
beneath his feet. Then he sang again, roaring new words to the
eternal old tune:

> 'A pound of gunshot tied to his feet,
> And a ragged bit of sail for a winding-sheet—
> Then out to the sharks with a horrible splash,
> And that's the end of Mister Rash.'

And with diabolical glee he leapt again with both feet upon his
victim's face.

All this time the girl stood still, like a statue, with the candle
high above her head; and the terrible parson went on with the
song:

> 'And all that isn't ripped by the sharks outside
> Stands up on its feet with the running tide.'

Taking the prostrate body, he lifted in on to its feet, and leered
into its face; then, letting it go, watched it fall and collapse into
a heap.

> 'And it kept a-bowing gently, and a-looking with surprise,
> At the little crabs a-scrambling from the sockets of its
> eyes.'

The Captain then shouted, shouted at the top of his voice,
and tore at the fast, firm shutter. The song ceased in the room.
The light once more went out of the jagged hole, and there was

the noise of a falling body. Probably the girl had fainted. The shutters were strong, and wouldn't give.

'The back door,' shrieked the terrified Jerry. 'The back door is open.' And round to the back rushed the Captain, followed by the boy. And as he ran he blew three shrill calls upon a silver whistle that he carried on a chain. The whistle was answered by another, and before the Captain had found and opened the back door, the Captain's bos'n had appeared from the bushes, followed by a strong party of the King's men. The bos'n made a light from his tinderbox, and as they were looking for a candle in the back kitchen, they could hear some one moving about in the sitting-room.

18

Behind the Shutters

'Thank God, somebody's brought a light, for I don't know what hasn't happened here. Ah, Captain, it's you, is it?' The speaker was Doctor Syn; he was calmly kneeling over the form of Mr. Rash. He had, in fact, propped his head upon his knee, and was dabbing the bleeding face with his clean handkerchief.

'Just get the brandy bottle out of that corner cupboard, will you, my man?' he said to the bos'n. 'The girl there has fainted. Nothing serious, just sheer fright.'

The bos'n did as he was ordered, and Imogene was quickly restored to consciousness.

The Captain, for the most part, stared at Syn and said nothing. Suddenly he passed his hand over his brow, and wiped away the great beads of perspiration that had gathered there; then, taking the brandy bottle from the bos'n's hand, he took a long pull, and with a sigh sat down in the arm-chair, still staring at Doctor Syn with unconcealed amazement.

'Feeling a bit squeamish, Captain?' said the latter, smiling. You're right; it's an ugly sight. More blood than necessary, though. Merely flesh cuts. Bruised a bit, too! Help yourself to brandy. Good-evening, Jerry; pleased to see you. Here's your poor schoolmaster got hurt. Feeling better, Captain? That's good. The sight of blood does turn one up. Was it Hannibal or Hamilcar who never could reconcile himself to the sight of it? I forget. Some great general it was, though. The girl here is the same. Better, Imogene? Surely it was Hannibal, wasn't it?'

'I am sure I don't know, or care,' thundered the Captain, standing up and turning desperately on the bos'n. 'Job Mallett, what in hell's name is all this business? I'm dazed.'

Doctor Syn went on speaking in his usual collected tones. 'It's all very horrible, I grant, but there's no mystery, I assure you. We were all three chatting here quite pleasantly, when in leaps that mulatto of yours, attacks my friend the schoolmaster, and all but kills him. I picked up a bottle and landed the brute a crack over the head. The bottle broke, and the madman turned on me, clapped a bit of broken glass in my mouth, which, I expect, is cut about a bit, and got away. I asked the girl to hold the light, and when she saw the schoolmaster's face, why, over she went, candle and all, into a dead faint. Never saw such a thing in my life. But I tell you this, Captain. It's your bounden duty to get hold of that maniac and string him up to the nearest tree, for there's not a man, woman, or child safe whilst he's at large.'

Then Doctor Syn helped them to move the still unconscious Rash into his own bedroom, leaving the bos'n and two seamen in charge, the rest of the sailors returning to the vicarage barn; and finally muffling himself in his great cloak, he proceeded to the inn to procure a room for the night. Supporting Imogene, he walked ahead, followed by the Captain, and Jerry Jerk bearing a lantern.

'Pot-boy?' said the Captain on the way.

'Sir,' said Jerry Jerk.

'Are we dreaming or what?'

'Blowed if I know; wish I did.'

On reaching the inn, they all agreed that it was none too safe to walk abroad that night again, for fear of the sinister mulatto out upon the Marsh; so they ordered the supper and the rooms to be got ready, and for an hour or so the Doctor chatted of indifferent things, just as if nothing had happened.

But the Captain kept silent that night. He had many things in his head that he couldn't understand, and the greatest of these was Doctor Syn, that pious old cleric, who was making himself so pleasant over a steaming bowl of punch; and as the parlour clock ticked on, and the room was filled with tobacco smoke, which the parson kept sending in thin rings across the fire-place, the Captain rubbed his eyes hard, fidgeted and shuffled in his chair, wondering when the dream would stop and he would find himself awake.

19

The Captain's Nightmare

Presently the Captain yawned, and Doctor Syn rose and summoned Mrs. Waggetts. He yawned again, and rubbed his eyes. Was he awake or dreaming? The last thing he remembered was drinking hot rum punch, and listening to a long story that he thought the Doctor would never finish. The punch seemed to have had a soothing effect on him, for after that he felt rather vague. He dreamt he was lifted up sleeping, lifted up by two men who had followed Mrs. Waggetts from the bar when Doctor Syn had called her. Was one of those men that insolent Sexton Mipps? He vaguely thought it was, though he couldn't be sure. No, he couldn't be sure of anything! He thought he had been carried up to bed, but that was too silly. Who would carry him up to bed? Was it Doctor Syn who had said to Mipps on the stairs that he wasn't going riding to-night for a thousand guineas, and that they must do without him for once? Then Mipps had answered:

'That yellow beast ain't a-lookin' out for Clegg's carpenter, is he? Well, I'll go. It don't want us both to-night.'

Then the dream got more confused than ever——There was a lonely reef in the coral seas, and on it was a weird figure calling. The Captain seemed to be on a ship that was standing away from the reef, and all the time the figure kept calling. There was a full ship's crew collected on the deck, who were threatening two men. One was a familiar figure, a figure he had not seen often out of his dreams; and so was his little companion; and still the voice kept calling. The crew pushed forward a spokesman; he was a Chinaman, they called him by a nickname—Pete. Pete sheepishly advanced, and stammered out to the familiar figure, whom he addressed as Captain, to put the ship about, and take up again the lonely form calling from the reef. Pete's argument was evidently useless, for as he turned to join his fellows, the tallest of the familiar figures stretched out his hand and caught the yellow man—he was clad in the scanty garb of a cook—and broke his naked back with a marline-spike that the little companion of the familiar figure had handed to him. Then the crew were commanded to throw the body overboard, or they would be served the same. They did this, and the sharks surrounded the ship, snapping their teeth. Then the breeze seemed to blow off the reef, and the familiar figure ordered the men aloft to unfurl the sails; they obeyed sullenly; and still the voice, getting fainter and fainter, yet called from the reef. The breeze increased, and the Captain and his mate ordered the men the quicker aloft.

'Get up aloft there, you dogs! Get up—get up—get up—' The familiar figure then caught sight of the dreamer,' (though he wasn't sure if he was still dreaming) and, striding up to him, ordered him aloft; and when he refused, he dragged him up by the arm. The dreamer felt dizzy, for the sails were blowing in his face, and he thought he must let go; and he begged the familiar figure to let him go down; but the voice went on crying, 'Up—get up—get up!'

Then the sail was pulled from his face, the wind blew through his hair, and he started up, catching hold of a stay (which turned out to be the bedpost), and letting the sail fall below the deck. In reality it was the bed-clothes slipping to the floor. Still the voice cried, 'Get up, get up.' He then recognized the familiar face and form of Doctor Syn, and beside him his companion, Sexton Mipps.

'Get up, get up,' the parson was crying. 'What a fellow to sleep you are! Like waking the dead, upon my soul, it is, Mr. Mipps.'

The Captain rubbed his eyes again.

The sun was streaming through the window, which was open, and a good stiff breeze was blowing in from the sea.

'What the devil—' said the Captain. 'Oh, it's Doctor Syn, is it? What's the time?'

'Just on ten o'clock,' said the cleric.

'Ten o' what?' bellowed the Captain, leaping out of bed,

'Clock,' repeated Mr. Mipps.

'I've overslept. Thing I've never done in my life. Been dreaming, too. Nightmares—horrible! But what do you want? Is anything the matter?'

'I think there is,' said the Doctor quietly.

'And so do I,' said Mr. Mipps.

'What! What's wrong—what's happened?'

'I don't quite know yet, but I don't like the look of it.'

'The look of what?' shouted the Captain.

'The vicarage,' replied the Vicar. 'Put on your clothes quickly, Captain, and come and see. I think there's something wrong.'

20

A Terrible Investigation

The Captain was not long in tumbling into his clothes. Meanwhile the sexton sat upon the bed, which neither of the other two seemed to think extraordinary. The Captain now and then addressed a sharp question to the Doctor; but the Doctor did not answer, nor, indeed, did the Captain seem to expect an answer. The Doctor was standing by the window, his grey hair blowing in the stiff sea-breeze that filled the room. Suddenly they heard a little shaking noise upon the bed, and, turning, perceived the little sexton with the tears rolling down his cheeks, given up to the most ungovernable laughter; and yet it was not laughter, for the sexton made no noise. He just let his body quiver and heave, and the tears roll on over his thin cheeks. It was a strange kind of laughter.

'What the thunder's amusing you?' roared the Captain; and he hurled the bolster at the sexton's head.

Mipps was himself again upon the instant.

'Blest if I knows,' he gasped; 'but thank you kindly for that bolster whack, for if something hadn't happened, I believe I should have bust.'

'But what is it? There must have been something to make you laugh like that.'

'If there was, I'm blest if I knows wot,' returned the sexton, 'for I gives you my word that I never felt solemner than I does now—no, not never in my life.'

Then the Captain was dressed, and they all three set out for the vicarage.

'Well, now, what is wrong with it?' said the Captain, surveying the little house that looked so pretty in the morning sun.

'That's just what we want to know,' answered Doctor Syn. 'In
the first place, short of forcing the door, I don't see how we're
going to get in. The place is all locked up, and though we have
battered and hammered on the doors and windows for a good
hour, we can get no answer from the sailors inside.'

'And my men in the barn, where are they?' said the Captain,
looking across at the building in question.

I'm afraid, Captain, that you are too liberal to your men, for
their rum barrel is empty, and the whole crew are still asleep.'

The Captain swore, and walked to the back door. He raised
his foot, and with one kick sent the door in, splintered and
cracked from the bolt sockets.

'Neatly done,' remarked Doctor Syn, 'though who's to pay for
a new door?'

But the Captain did not heed him, or care a brass farthing
for the door. He was bent on investigating the house. Mipps
and the Doctor, and Jerry Jerk, who had appeared from somewhere followed him.

The kitchen was empty, so the Captain opened the door of the
sitting-room, which was very dark because of the closed shutters.

He strode across to the broken window, threw it wide open,
and unbolted the shutters, which, swinging back, let in the light
of day. In the corner of the room opposite the window lay the
two sailors who had been left to watch with the bos'n. Both
were bound and gagged, and one of them was moving. The
Captain loosed his bonds with a clasp knife, and the fellow
seemed to recover his senses.

'What does this mean, my man?' said the Captain.

The sailor turned and pointed to the body of his friend. It lay
half propped up against the wall, and above it was a large splintered tear in the white plaster. There were blood marks, too, on
the wall. The Captain saw and understood, for the neck of the
propped-up body had been cruelly pierced, although there was
no sign of a weapon. Some missile had transfixed it to the wall,

and then been plucked out, so that the body had collapsed amidst a mess of broken plaster.

'It's Bill Spiker, sir,' said the sailor. 'He's dead! He was a good gunner, sir. We wanted Spiker, sir, to fight the French—and he's dead,' and the sailor fell to blubbering.

Just then they all became aware of a moaning overhead.

'What's that?' said Mipps, beginning to giggle.

Indeed, the uncanny atmosphere of the vicarage that morning had upset them all.

'I'm sure I don't know,' said the Captain, 'for I've had my fill of horrors. I don't mind blood and I don't mind fighting, but these mysteries are horrible. What the devil is that moaning?'

'That'll be Job Mallett, Captain's bos'n,' said the sailor.

'Or Rash, the sick schoolmaster,' said Doctor Syn.

But Mipps said nothing; he had left the room and was now in the passage, giggling.

'Damn that sexton's body and soul!' ejaculated the Captain. 'His giggling gives one the creeps. What's tickling him now?'

'Unstrung,' muttered the Vicar, as he followed the Captain up the dark stairs to the bedroom.

There in the bed, last night occupied by Mr. Rash, lay the fat bos'n on his back, with his face gagged up and covered with a nightcap. He was making dreadful moans.

The Captain pulled the bedclothes off, and discovered that the faithful fellow was tied to the bed. Grateful he looked, though troubled, when the Captain cut his bonds and pulled him up; and he owned in a shamefaced manner that he never had endured such a horrible night in his life, and that Parson Syn (saving his presence) must be the foul fiend himself to be able to sleep in such a devil-haunted house.

Doctor Syn went downstairs, fetched the brandy bottle, and administered a good dose to the bos'n, and also to the other seaman who had followed them upstairs.

'And where's the schoolmaster got to?' said the Captain.

'He's gone.'

'Gone!' they all repeated together.

'Ay, sir, gone! And if ever a man has gone body and soul, I declares he has; for I solemnly and soberly declares that I see'd him hoisted up and removed downstairs by a couple of horrible light-faces.'

'Light-faces?' roared the Captain.

Yes, sir, coves with faces all a-shine. Why, I wouldn't settle down and live within a hundred miles of Romney Marsh for a thousand guineas a year pension, I wouldn't. For, talk about devils—the place stinks of them.'

'Now, look here, my man,' said the Captain, 'just pull yourself in a brace or two, and tell me what happened.'

'Why, so I will,' said the bos'n, 'for queer, most queer it be.'

21

The Bos'n's Story

'Nothing happened, sir, for some hour or so after you left, and then things made up for lost time, as it were, and came fast and quick. I was sitting outside this here room, with the door on the jar; outside I was, because I couldn't bear the sight of that schoolmaster's face. I think you'll own yourself, sir, that it wasn't just exactly wot you might call a pleasant evening face, especially a-battered about as it was. Poor Bill Spiker and Morgan Walters here was asleep downstairs, for we'd agreed that I should stand first watch.

'Well, the boys had brought us over our allowance of rum from the barn, and we'd all had a drop, though I kept most of mine to the end of my watch, thinking to use it for a night-cap, as 'twere. But the little drop I did get was making me feel very drowsy, and I began to think the next hour would never come, when I could wake up Bill Spiker. Presently I hears a noise of galloping horses. I goes to the window on the stairs there, and looks out. Right along the road I could see those same riders with lit-up faces wot I'd see'd the night before last. I know it was them, 'cause I could see their faces, you understand—when quite sudden I was seized from behind, and pulled over backwards down the stairs. I fought the best I could; but there was a sort of overpowering 'kerchief pulled over my mouth, and I was lifted up on four men's shoulders. I couldn't see anything of their faces, but as I went up the stairway on their shoulders, I just remember a-seein' that schoolmaster a-comin' down in the same fashion as I was a-goin' up, only that he only required two to hold him. Now, whether this was because I was heavier, I don't know,

or whether 'cos he was only a-comin' down while I was a-goin'
up, or whether the things wot had got hold of me was real or
sham as it were, but certain am I, the two things wot had the
schoolmaster (and things I must call 'em though they was a bit
like men) had got the same shiny faces all alight, just like them
demon riders had. Then I don't remember nothing else, till I
was woke up by hearin' a sort of horrible shriek downstairs
which I thought was just a dream, but now suppose was poor
Bill a-voicin' his last opinion in this world. After that I went to
sleep again, till I was waked up again by a sort of groanin',
which I finds was myself, and then in comes you after a long
time and lets me go, as it were. And that's all I knows, so help
me God, sir; but quite enough for one night, as I thinks you'll
agree.'

Morgan Walters then gave his version of what happened in
the night, which bore out certain points of the bos'n's story.

He had soon fallen into a deep sleep, but was awakened with
a feeling that something was wrong. He tried to move, but
couldn't; indeed, he could scarcely breathe. The only things he
could see were two dark forms moving about the room, with
their faces lit up by a curious light. These two things passed out
of the room, and then, for what seemed an interminable time,
Morgan Walters worked away at his bonds, and presently
became aware that his companion was doing likewise. They
couldn't talk for the bandages over their mouths. Presently
Morgan Walters thought that he could hear the sound of horses. It sounded like a regiment of pack ponies trotting on the
high-road. ' "Tlip tlop" they went,' he said; 'a slow "tlip tlop,"
and a lot of them too.' Then he heard a sigh of satisfaction from
his companion, and saw him stand up, for he had partially
unbound himself. Whether to let in the refreshing sea air, or
whether he had also heard the horses and wanted to locate them,
Morgan Walters couldn't say, but Bill Spiker had got to the broken window and unbolted the shutters. He felt the cold air come
into the room with a great gasp, and then he seemed to have
dozed off again; but the next thing he heard was a great scream
of agony, and turning over he beheld Bill Spiker embracing the

wall. The wall held him up, for there was a weapon transfixed
to it through his neck. The very horror gave Morgan Walters a
wild strength, and he somehow stood upon his feet. Then came
a curious thing. He saw between himself and the form of his
fellow, a man—a yellow-faced man—the mulatto seaman. With
one hand the creature plucked the weapon from the wall, and
drew it back through the bleeding neck that held it. This was
strangely vivid to Morgan Walters, and he could recall his
thought of wonder that the blood in no way stained the yellow
hand that drew the steel from the flesh. The body of Bill Spiker
fell from the wall and collapsed in a heap; and a hand seemed to
strike Morgan Walters at the same time, for he lost consciousness again and remembered no more

'Did the mulatto touch you?' said the Captain, speaking suddenly and rather loud, so that all in the room gave a perceptible
start. 'Think well, my man.'

'I am quite certain of that, sir; I know he did not.'

'And yet you were knocked down!'

'So it seems, sir, but it may have been just losing my senses
again. I've never fainted before, so perhaps it was that, or the
effects of the suffocatin' 'kerchief.'

'And you remember nothing else?'

'One thing, though whether I dreamt that or not I couldn't
swear to. It seemed that, when I came to something like myself,
the dawn was breaking, for the room was filled with a grey
light. Suddenly something came into the room and closed those
shutters. Then I fell off into another sort of sleep, and dreamt
that people were trying to wake me up by banging on the shutters; and then at last, hours after, you came, sir, and freed me.'

'One moment,' said the Captain; 'this something that closed
the shutters—a man?'

'Yes, like a man.'

'Like what man?'

'Well, sir, it was like one of them devils that I'd seen leaving
the room. It also reminded me—yes, it reminded me of that gentleman there, a-standing at that door—that sexton. In fact, now

I comes to think of it and look at him, I remembers dreaming a lot about him in the night.'

'Thank you kindly,' said Mr. Mipps, who was listening to the narrative from the door, 'but don't trouble to drag me into it, mate. I gives you my word that we were all as merry as crickets till you King's men come nigh the place; and as for talks of demons and such like—well, there's always gossip of such, o' course, but since you fellows come abroad, the talk's been of nothing else. And murders, too! Why, we'd never heard of mur-ders—except, of course, in church. We was a happy a content-ed pleasant-going little village as you could have wished, we was; but now, so help me God, you fellows have turned our lit-tle spot into a regular witches' kitchen, that you have. Two days you've been here, and two murders we've had—one a day; and if you stays here for a year, as you can calculate for yourself, we'll have three hundred and sixty-five at the present rate. Of course, it's good for my trade, so I says nothing. Go on mur-dering to your hearts' content, for I can knock up one a day all right. But I ain't a-goin' to take any blame about it, and wot's more, I object to bein' dreamt about; so another night kindly leave me out of your adventures, 'cos I don't like bein' mixed up with such traffic.'

Saying which, Mipps stepped across to the corpse of Bill Spiker, and producing his foot-rule, measured him up, and entered the results in a dirty note-book.

The Captain then proceeded to the barn, and soundly rated his still drowsy men; and putting the bos'n in charge of the corpse, he asked Doctor Syn to join him for breakfast at the 'Ship.' And as there was no schoolmaster, and consequently no school, Jerry Jerk had the extreme pleasure of waiting upon them.

22

A Curious Breakfast Party

During the meal Jerry took good stock of both men. The
Captain's manner was sullen and grumpy. He was turning things
over in his mind that he was incapable of solving, things altogether out of his ken. Doctor Syn, on the other hand, seemed
eager to discuss all these curious events; but, underlying his quiet
conversation, there seemed to smoulder a nameless fear, which
now and then burst into flames of fury—fury against the
Captain's inactivity in taking measures to find and capture the
mulatto. But he never went too far, never said anything that his
tact could not smooth over; in fact, he was at great pains not to
quarrel with the Captain as the Squire had done.

So Jerry watched them as they breakfasted in the sanded parlour of the 'Ship,' keeping as much in the room as he could, and
dreading to be dismissed.

Presently the Captain turned to him and inquired whether he
had breakfasted. Jerry replied that he certainly had had a snack
or two, but that broiled fish always did go down very pleasant
with bread and butter and fresh milk, and accepted with alacrity
the invitation from the Captain to bring a chair and help himself.

The Captain got up, filled a pipe, and lit it; the Doctor did the
same; both men pushed their plates to the centre of the table,
leaning their elbows on the cleared space; and Jerry in the centre, for all the world like a judge of some quaint game of skill,
watched the opponents. They drew deliberately at their pipes,
sending preliminary battle clouds across the table before the
real tussle began, each desirous of ascertaining how much the

other knew or guessed about the strange events, but each very fearful of betraying what he guessed. So Jerry watched them, feeling certain that a battle was imminent, wondering upon what side he would be called to fight, and what the end of it all would be; but with all his watching and wondering, he didn't forget to eat, and eat heartily, too, for his maxim was, 'Eat when you can, and only think when you've got to.'

The Captain spoke first.

'Doctor Syn, you heard me say at that inquiry yesterday that I was no strategist—that I was only a fighter.'

'I did,' returned the parson.

'I know everything inside, outside, and around about a ship, but I don't know much else, and certainly nothing else thoroughly, so to speak. But I have seen other things in my time for all that, just as any one who travels is bound to see things, and have remembered a few things outside my business. Now, you're different from that, for you're a scholar, and have travelled far; and a man who can use his book knowledge on what he comes in contact with in the world is the sort of man who might perhaps explain what's bothering me at the present moment. For I am dense, and you are not.'

'What is bothering you, Captain? Of course, something to do with these murders that are uppermost in our minds?'

'Something, I dare say,' replied the Captain, slowly weighing his every word; 'but, on the other hand, maybe it's nothing. I can't connect the two things myself, and yet I've a feeling that I ought to be able to. I've tried though, tried hard, been trying all through breakfast, and it worries me because, as a fighting man, thinking always does worry me sorely. You may laugh at what I'm going to tell you, and if you do, I shan't take offence, because it's precisely what I should have done had any one told me about what I'm going to tell you. Something' (the Captain hesitated, speaking as if he longed to keep silent; speaking as if afraid of being disbelieved)—'something—well—I'll tell you first that it sounds ridiculous on the face of it, but something which—well, *which I saw myself.*'

'Tell me,' said the parson, leaning further forward over the table.

The Captain sat up rigid in his chair, took his pipe from between his lips, and spoke as if repeating a lesson that he didn't understand.

'Once in a Cuban town, in a little Cuban town—can't remember the precise longitude and latitude, but that's no matter, and I can't even remember the name of the town or what I was doing there exactly, but that has no odds on the story.'

'Go on,' said the Vicar.

'Well, in this little Cuban town I saw a priest die. He was as dead as this table, you understand; the doctor said so, and I knew it. Well, imagine my feelings when, half an hour after death, this man arose, entered the next hut, and deliberately, brutally, and carefully stabbed a sleeping child to death.'

The Doctor said nothing, but looked at the Captain.

Jerry stopped eating, and looked at Doctor Syn. He was pale, very pale.

Then the Captain leant over the table and continued speaking, but not like a lesson, for there was a thrill in his voice.

'I found out afterwards that the dead fellow had borne a life-long grudge against his neighbour. The revenge that he had somehow failed to get during his lifetime he accomplished after death. It was devilish curious.

'It was a devilish trick,' said the Doctor. 'The fellow was feigning death for a purpose—namely, to put his neighbour off his guard. He was not really dead. It would be against all laws of nature—why, of course, it would—for a man to arise and walk and commit a foul murder, and all this half an hour after his decease! Nonsense, fanciful nonsense!'

'Again the laws of nature, I'll allow,' went on the Captain, as if he had fully expected that his story would be disbelieved; 'but if you'll excuse me saying so, who are you, Doctor Syn, and, for the matter of that, who am I, to say what the laws of nature are, or how far they extend? For my own part, I should prefer to question mine own ignorance rather than the laws of nature.'

'But what connection is there between this story and our present trouble in the village owing to this murdering-mad seaman?'

'Why, just this,' went on the Captain deliberately. 'When you first caught sight of this same murdering-mad seaman—you remember, outside the barn—I noticed that you took cold all of a sudden. You got the shivers.'

'Marsh ague—marsh ague,' put in the parson quickly. 'Get it often in this place. Poor old Pepper used to tell me that it was the result of fever I once had badly in Charleston, Carolina. Nearly lost my life with it. I dare say he was right. I'm a frequent sufferer; as soon as the mists rise from the Marsh I get the shivers.'

'Ah, then there falls one of my points to the ground. Still, I have another ready. Suppose we grant that your attack of ague had nothing to do with your sudden meeting with this man.'

'Of course it hadn't,' muttered the Doctor. 'Absurd.'

'Very well, then. Did you notice that the entire weight of the rum barrel was carried by Bill Spiker, the gunner?'

'No,' said the Doctor, 'I didn't notice that.'

'No more did Bill Spiker,' cried the Captain. 'You can lay to that, or he would have soon raised objections; but I did, because it's my business to note which of my men work hardest.'

'I don't see what that has to do with the case,' said the Doctor. 'It's a common enough complaint to find a man shirking work.'

'Not when the man who shirks is a willing worker. That's what made me wonder in the first place, and I've now come to the conclusion that whenever the mulatto was ordered to work alone—alone, mind you, without the help of the other seamen— why, he could accomplish anything; but when he was working with anybody he seemed, in spite of himself, to become singularly useless.'

'You call yourself dense, Captain, and you affirm that I am not; but you seem to have a keener perception of the abstruse and vague than I have. I cannot follow you.'

'You will be able to follow me in a moment,' said the Captain humbly. 'I fear it is the poor way in which I am getting to the

point. But I have to tell things in my own way, not being given
to talk much.'

'Go on, then, in your own way,' said the parson.

'I then recollected that in my short acquaintance with the
mulatto I never remember to have seen him in actual contact
with any one or anything. And I also recollected a strong ten-
dency amongst the men to avoid him, and keep out of any personal touch with him.'

'Natural enough,' explained the parson. 'It is the white man's
antipathy towards a black. Perfectly natural.'

'Perfectly,' agreed the Captain. 'And I think we may add the
Englishman's antipathy towards the uncanny and mysterious.'

'I dare say,' said Doctor Syn.

'I am sure of it,' went on the Captain. 'Indeed, I went so far
as to ask the bos'n, who has had most dealings with the fellow,
whether he had ever touched him.'

'*Touched* him? What do you mean?' asked the parson, who
began dimly to see what the other was driving at.

'*Touched—touched* him,' repeated the Captain, with emphasis. 'The bos'n told me "no," and that he wouldn't care about it,
for he considered that "a weird-looking cove" (I'll use his precise way of expressing it)—that "a weird-looking cove, with a
face like a dead 'un, what never took food or drink to his knowledge, weren't the sort of cove that a respectable seaman wanted to touch." '

Jerry looked at the Doctor. He was as white as the snowy
tablecloth before him. Yet he feigned not to follow the Captain's
meaning.

'And now,' cried Captain, 'mad as it sounds, do you see any
connection between the two cases? It's plain to any traveller
that some of these foreign rascals, especially the priests, possess
strange gifts that the white man's brain runs short of, and I want
to know if you see any connection between the two cases.'

Doctor Syn's hand was trembling; so much so that the long
clay pipe stem snapped between his finger and thumb. Neither
seemed to notice this, though the lighted ashes had fallen out of
the bowl upon the tablecloth, and were burning little holes in it.

'Do you see any connection, Doctor Syn?' said the Captain, leaning right over the table, and bringing his face close to the cleric.

Doctor Syn did not answer.

The Captain repeated the sentence with more force, with all the stubborn and combative force that he could muster into his voice.

'Any connection between the Cuban priest who was able to commit deliberate murder after death by centring the enormous will power of his revenge upon that one object? Do you see any connection, I say, between that man and a man who was marooned upon a coral reef in the Southern Pacific being able to follow his murderer across the world in the beastly hulk of his dead self? I don't understand it, nor do you, perhaps; but I fancy that I see the semblance of a connection, and what I want to know is, do you?'

Then Doctor Syn did a surprising thing. He slowly raised his face to the level of the Captain's, slowly raised his eyes to meet the Captain's gaze, and then, drawing his lips apart, laying his white teeth bare, he drew over his face from the very depths of his soul it seemed, a smile, a fixed smile that steadily beamed for at least a quarter of a minute. Then he said:

'You most remarkable man! A King's captain, eh? I vow you have mistaken your calling.'

And he deliberately, and with the flat of his white hand, patted the Captain's rough cheek—patted it as though the Captain were a child being petted or a puppy being teased.

'What the thunder do you mean,' roared the infuriated officer, 'by *calling*? Mistake my *calling*?'

'Your profession,' said Doctor Syn, calmly putting on his cloak and hat.

'What would you have me, then,' cried the seaman.

'I wouldn't have you any other than what you are, sir.' replied Doctor Syn, with his hand on the door latch 'A thoroughly entertaining and vastly amusing old sea-dog, mahogany as a dinner-wagon, and loaded with so many fancies as to be near the breaking-point.'

The Captain was so taken aback at the manner of the Doctor that he could only look and gasp. Doctor Syn, perfectly at ease, opened the door.

'I wonder,' he said, in a low voice—almost tenderly, Jerry thought.

The Captain, with a great effort, managed to ejaculate, 'What?'

'Why your mother sent you to sea—for as an apothecary, an apothecary—ay, yes, indeed, what a magnificent apothecary the world has missed in you, sir.' And the Vicar went out, closing the door behind him.

The Captain could do nothing but stare at the closed door; whilst Jerry, perceiving nothing entertaining in that, stared at the Captain, who suddenly exploded out in his great sea voice:

'An apothecary—an apothecary? What, in the devil's name, does he mean by that?'

Jerry still looked at the Captain. Certainly he had never beheld any one more unlike an apothecary. By the wildest stretch of his imagination he could not picture the Captain mixing drugs.

'It's my opinion—' he said at last, and then hesitated.

'Yes,' thundered the Captain, with an eagerness that seemed to welcome any opinion.

'Well, it's my opinion, sir, that Doctor Syn is off his head. Mad, sir.'

'And it's my opinion, pot-boy,' said the Captain as if he valued his own opinion as highly as Jerry Jerk's; 'it's my opinion that he's nothing of the kind. He's feigning madness. He had to do something, you see, to get out of the room, so he called me something that he knew would take my breath away for the moment, knowing me to be dense, and he succeeded. For if any man was unqualified to be an apothecary, I'm the fellow. An apothecary!'

Then the Captain sat down in the armchair, and laughed till the tears rolled down his cheeks, and Jerry was obliged to join in, though he didn't know what he was laughing at. At length he stopped and became suddenly grave. Getting up, he placed his hands on Jerry's shoulders.

'Look here, pot-boy,' he said, 'you and I have common secrets. That I know. What the devil you were doing out on the Marsh the night before last I don't know, but that you saw the school-master kill Pepper I *do* know.'

'You know?' cried Jerk, utterly astonished. 'Then Doctor Syn must have told you, for I never breathed a word.'

'I know all about it, my boy, because I was hiding in the same dyke as you. Now, see here, from what I've seen of you, I imagine you can be relied upon. We'll pluck a leaf out of that parson's book. We'll find out his mystery. We'll find out the whole mystery of this damned Marsh, and as to being apothecaries, why, damme, so we will. We'll take him at his word.'

'And be apothecaries, sir?' asked Jerry, more puzzled now than ever.

'Yes,' cried the Captain, slapping his great hands up and down upon Jerry's shoulders. 'Apothecaries make experiments, don't they?'

'I dare say they do, sir,' replied Jerk.

'Well, so will we, lad,' went on the Captain, as happy as a sand-boy. 'We'll set a trap for all this mystery to walk into. We'll set a big trap, my lad; big enough to hold all the murderers and mulattoes on the Marsh, the demon riders as well, and certain-ly not forgetting the coffins in Mipps's shop or the bottles of Alsace beneath this floor. We'll catch the lot, my boy, and exam-ine 'em. Yes, damn 'em, we'll examine 'em, inside and outside, by night and by day. And when we've examined thoroughly, why, we'll give 'em to Jack Ketch—to old Jack Ketch who'll hang 'em up to dry. Not a word, my boy, to any one; not a word. Here's a guinea bit to hold your tongue; and look to hear from me before the day's out, for I shall want your help tomor-row night.'

The Captain was gone. He had literally rushed out of the door, leaving Jerk alone in a whirl.

'Well,' he said to himself, 'if a man ever deserved a third breakfast, I'm the one, and here goes; for both of these fellows is stark staring mad, though it's wonderful the way they all seems to take to me.'

And thrusting the precious guinea bit into his pocket, Jerk again vigorously attacked the victuals.

23

A Young Recruit

'Talk about an 'ealthy child, and there he is,' said Mrs. Waggetts, entering the sanded parlour with Sexton Mipps. 'And eat! Nothing like eating to increase your fat, is there, Mister Mipps? But there, I suppose you never had no fat on you to speak of' 'cos if ever a man was one of Pharaoh's lean kine, you was.'

'It's hard work what's kept me thin, Missus Waggetts,' replied the sinister sexton— 'hard work and scheming; and a little of both would do our young Jerry here no harm.'

'As to work,' replied Jerry, gulping down more food, 'there ain't been no complaints against me, I believes; Missus Waggetts?'

'Certainly not, Jerry,' replied that lady affably.

'That's good,' said Jerk. Then, turning to the sexton, he added, 'And as to scheming, Mister Sexton, how do you know I don't scheme? Some folks are so took up with their own schemes that p'raps they don't get time to notice wot others are a-doing. I has lots of schemes, I has. I thinks about 'em by day, and dreams of 'em at night.'

'And they gives you a rare knack of putting away Missus Waggetts's victuals, I'm a-noticing,' dryly remarked the sexton.

'Lor', I'm sure he's heartily welcome to anything I've got,' returned the landlady. 'It fair cheers me up to see him eat well, and it'll be a fine man he'll be making in a year or So.'

'Ay, that I will,' cried young Jerk. 'And when I'm a hangman I ain't a-goin' to forget my old friend. I'll come along from the town every Sunday, I will, and we'll go and hear Parson Syn preach just the same as we does now, and Mister Mipps will show us into the pew, and everybody will turn round and stare at us, and say, "Why, there goes Hangman Jerk!" Then we'll come back and have a bite of supper together, providing I don't have to sup with the Squire at the Court House.'

'That 'ud be likely,' interrupted Mipps.

'And after we've had supper I'll tell you stories about horrible sights I've seen in the week, and terrible things I've done, and it'll go hard with Sexton Mipps to keep even with me with his yarns, I tell you.'

'Ha, ha!' chuckled Mipps, 'strike me dead and knock me up slipshod in a buckram coffin if this lad Jerry Jerk don't please me! Look at him, Missus Waggetts. Will you do me the favour of looking at him hard—though don't let it put you off your feed, Jerry. Why, at your age I had just such notions as you've got; but there, I never had your advantages. Why, at thirteen years of age I was as grow'd up in my fancies as this Jerk. Sweetmeats to the devil, eh, Jerry? for it's some who grows above such garbage from their first rocking in the cradle. This Jerry Jerk is a man. Why, bless you, he's more a man than some of 'em wot's a-doin man's work.'

'That's so,' said Mrs. Waggetts, enthusiastically backing the sexton up. 'And don't you forget that he owns a bit of land on the Marsh, and so he a Marsh man proper.

'I doesn't forget it,' cried Mipps, 'and I've been telling certain folk how things were going with Hangman Jerk, and I've made 'em see that, although only a child in regard to age, he ain't no child in his deeds. And so they agreed with me, Missus Waggetts, that it 'ud be unjust not to let him have full Marsh man's privileges, and I'll go bail that Jerk won't disgrace me by not living up to them privileges.'

'P'raps I won't, Mister Sexton, when I knows what them privileges are.'

'You listen and I'll tell you,' answered the sexton.

'And listen well, Jerry,' added Mrs. Waggetts, 'for what Mister Mipps is a-goin' to say will like as not be the makin' of you.'

'Jerry,' cried the Sexton, 'you're just one after my own heart. You ought to have lived in my days, when I was a lad; gone to

sea, and got amongst the interestin' gentlemen, like I did. Ay,
they was interestin'. And reckless they was, too. They was
rough—none rougher—but I don't grudge 'em all the kicks they
gave me. Why, it made a man o' me, young Jerk. I tell you,
Master Jerry, that, bad as them sea adventures was, they did
some good, for they made a man o' me, Jerry. I should never
have been the sort o' man I is now if them ruffians hadn't kindly knocked the nonsense out o' me.'

'Shouldn't you, though!' said Jerry.

'Never, never!' said the sexton with conviction. 'But mind
you,' he went on, 'you has advantages wot I never had. I had to
learn all the tricks o' my trade, and I had to buy my experience.
There was no kind friend to teach me any lesson, no benevolent
old cove wot 'ud pay for my experience. No, I had to buy and
learn for myself, but, my stars and garters! afore they'd done
with me I had 'em all scared of me. Even England hisself didn't
a-relish my tantrums, and when I was in a regular blinder, why
I solemnly believes he was scared froze o' me. There was only
one man my superior in all the time I sailed them golden seas,
and that man was Clegg hisself. I served on his ship, you know,
Jerk. I was carpenter—master carpenter, mind you, to Clegg—
to no less a man than Clegg. And on Clegg's own ship it were,
too. She was called the *Imogene*. I never knew why she was
called so. It sounds a high, fiddaddley sort o' name for a pirate
ship, but then Clegg was a regular gentleman in his tastes. Why,
I remember him sitting so peacefully on the roundhouse roof
one day a-reading of Virgil—and not in the vulgar tongue neither—he was a-readin' it in the foreign language wot it was first
wrote in, so he told me; and you couldn't somehow get hold of
the fact that that benign-lookin' cove wot was sitting there so
peaceful a-readin' learned books had, maybe half an hour
before, strung up a mutineer to the yardarm, or made some old
cove walk the dirty plank. He was a rum 'un, and no mistake,
was that damned old pirate Clegg. But I'd pull my forelock—
supposing I had one—all day long to old Clegg, even were I the
Archbishop of Canterbury and he only an out-at-heel sea-dog.
Now with England it was different. Though I'll own he could

beat the Devil hisself for blasphemy, I wasn't afraid of him: he was one you could size up, like. But Clegg—oh, he was different. Show me the man wot could size up Clegg, and I'll make him Leveller of Romney Marsh—ay, King of England, supposing I had the power. There was only one man wot I ever see'd wot made Clegg turn a hair, and that was a rascally priest; but then he had devil powers, he had—ugh!' And the sexton relapsed into silence.

His listeners watched him, and, watching, they saw him shiver. What old scene of horror was flashing before that curious little man's mind? Ah, who could tell? No living body; for the crew of the *Imogene* had all died violent deaths one after another in different lands, and since Clegg was hanged at Rye—why, Mr. Mipps was the only veteran left.

'Pray get on with the business in hand, Mister Mipps,' said Mrs. Waggetts; 'for though I declare I could a-listen to you a-philosophizin' and a-moralizin' all day long, young Jerk is all agog, ain't you, Jerry?'

'That's so,' replied Jerk. 'Please get on, Mister Sexton.'

'I will,' said. Mr. Mipps. 'You may wonder now, Jerry Jerk, how it has been possible for an adventurer like I be, or rather was one time, when I was a handsome, fine-standing young fellow aboard the *Imogene*—I say you may fall to wondering how I come to be a sexton, and to live the dull, dreary life of a villager. Well, I'll tell you now straight out, man to man, and when I've told you, why, you'll understand all the mystery wot I'm a-gettin' at.' The sexton smote his hand upon the table so that all the breakfast dishes jumped into different positions on the table, and the two words he said as his fist crashed down were these: 'I couldn't!'

'Couldn't what?' asked Jerk, whose anxiety for the breakfast dishes' safety had driven the context of the sexton's speech from his mind. 'Couldn't like a humdrum life, after the high jinks I had at sea.'

'But you did, Mister Sexton, and, what's more, you're a-doin' it now,' replied young Jerk.

'And very prettily you can act, can't you, Hangman Jerk!' said Mr. Mipps, winking. 'I declare you're a master in the way of pretendin'. Well, pretendin's all very well, but it's often plain-spoken truth wot serves as a safer weapon for roguish fellows, and it's plain-spoken truth I'm a-goin' to use to you, believin' in my heart that if ever there was a roguish fellow livin', and one after my old heart, why, Hangman Jerk is that fellow.'

'Please get on, Mister Sexton,' said Jerry, feeling very important.

'Yes, get on, get on,' repeated Mrs. Waggetts, 'for I'm a-longin' to hear how he takes it.'

'Can you doubt? I don't,' replied Mipps. 'I bet my head he'll take it as a man, won't you, Jerry Jerk, eh?'

'I'll tell you when I knows wot it is,' replied the boy.

'Why, what a talky old party I've become. Time was when I never uttered a word; but do—ah, I was one to do. And much and quick I did, too.'

'We knows that very well, thank you, Mister Sexton,' said Jerry— 'that is, we knows it if we knows your word can be relied upon.'

'You may lay to that,' said Mipps, 'and you may lay that, in our future dealings together, you can depend on me a-standin' by you as long as you lay the straight course with me.'

'I'll take your word for that,' responded Jerk. 'Now, p'raps, you will get on.'

'Well,' said the sexton, 'I must begin with the Marsh—the Romney Marsh. No one knows better than you do that she's a queer sort of a corner, is Romney Marsh. I've seen you a-prowlin' and a-nosin' about on her. You scented excitement, you did, on the Marsh. You smelt out a mystery, and, like a lad of spirit, you wanted to find out the meanin' of it all. Very natural. I should have done the same when I was a lad. Well, now, the whole business is this the Marsh don't approve of folk a-nosin' and a-prowlin' after her secrets, see?' And the sexton's face grew suddenly fierce. All the lines of quizzical humour vanished from around that peculiar mouth, and left a face of diabolical cruelty, cunning, and malice.

But Jerk was not easily unnerved or put out of countenance. There was something about Mipps that put him on his mettle. He liked Mipps, but he liked to keep even with him, for his own self-respect, which was very great. In some things Jerry Jerk was most inordinately proud.

'Oh, the Marsh don't approve, eh? And who or what might be the power on the Marsh to tell you so?'

'The great ruler of the Marsh—the man with no name who runs his schemes and makes his sons prosperous.'

'That'll be the Squire, then,' said Jerry promptly, 'for he's the Leveller of Marsh Scotts, ain't he? He makes the laws for the Marsh men, don't he?'

'He does that, certainly,' agreed the sexton. 'But whether or no he's the power what brings luck to the Marsh men neither you nor me nor nobody can tell. Sufficient for us that the Marsh is ruled by a power—a mysterious power—wot brings gold and to spare to the Marsh men's pockets.'

'Ah, then,' said Jerry, with his eyes blazing, 'then I was right. There are smugglers on the Marsh.'

'There are,' said the sexton, 'and it's wealthy men they be, though you'd never guess at it, and darin', adventurous cusses they be, and rollicky good times they gets, and no danger to speak of, 'cos the whole blessed concern is run by a master brain wot never seems to make mistakes. 'Twas this same master brain wot agreed that you should share the privileges of the Marsh, and I was ordered to recruit you.'

'Oh, and what'll be required o' me,' asked Jerk, 'supposin' I thinks about it?'

'You'll be given a horse, and you'll ride with the Marsh witches, learn their trade and be apprenticed to their callin'.'

'And how do you know I won't blab, and get you and your fellows the rope?' asked Jerry bravely.

'Because we've sized you up, we 'as, and we don't suspect you of treachery. If we did it wouldn't much matter to us, though I should be right sorry to have been disappointed in you; for I declare I don't know when I took to a young man like I 'as to you. You're my fancy, you are, Jerry. Just like I was at your age.'

'Yes, but just supposin' that I did disappoint you, mister Sexton? It's well to hear all sides, you know.'

'Ay, it's well, and wise too, and I'll tell you. If it was to your advantage to betray us to that Captain, perhaps, well, I dare say you'd do it.'

'I don't know,' said Jerk. 'All depends. P'raps I might, though. You never knows.'

'No, you never knows. Quite right. But you'd know one thing—that, go where you would or hide where you liked, we'd get you in time, and when we did get you it 'ud be short shift for you—you may lay to that.'

'I dare say,' said Jerry— 'unless, of course, I got you first.'

'You'd have a good number to get, my lad,' laughed the sexton. 'But it's no use a-harguing like this. You won't betray us when it don't serve your turn to do so, and it won't do that, 'cos we has very fine prospects open for you. Why, we can set you in the way of rolling in a coach before we've done with you, and who knows, years hence, when you're older than you be now—who knows but what you might not succeed to the headship. If anything was to happen to the great chief, what's to prevent you from taking his place, eh? You're smart, ain't you?— there's no gainsaying that, now, is there, Missus Waggetts?'

'No, indeed,' replied that lady.

'Then take my tip, the straight tip of an old gentleman o' fortune, and you join us.'

'What'll I have to do, and what is it I'm a-joinin', though?' asked the boy.

'The great scheme of wool-running,' said Mr. Mipps.

'Ah!' sighed Jerry, 'I thought as much, And what am I to do, always supposin' that I'm willin' to join?'

'We've a vacancy in the horsemen—a man short, you see, though we've got the horse. It's Mr. Rash's horse, but we've turned out the schoolmaster and kept his horse. He weren't one of us, you see, so we found that we didn't want him no more.'

'"You've killed him!' cried the Hangman, starting up.

'I didn't say that,' retorted the sexton. 'I merely remarked that we didn't want him no more. And now just give me your attention. I've every reason to believe, and so has the great chief that I work for, that you are getting very thick with that swab of a King's Captain. Well, now, don't go a-suddenly a-givin' him the cold shoulder, do you see? You can't drop a friend all at once like a hot potato without exciting the gossip of folk. So remember what I says, and keep civil to him. But it's my opinion that after to-night you'll know which side you be on, for once get the thrill of the Demon Ride, and you'll not want to get dismissed. Besides, gettin' dismissed by our chief ain't exactly what you might term a pleasant form of bein' entertained.'

'And what do I do, Mister Sexton?'

'You'll get told all in good time.'

'Well, what do the demon riders do?' persisted the boy. 'Frighten folk from the Marsh when the ponies are trotting under the woolpacks.'

'And where do the woolpacks come from?'

'From nearly every farm on the Marsh.'

'And they put it all in packs and send 'em down to the coast?'

'That's the ticket, my lad. Pack 'em all up on ponies, and bring back coffins full of spirit from France.'

'Coffins full of spirit from France?' repeated the amazed boy.

'Yes, that's why I'm a coffin-maker. What would you expect to see inside a nailed-up coffin, eh?'

'Why, a dead 'un,' said the boy.

'Exactly, and as folk ain't particular fond of amusin' themselves with a sight of dead 'uns, they lets my coffins alone, do you see, and the spirit is treated with every respect, and is allowed to go on its way very snug and all knocked up most particular solid.'

'And the head of it all's the Squire, is it?'

'I never said so,' replied the Sexton quickly; 'but the less you think and say on that subject the better. So don't you hamper your young career with thinking about it. All you've got to do is to obey.'

'And what do I get out of it?'

'Gold and the fun of your life.'

'And when do I start?'

'To-night.'

'To-night?' faltered Jerk, much relieved, for he had thought of his promise to help the Captain, and was greatly thankful that the dates had not clashed.

'At half-past twelve at Old Tree Cottage. But don't go to the coffin-shop side—tap at the back kitchen window.'

'Half-past twelve, you say?'

'That's the time,' answered Mipps, holding out his hands and seizing Jerk's in both his, 'and I can tell at a glance that you're a-going to be a credit to the undertakin'.'

A minute afterwards he was gone, and Jerk was sent by Mrs. Waggetts into the bar to polish up the tankards.

24

The Coffin-maker has a Visitor

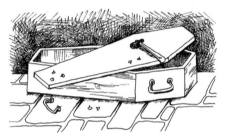

About noon of the same day Captain Collyer in walking through the village found himself passing Old Tree Cottage, the low-lying residence of Sexton Mipps, with its coffin shop facing the street and its small farmhouse behind. Attracted by a great noise of hammering, the Captain stepped up to the window and glanced in. Rows of coffins lined the wall, and coffin planks were propped up against shelves containing everything imaginable. In the centre of the shop stood two black trestle-stools, and upon these funeral relics reposed a large coffin with no lid. Inside this gloomy thing sat Mr. Mipps. He was sitting straight up and hammering lustily upon the coffin sides, singing away with much spirit to the rhyme:

> 'O hammer, hammer, hammer,
> And damn her, damn her, damn her,
> For I don't fear my wife now she's dead.'

The Captain, amused at the words, pushed open the casement and leant into the room. Whether the sexton saw him or not the Captain did not know, but the song changed immediately to a song of the sea:

'There's no swab like the captain,
There's no swab like the captain.
Of all the swabs I've ever seen
With a diddle diddle diddle diddle diddle diddle dee,
No swab like the captain.'

'A very appropriate song, Master Sexton,' laughed the Captain.

Mipps turned round and surveyed the intruder. 'Why, knock me up solid if it ain't the good Captain. The gold of the high noon to you, sir—though there ain't much gold in the sky to-day. I take it as a very friendly piece of impertinence that you should come and look me up so unexpected. Had I know'd of your arrival, I'd have had these grisly relics stowed away, for some folk has a distinct dislike to lookin' at their last dewelling-houses.'

'You are used to 'em, I suppose, by now,' said the Captain.

'Oh, love you, yes, I don't mind 'em. Some undertakers has fearful superstitions about coffins. Some won't get in 'em to measure 'em. Lord, I always does, and lies down inside 'em and pops the lid on the top to see if it's airtight.'

'Awkward if the lid was to stick.'

'You may well say that, 'cos once it did. But it weren't so much awkward as peaceful, for after I'd pushed and struggled for a power o' time, I just resigned myself to my fate, feeling thankful that at any rate I had the privilege of being my own undertaker. I shall never forget my feelin's when my last bit of breath came up and went out. It was just the sort of feelin' you gets when you drowns, only more so. 'Cos when you drowns you sees all the bad actions of your life a-troopin' before you; but gettin' buried alive is different, 'cos you sees all the good actions wot you've done. Mind you, things I'd clean forgot—little acts of kindness wot I thought could never have been record-ed anywhere—why, they all walked out, and I seemed to be greatly comforted, 'cos I thought as how I was quite in the running for heaven. In fact, I was so pleased with my past self that I fairly kicked with delight, and that was the means of bringing

me back to earth, 'cos over went these trestles, and the jar I got
knocked the stuck lid off. No, I've been near gone these many
times, but never so near gone as that—for, as you see, I was finished with the undertaker, having undertook myself, and I only
had to be passed through the parson's hands and get knocked
over the sconce with the sexton's shovel.'

'A horrible experience, Master Sexton,' returned the Captain.

'It was. But I could tell you horribler. I takes a pride in my
business, same as you might in yours. That's why I went round
the world.'

'Oh, you've been round the world, have you?' said the
Captain.

'Not once nor twice, but many times—and do you know
why?'

'Buccaneering?' said the Captain casually.

'There you go, suspicious! Can't you mind your manners for
five minutes. Can't you make an effort, when you're agossipin'
with honest folk, to forget that there is dishonest ones. I never
did see the like. Here we be chatting quite friendly, and forgetting our little differences, when you starts accusin' me of bein'
a Captain Clegg or an England. Do I look like a bold pirate
now? Looking at me straight sitting up in this 'ere coffin, could
you say that I looked like a swaggerin' gentleman o' fortune?
No, you couldn't. Very well, then, why go and make unpleasant
insinuations against a respectable sexton o' the realm! Mind
you, I don't say as how I didn't come across some of that breed
during my travels, and I don't say as how circumstances didn't
at times make me work for 'em. But not for long. I held no sort
of likes with the likes of them, and though some of 'em had
most engaging ways, it was easy to see that they was all of 'em
unadulterated sinners. And swear! God bless your eyes, Captain,
it made you blush like a woman to hear 'em.'

'And if it was not for gold and adventure that you went, may
I ask what tempted you abroad?'

'Certainly, Captain. It was the 'love of my work—the zeal to
have a look at other sextons, vergers, and undertakers, and see
what they were a-doin' with the business. But, Lord love you,

Captain! I soon found as how funerals was done on different plans abroad. Why, I could tell you some things I see'd with regard to burials abroad what 'ud make your flesh creep, though the sun is high in the heaven.'

'Well, I've an hour to spare, Master Sexton. What do you say to coming along to the "Ship" and enjoying a drink and a friendly pipe?'

'I thinks I can do one better than that, thanking you kindly,' said the sexton, vaulting with marvellous dexterity out of the lofty coffin to the floor. 'For I've baccy, pipes, and good brandy all to hand, and if you'd care to spend an hour with Sexton Mipps and listen to his babbles, why, light your "strike me dead" and gulp your spirits and settle your hulk in that there coffin, what hasn't got no passenger inside. We'll shut the window for it's a-blowin' the fire out, and if you ain't cosy-well, it's not the fault of the sexton.'

Mr. Mipps, after busily providing his guest with the requisites for smoke and drink, and after splitting up a coffin plank to renew the fire, sprang back into the coffin, sitting snug with a glass of brandy and his churchwarden. The Captain also was ensconced on a coffin in the corner, and to the crackle of the split coffin plank upon the fire the sexton began to yarn.

25

The Sexton Speaks

'Funerals may be divided into three classes, for there be solemn funerals, there be grisly funerals, and there be funny 'uns. The funniest funeral I ever did see was in China. Do you know, Captain, they very seldom buries out there. They leaves the blessed coffins above ground. The whole of the country-side is a littered with 'em, and they has other very funny customs about funerals out there. When a fellow goes and dies, it's a devil of a business he has to go through before he gets fixed up final. Every family 'as their own particular priest, you understand, and this particular priest is always a very sly sort of dog. The dead 'un is put into the coffin, and then the family pays their sly dog a considerable sum of money in exchange for very hard prayers wot the sly dog makes for 'em to his gods. He goes away and prays for weeks on end, asking his gods just where exactly the family ought to bury their dead 'un to enable him to get into heaven by the most convenient road. And as the sly dog gets paid all the time he's a-praying, you can bet your wig that he strings them prayers out to some length. I'll tell you about a certain Ling Fu Quong—well, if I hadn't rung the curtain down, as the stage' players say, upon that gent's little comedy, I believes he'd be drawin' in a salary now for a fellow what died some forty years ago. You see, it happened like this. I had had dealings with a smug-faced Chinese merchant wot did business at Shanghai. When I was about to sail for the old country, old smug face came to say how sorry he was I was a-goin' to leave, and hoped he'd have the pleasure of doin' business with me again when I come back. We started talking, and I told him that

I should very much like to see a Chinese funeral, and old smug face said that he would gladly oblige me, because a very particular old uncle of his had died, and his funeral was shortly to take place. Well, the upshot of it all was that I was invited to go up the river on smug face's boat to Soochow, where he lived and where his uncle had died, a city some sixty miles away or thereabouts.

'Have you ever been on one o' them large sampans, Captain? No. Well, it's a long sort o' boat, fitted up very snug indeed, with flowers all trailing over the side, and all fixed up to look like an old homestead sailin' on the river. After a very pleasant trip— and, Lord luv you, I did make that old Chinaman laugh telling him things, for I could speak their lingo a bit—well, after a very pleasant trip we gets to Soochow, and a rummy old place it was. It stood right on top of the river, with its old walls running straight down into the muddy water. It was a strong town, full of fighters and wealthy merchantmen. They was all pleased to see me, and received me very proper. Most of 'em was a-lookin' over the wall a-wavin' flags at me, and them as hadn't got none were a'wavin' their pigtails. I might have been the great Cham for all the fuss they made o' me. O' course, mind you, I had my enemies. There was a sort o' lord mayor of the place wot I could see didn't quite approve of me being the nine days' wonder, for he was one of them jealous coves wot don't like any one to have a fling but himself. But I didn't mind him, for although I was only a little fellow, I had an eye like a vulture, a nose like a sword-fish, and when I was put out a way of lashing myself about like a tiger's tail wot used to scare them natives. O' course, it wasn't pleasant when, you come to think of it, 'cos there I was the only Englishman amongst them millions of yellow jacks. But an Englishman's an Englishman all the world over, ain't he, Captain? and he wants a bit of squashing, and so that lord mayor discovered, 'cos one day I walked right up to him in the street and I clacked my teeth at him so very loud that he ran home and never annoyed me no more.

'But I was a-goin' to tell you about that funeral. When we got to the front door of old smug face's house, we discovered his uncle's coffin reposing upon the doorstep, very peaceful, but in a most awkward sort of position, 'cos you had to crawl over the blessed thing to get in or out o' the door.

' "Lord love you, my most excellent Mipps," cried old smug face when he saw it, "why, this'll never do. My late lamented uncle"—I forget the uncle's name, but it was Ling something— "is fairly blocking up the fairway.'

' "Ling Fu Quong,' I replied, "you've hit it; for if we 'as to do steeplechase over that there thing every time we wants to get out o' doors for a breather—well, we'll fair tire ourselves." And so old smug face agreed, and he accordingly sent for the family parson. Well, old sly dog arrived, and of all the fat, self-satisfied coves I ever see'd, he was the king. It was easy to see as how he made a good thing out of his job. My old friend smug face begins telling him how awkward it was having a coffin right across the front door, and old sly dog said as how he was very sorry, but it were just in that place wot the gods had told him to put it.

' "Don't you think that if we were to offer sacred crackers to the gods that they might find as how they've been mistook," suggested smug face.

' "I'll have a try, O bereaved one," answered sly dog.

'So my friend unlocks his treasure chest, and forks out a regular king's ransom, which he gives to the priest to buy crackers with, just to persuade the gods to change their minds. I tell you that if old sly dog had really spent all that money in crackers, why, Gunpowder Plot wouldn't have been in it. Anyhow, the priest left with the money, and we spent the next few days a-climbin' over that inconvenience whenever we wanted to go out or in doors. You must understand also that coffins out in China ain't the neat sort of contrivance like we've got here. Oh, Lord luv you, no! for them Chinese ones beat all the great cumbersome family coaches I ever see'd in the coffin line.

'Well, in a few days back comes sly dog lookin' more prosperous than ever. It was very plain to me that he'd been having a good time with that money, and if he had spent five minutes in prayer to his gods, I should be very much surprised. Well, he tells my old friend to turn out of the house for that night, because the gods had promised to visit him if he stayed all alone along of the coffin. I wasn't particular about where we stopped, though I could see smug face didn't like turning out his house, but I felt annoyed to see how very easily he knuckled under to whatever the priest said.

'So we went away, as I say, for that night. Now, the nights come up cold in China, and we both got two very snivelly colds wot had been brought on by the draughts through not being able to shut that front door. Next morning sly dog came round to say that the gods would visit the house every night and see just where they could order the coffin to be moved to, and in the meantime sly dog was to spend his days and nights in the house. A comfortable time he had of it, you may be sure, for my friend had got a house well stored with very good things.

'At the end of a week sly dog comes round to say that the gods had decided to move the coffin, and that he had seen their orders carried out. So, after giving him more money, much to my indignation, for I couldn't bear to see my friend imposed upon, we left him and set off for the house. And where do you think that dirty priest had put that coffin?'

'Where?' queried the Captain.

'Why, in the bed where I was going to sleep. This roused the devil in me, and I determined to get even with that gent. But I had to think things over very carefully. You see, if I objected to sleepin' in the same bed as the coffin, my friend might think I thought myself superior to sleepin' with his uncle, and that I knew would offend him, 'cos the Chinese seem to bear a most ridiculous respect towards their dead relations. So I decided that, come what might, I would certainly sleep there, and at the same time I hit upon a scheme for the undoin' of that priest.

'Next morning I woke up after a very pleasant sleep alongside that coffin, and felt much refreshed, though, o' course, I wasn't goin' to let 'em know that. When my friend asked me how I had slept, I told him very badly, because all through the night the old uncle in the coffin kept a waking up and asking if I would go and fetch the priest. So smug face sends round at once to sly dog for me to tell him all about it.

' "Did the late lamented uncle of this bereaved man really converse with thee in the night, O Englishman?" asked the priest, trying to look very knowing. I was longing to reply by giving him one in his mouth, but I pulled myself together, and answered very respectfully.

' "Of a truth did the late lamented uncle of this bereaved one"—a-jerking my thumb towards smug face—"converse with my contemptible self in the small hours of the dawn previous to the inestimable crowing of the invaluable cock upon the temple roof. Of a truth did he converse with me, and say unto me"—I could speak their lingo very well in those days—" 'Send for the wise and learned priest of the family, and tell him that I have much to say unto him on matters of most heavenly import, and command him to sleep upon the very spot where thou art now sleeping, O foreigner of the white face. Let him sleep there tomorrow night alone. Let none other be in the house, for it is to the priest alone that I can confide my troubles. Urge also my dutiful nephew to pay large sums of money to the priest, so that he may not fail to come to me in my sore and troubled hour.' "

'Well, o' course, they all thought it very wonderful, and, provided with more money by my friend, the priest went off to sleep the night with the coffin. I had pretended to be tired that night, and had retired to my sleepin' room early, so they thought, for we were spending that night with the friends of my friend. But no sooner had I fastened the entrance of my room than I had got out of the window, which looked out upon the city wall, and climbing along the parapet, I safely reached the ground, and set off at a good run to the empty house, getting there well before the priest. Now, I had told the merchant to be sure and see the priest safe at the house himself, for I feared that fright might keep the rascal away. The merchant promised to do this, for I believe that by this time me was 'losing confidence in the family confessor. As soon as I got into my old bedroom I opened the coffin, lifted out the corpse, stripping him of his funeral clothes, which I donned. Then I hid the corpse in a dark corner of the room behind a screen, and got into the great coffin.' Now, the lids were not screwed down in China, but merely allowed to rest upon the top. Presently I hears the priest arrive, and my friend bid him good-night, and leaves him.

'Well, the fellow possessed more courage than I had credited him with, 'cos he comes promptly into the room, counts out his fresh money on the top of the coffin itself, and then curls himself up alongside it upon the mattress. Just as soon as I heard him beginning to breathe heavy I pushed open the coffin lid, calling upon him by name in most sepulchral tones. He woke up, o' course, and sits up on his side of the bed, and looked at the coffin. There he beheld me a-sitting up inside the coffin a-lookin' at him, only, o' course, he didn't think it was me but the dead uncle. Well, he was so frightened that I just had an easy walk over him. I jumped at him, I kicked him, I made him swear that he would return every penny of his false gotten gains to the merchant, and that, if the merchant refused, he was to give it to the white stranger that sojourned there; and finally, after thrashing the stuffing out of him, I popped him bodily into the coffin, jammed the corpse from behind the screen in on top of him, and over 'em both I closed the lid. Then, seeing as how he was unconscious 'through the drubbing he had had, and the awful fright, I left him, and went home to bed at the house of the friends of my friend, getting in as I had got out, through the window.

'Well, next morning, sly dog turned up, and said that the gods had visited him in the night, and that the coffin was to be buried twelve feet deep in the merchant's field, and that he was so over-joyed at having conversed so very pleasantly with the gods that he must insist on returning the gold to the merchant. This the good merchant, of course, refused to accept; so the priest was obliged, according as he had been commanded, to hand it to the white stranger wot sojourned with the merchant, and who was your humble servant, Captain. That day I went back to Shanghai loaded with presents not only from my friend but from the friends of my friend, at whose house we had sojourned, and with every gold piece out of that sly dog's pocket. And that's the story of the funniest funeral I was ever at, and there ain't many wot ever see'd a funnier one, I should say.'

Mr. Mipps finished his glass of brandy, and, jumping out of the coffin, refilled it again, relit his pipe at the fire, and vaulted back again with such spirit that the black trestles rocked backwards and forwards. He addressed the Captain again with a yarn which he called the grisliest funeral he was ever at, which was a tale about the Parsees and one of the Towers of Silence.

26

The Tower of Silence

'The Parsees, or Guelirs, as they is called sometimes, is the queerest mild-lookin' fish you could wish to see. For fire-worshippin' savages they is most respectable, polite, and Christian in their behaviour. Most of the men is very fat indeed, and they wears japanned hats on their heads made in the shape of a "cloven hoof," what gives 'em a very rum look. They lives very decent with their wives, only being allowed by their religion to have one at a time, which, to my way o' thinkin' is more than enough too. But if the wife don't bear no child for nine years, the husband can marry another, which in my opinion would be a silly thing to do

'But I ain't a-givin' you a lecture on these folk. I wants just to give you an idea of the way they buries their dead, or rather the way they don't bury 'em, for, you see, they altogether dispense with wottumps. They has birds instead. Can you imagine the horrible feeling of waking up out of a trance and seeing yourself divided up amongst a thousand birds, all a-flyin' off with bits o' you in different directions? That's the sort o' thing them Parsees 'as to put up with in the undertaking line.

'I'll tell you the story of an old man wot I see'd knocked over in a Bombay street one day by a runaway horse and nearly killed. I was close by when the accident happened. I happened to notice the old gent crossin' the road just before it did happen. He had a very beautiful young girl awalkin' with him, and she seemed very particular struck all of a sudden with me, for she turned round and tipped me the wink in as modest a way as she could possibly manage. Mind you, I don't blame the girl, 'cos

I always did seem to attract the admiration of the females, probably because they never attracted me. That shows the contrari-
ness of fate, don't it. Well, her old father turned round and saw
his daughter smilin' at me. And that was just why he didn't get
out of the way of the runaway horse. Feelin' as how I was part-
ly to blame in the matter, though in all innocence, o' course, I
offered to help to carry the old gent to his house. Two other
coves come along to help too, but I could see that the young
girl took no notice of them, though she thanked them very prettily, 'cos all the way her attention was divided between weepin'
over her poor old father, wot was so badly hurt, and smilin' at
me.

' "He's a-goin' to die plain enough," says one of the coves
what was helpin'.

' "You're a cheerful sort o' fellow, ain't you?" says I, in his
lingo. "And who might you be that knows such a lot?"

' " 'Tain't me," answered the cove, "but the bird knows."

'And now, strike me dead, Captain, if I didn't see a great
black beastly vulture a-followin' up the street. He went on in the
most indecent way a-flappin' round us, then flyin' on ahead and
sitting on a housetop to wait till we come up. When we reached
the old gent's house, that horrible creature, with its disgusting
long red neck, like a sort of snake, set on the balcony opposite
the sick-room lattice, and nobody could budge him. I proposed
shooting the damned thing there and then with my pistol, but the
old gent wouldn't hear of it. "I'm a-dyin', he said; "that's plain
enough, and well that there bird knows it. He'll wait there till I
die, and when he sees the bearers come for my body, he'll be off
to the Tower of Silence to warn his fellows of my coming. Then
the birds will devour my body, and will lift me high above the
earth." Well, although he put it very poetical, I couldn't help
thinkin' how very nasty it all was. But it were just as he said, for
I used to call in every day and inquire after him, and so it happened that I was there when he passed away.

'Now, the moment he had passed away, that weird bird gave
a sort of cry; and if ever I heard a death-cry, it was the cry of that
there vulture. Immediately another bird of the same kind came

flying along and perched itself alongside. The first bird evidently told his chum that the old 'un was dead, 'cos away flew the second bird, after having a good look through the lattice, away he flew to the Tower of Silence, wot stood on a hill outside the city. The first bird he stopped there till the bearers came for the body, which was the same day, 'cos they undertakes very prompt in the East on account of the heat. He was to be buried in the evening, or rather eaten, and I never shall forget those humpty-backed birds lookin' so ugly on the walls of the great round open Tower. About twenty of 'em were perched on the branch of a grey old blasted tree, what looked over the outer wall of the cemetery, and as soon as the procession mounted the hill, these fellows flew back to the wall of the Tower, and their friends (there was about four hundred of 'em perched along the wall) sort of squashed up, you understand, to give them room. Now, as a rule, you aren't supposed to look at the body being eaten. They lay it inside the Tower on a grating, and as soon as the bearers has clanged the iron door behind 'em, them birds drop down like a lot of dead weights and fight for the choice bits. In the space of an hour they've picked the dead 'un clean, and the bones fall into a lime-pit, so that there's nothing left.

'Now, o' course, I was very anxious to see the whole performance, and one o' the bearers thought he could manage it for me. I paid him a goodly sum, and he got hold of a ladder, and when all the mourners had gone home we both climbed up and looked over the wall. I never have seen such a sight. Them birds was having a regular rough-and-tumble, but they didn't make no noise over it, 'cos their mouths was too full, you see.

'Now, I hadn't suspected nothing, but presently the bearer, who sat with me on the top of the wall, says, "Our religion don't allow us to look at this sight."

' "Well, we are a-lookin', ain't we?" says I in the lingo, "and it's very interestin', I considers."

' "No one shall see this and live," says he,

' "Oh," says I, "really, now, and what's to prevent me from living?"

' "This," says he, and he whips out a knife and aims a blow at me.'

'I dodged as best I could, knocking over an old vulture on the wall what couldn't move, as he had eaten so much of my old friend the gent down below. But the knife did graze me in the arm for all that. See, here's the scar still,' and the sexton rolled up his sleeve and showed a livid mark upon his dirty tattooed arm. 'That put my monkey up, I tells you, but I didn't want to lose my temper for fear I might so lose my balance on the wall, so I just asked him what the devil he thought he was a-doin'.

' "That man down there," says he, pointing with his knife down into the great hollow of the Tower, "had a daughter."

' "I knows her very well," says I, "and a fine, upstanding young party she is, too."

' "I love her," screamed the man, "and she loved me till her eyes fell on you—you dog of a white man! and now, she won't marry me. But you shan't marry her, you white scum."

' "I don't know that I'm particular desirous to," said I.

' "You insult her!" he screams, in a most unreasonable rage, and he jumps up on to his feet, and rushes at me along the wall.

'Well, I caught his ankle and twisted it. Over he falls on top of me, just missing me with the knife. But he missed more, for he missed his hold on the wall, and down he went crash inside that Tower, right on top of the vultures. They shambled away, frightened and screaming, and I could see him writhing there below me, all smashed up but still alive, and suffering the tortures of the damned. He was trying to put an end to his misery by reaching out for the. knife, which had lodged just within his reach upon the grating; but as soon as he touched it, it slipped through into the lime-pit. Blackguard though he was, I didn't like to think of his lingering there for hours waiting for them birds to finish him off when he got too weak to move, so I drew out my pistol, what I always carried, and put him out of his troubles with a very good shot what hit him full in the head. And that was the end of that. I had to get out of Bombay as quick as I could in case of trouble; but I thinks that I attended a very weird and grisly funeral that day, don't you, Captain?'

'I think so too,' said the Captain, and filling their glasses once more, they pledged each other.

The Captain left the sexton to his hammering, and walked out over the Marsh. He had taken good stock of that coffin shop whilst Mr. Mipps had been yarning, and he was putting two and two together, and the result was four black marks against the sexton. He knew him to be out of his own mouth an adventurer, and, when it came to the push, an unscrupulous one. Also, he had confessed to having had dealings with bucca-neers, and the Captain was quick enough to see that he must have been hand-in-glove with the ringleaders, probably a ring-leader himself. Then he had counted no less than thirteen coffins—finished coffins, with closed lids—in the shop, and he knew that there were only two bodies awaiting burial in the place: the doctor, Sennacherib Pepper, and the sailor killed at the vicarage. Therefore, what were the others for? That they were misfits was out of the question, for Mipps was too shrewd a man to make eleven misfits; besides, he would have broken them up for fresh material. No, those eleven coffins were des-tined for other things besides corpses. And the fourth black mark against the sexton was his hypocrisy, and the ready wit that did it. If any man was interested, and deeply interested, in the great smuggling scheme of Romney Marsh, he felt that Mipps was the man—the tool of another's brain, another might-ier than he. The Squire probably, Doctor Syn possibly, though he had yet to bring the test to bear upon that enigmatical Vicar.

But although as yet Doctor Syn was beyond his grasp, Sexton Mipps was within it. He was sure of his guilt, and, knowing all he did of the man's character, he fell to wondering how it had been possible to fall under his spell; for, apart from Doctor Syn, he would rather have have Mipps for his friend than the rest of the village put together. That odd little man had a rare way of making you like him, for over all his astute cunning hung an imperceptible something that was nearly, if not altogether, lov-able. But the hunter goes to no pains to rehearse the beauty of an animal he is stalking. The Captain puzzled out his plans for cornering not only Mipps, but every wrong 'un on the Marsh;

and if the Squire and Doctor Syn were in the bag—well, so much the better for the bag.

27

The Devil's Tiring-house

If the village was abed by ten o'clock, the coffin shop was very much alive by half an hour after midnight. Jerk, according to his instructions, found himself tapping upon the back window at that very hour, and immediately was hauled into the house by Mr. Mipps himself. The sexton wore a voluminous riding-cloak, heavily tippeted, and a black mask hid the upper part of his face; but Jerk could see by a glance at the fine sharp jaws that Mipps had laid aside his oiliness of manner, his sarcastic wit, and cringing self-complacency, and was allowing the real man that was in him to shine forth for once in a way. Jerk saw the iron qualities in the sexton that had struck the spark upon the flinty bosom of Mrs. Waggetts, for as Mipps walked about amongst his men, from room to room, and in and out of the coffin shop, which was heavily shuttered, there was mastery in his air.

And the company that Jerk found himself among—well, if he had suddenly found himself in the green-room of Drury Lane Theatre in the midst of the great play-actors, he could not have been more surprised, for there collected together were the Jack-o'-lanterns, the Marsh witches, and the demon riders all preparing themselves as for a country fair. Grisly old men, fishermen and labourers, as the case might be, were arranging themselves in torn rags of women's garments, and with a few deft touches from Mipp's hand, lo! the fishermen and labourers were no more, and Marsh witches took their place. Similarly were the big fellows, hulking great men of Kent, metamorphosed into demons, enormous demons, upon whose faces Mipps stuck heavy mustachios and hairy eyebrows of a most terrible aspect. The grisled ones likewise used horsehair in long streamers from their conical hats, so that their appearance as witch folk should be the more pronounced. There were also three little boys and two little girls, dressed as Jack-o'-lanterns. They were much younger than Jerk, but their rig-outs filled him with envy.

'Gentlemen,' said Mipps, leading Jerry into this motley throng of eccentrics, 'the new recruit. A young man wot has the eye of an eagle and the nerves of a steel blade. Those who quarrels with this young gent'll come off worst, if I'm not mistook; but them wot be his friends can bank on his good faith, for he's as staunch as a dog. Get your brandy flasks out, my devils, and let's drink to our new recruit. Jerry Jerk, his name is, but, accordin' to custom, we drops all mention of private names in this business, so up with your glasses whilst I rechristen him. We has power, we has; we has devils amongst us of very great power, for we has lawyers, and farmers, and squires, and parsons wot be in league with us. But the greatest enemy we has is not the Revenue swabs, nor the Admiralty uniforms, nor the bloody redcoats, nor the Prince Regent (God bless him for a vagabond and a "rip"). No, I think you knows who we fears more than all that ruck?'

'Jack Ketch! Jack Ketch!' whispered the horrible creatures.

'Why, right you are, for Jack Ketch it be,' retorted the sexton. 'And here's a man wot's goin' sooner or later to be a Jack Ketch. He's got all the gifts of the hangman, he has, just that jolly way with him he has, and so you'll all be delighted to hear as how he's joined us; for with Jack Ketch as our friend, we'll cheat the black cap on the gallows. Gentlemen, Jack Ketch.' Therefore, they all drank to Jerk with much spirit; and Jerk, having been presented with a flask, pledged them in return, and was introduced to all severally by the sexton. 'This is Beelzebub. Knocked over a good round dozen Revenue swabs in your time, ain't you, Beelzebub? And this is Belch the Demon, the finest rider we ever had in our demon horse. And here's Satan; and this be Catseyes, the weirdest old witch you ever met with in a story-book.' And so on, until such a vast collection of weird names had been rammed into Jerk's brains that he felt quite overpow-ered. However, when his own particular uniform was produced for him to don, his interests were requickened, and before Mipps had half finished attiring him in the strange rags, Jerk would have gone bail that it wasn't himself he saw in the old cracked mirror.

'And now, Jack Ketch,' says Mipps, 'you only has to follow me into the coffin shop to get your allowance of Devil's Pomade. Then I thinks you'll feel real pleased with yourself.' Into the weird coffin shop accordingly Jerry followed the sexton, and there was that black cauldron that he remembered so well. Now he would discover its use. Mipps stirred the contents, and with a great brush began daubing Jerry's face. The curious smell made the youngster close his eyes, and he felt the brush pass over them.

'Now,' said the sexton, 'I blows out the candles, and you shall see.' Jerry opened his eyes as the sexton blew out the lights. 'Bring in the mirror,' called the sexton. And then into the coffin shop came the other members of the company, and the mystery of the demon riders was explained, for in the dark room each diabolical face glistened like the moon, and when the cracked mirror had been held up before him, he saw that he in his turn burned with the same hell-fire. 'It's time, Satan, to get the Scarecrow in; and you, Beelzebub, go and paint the horses with what's left in the cauldron.'

Beelzebub obeyed the sexton promptly, and, picking up the cauldron, went to the back of the house, Satan accompanying him on his different errand—namely, that of bringing in the Scarecrow, a thing that puzzled Jerry exceedingly.

Mipps seemed to read his thoughts, for he approached and whispered, 'Jack Ketch, you're a-wonderin' about the Scarecrow now, ain't you? Well, you've noticed him, I dare say, all dressed in black at the bottom of my turnip field, ain't you?'

'Yes,' replied the new-christened Jack Ketch, 'I've noticed him as long as I can remember, and a very life-like Scarecrow I considers him to be.'

'You're right,' replied the sexton. 'It's the best Scarecrow I ever see'd, for it's life-like and no mistake; and if you keeps your eyes open, you'll see him a bit more life-like to-night. You wait.'

Satan soon reappeared bearing on his shoulder the dead lump of the Scarecrow. Mipps indicated an old coffin that lay on the floor behind the counter of the shop, and Satan at one pushed the Scarecrow into it, and covered him with a lid.

'He'll be there till the work's done,' said Mipps, 'for, you see, the great man himself rides out at nights as the Scarecrow, and if you keep your eyes open, you'll spot him. Now, Beelzebub,' as that terror appeared, 'I take it that them horses is all ready, so bear in mind that my friend Jack Ketch is new to the game, and stick by him. Good luck to you, devils, and may the mist guard the legion from all damned swabs.' And so the company filed Out of the Devil's Tiring-house.

'Ain't you coming along, Hellspite?' said one of the ghastly crew to the sexton.

'No, Pontius Pilate, I ain't,' replied Mipps; 'for me and blunderbuss is a-goin' to watch that damned meddlesome Captain.'

And so they left him there, Beelzebub leading Jerry by the hand out of the back door of Old Tree Cottage.

28

The Scarecrow's Legion

The company found their steeds in the turnip field at the back of the house, guarded so religiously during the daytime by the old Scarecrow that now reposed in the coffin. Horses and ponies were decked out with weird trappings, and all tethered to a low fence that bordered one of the dykes. Jerry's horse, or rather the missing schoolmaster's horse, was brought to him by Beelzebub himself, whom Jerry very soon discovered to be a most entertaining and affable devil. It was fortunate indeed for Jerry that he was a good rider, and had a knowledge of the Marsh, for the cavalcade immediately set out across the fields, breaking into a wild gallop, leaping dykes and sluices so madly that it was a marvel indeed to the boy that his old scragbone could keep pace with them. Beelzebub rode at his side on a strong farm horse, and kept urging him to a higher speed. It was nothing more nor less than a haphazard cross country steeple-chase, and the young adventurer was caught in the thrill of it.

'Heels in hard, Jack Ketch, when I tell you. Now!' and hard went the heels in, and neck to neck went the horse straight at the broad dyke. 'Yoikes!' and up they would go, crashing down again into the rush tops on the far side. Thus they traversed the Marsh for six miles till they reached the highroad under Lympne Hill. There they drew rein at a spot where three roads meet. At the bend of these roads Jerry could see a man on a tall grey horse.

'That's the Scarecrow,' whispered Beelzebub. 'That's the great man hisself.'

One of the Jack-o'-lanterns trotted off on his pony towards this figure, and Jerk saw him salute the Scarecrow, who handed him a paper. Saluting again, the youngster came back to Beelzebub, who took the paper from him, and read it carefully by the light of the young Jack's lantern (For these boys carried lanterns fixed upon long poles, bearing them standard fashion as they rode.)

As he was reading, Beelzebub kept catching his breath excitedly, and he tucked the paper away in his belt, he muttered, 'May the Marsh be good to the Scarecrow to night.' Jerry instinctively looked down the road to where the Scarecrow had been standing, but horse and rider had disappeared. 'Ah, Jack Ketch,' said Beelzebub, 'you are wondering wot's of him, eh? You'd need an eye of quick-silver to keep sight of him. Here, there, and everywhere, and all at once, he is, and astride the finest horse on Romney Marsh, a horse wot 'ud make the Prince Regent's mouth water, a horse more valuable than the Bank of England.'

'But where he's gone to?' asked Jerry.

'About his business and thine, Jack Ketch,' answered the devil.

'I wish I'd seen him go,' returned Jerry, 'for I likes to see a good horse on the move. He went very silent, didn't he?'

'You'll never hear the noise of the Scarecrow's horse a-trottin', Jack Ketch, 'cos he's got pads on his hoofs. Ah, he's up to some tricks is the Scarecrow, and, by hell, he'll need 'em tonight.'

'Why?' asked Jerk.

'Because he's had word passed from Hellspite that the King's men are out, and Scarecrow thinks as how we may have to fight 'em.'

'And don't you want to do that?'

'Why, you see, it 'ud be awkward if any of us got wounded, and wounded men ain't easy things to hide in a village, is they? and it 'ud be a difficult business to explain. Though, come to that, the Scarecrow ain't never put out for an explanation o' nothing.'

As he was speaking, Beelzebub took Jerry's rein and started off again at the head of the cavalcade. Their way was now along the road where the Scarecrow had appeared, and when they had ridden for about half a mile they again sighted him, sitting his horse stock still in the middle of the way. But this time he was not alone, for there were some half-dozen men leading pack ponies from the road into a large field. Towards this field Beelzebub led his cavalcade, and consequently they had to pass the grim figure called the Scarecrow. Jerry, you may be sure, was ambitious to get a near view of this strange personage, for he wanted, if possible, to pierce his disguise, and see if he could recognise the features. But the nearer he got, the stranger became the strange figure. If it was any one that he knew, then it was only the Scarecrow in Mipp's turnip field, for he was as like as two peas are like each other.

And the voice was not like any voice he could put an owner to, although there was something familiar in it. It was a hard, metallic voice, the voice of a commander.

'The King's men are watching the Mill House Farm, so, Beelzebub, you will circle the pack ponies as usual till we get half a mile from the house, then you will cut off and decoy them from the rear. If your attack is sudden and fierce, they will have all they can do to defend themselves, and that will give the Mill House Farm men time to get their pack ponies in with the others. I will see that they get them away safely; and when you have shaken off the King's men, pick us up again on the Romney Road opposite Littlestone Beach. Understood?'

'Understood, Scarecrow, understood,' replied Beelzebub promptly.

'And,' went on the strange man, 'you will stick by Jack Ketch as far as possibly, and don't let him get into any needless danger. I want him to see all the fun that is possible, but I don't want any hurt to come to him. If I alter the plans, I'll pass the word. Understood?'

'Understood, Scarecrow, understood,' repeated Beelzebub.

'Then off you go.'

And off they did go, the pack ponies trotting under their heavy loads of wool keeping along the edges of the fields. This was done with a very good purpose, for where the dykes run

zigzag over Romney Marsh, a thick mist arises some eight feet
high, and even upon nights of full moon these mists yet hang
about like heavy rolls of spider's web, contrasting strangely with
the rest of the country, which is all bright and clear. Jerk had to
ride even faster than before, for the pack ponies, entirely hidden
by the mist curtains, were circled and circled all the way by the
galloping demons and Jack-o'-lanterns, these last swinging their
pole lights round their heads, and uttering strange cries like
those of the marsh fowl. This accounted, then, for all the ghost
tales he had heard. Belated travellers crossing the Marsh, or villagers who were not in the secret, had seen and heard these
ghostly things upon the Marsh. A very clever scheme Jerk
thought it was, and a very good way of clearing the ground of
the curious. So on they road in wild circles round and round
the pack ponies. Beelzebub was the actual leader. He it was who
gave the orders, but the mysterious Scarecrow would dash out
of the mist every now and again just to see that all was well
with the legion, and then as quickly would he disappear, borne
away like a ghost upon that spectral grey thoroughbred.

On they dashed, stopping at numerous farms on the way,
where they always found more pack ponies waiting to join the
cavalcade. And the Scarecrow was always somewhere. As soon
as any little hitch occurred, as one frequently did when the men
placed the temporary bridge over the dykes for the transit of
the pack ponies, the Scarecrow would suddenly appear in their
midst giving sharp orders, whose prompt obedience meant an
instant end to the difficulty, whatever it chanced to be. It was the
laying of this same temporary bridge that caused most of the
delays, for it was a cumbersome thing to move about, and it
had to be built strong enough to support the weight of the pack
ponies. These ponies, too, caused at some periods of the march
a considerably bother, for their packs of wool would sometimes
shake loose from the harness, and the cavalcade would be fain
to stop whilst this was remedied. But although the pack ponies
stopped often, the demon riders were never allowed that luxury. Beelzebub untiringly flogged the horse round and round,
now in large circuits, now in small circles, always ringing in the

pack ponies. from any prying eyes. It would have meant death to any one who got a view within that sweeping scythe of cavalry. And as murders on the Marsh were all put down to Marsh devils, and because of the dreaded, superstition that had grown in the minds of Kentish folk, the smugglers were utterly callous as to what crimes they perpetrated. They were as safe from the law as the most law-abiding citizen; for those who didn't credit the existence of murdering hobgoblins, at least possessed sufficient fear of the smugglers themselves, and left them religiously alone. After all, it was no business of any one's but the Revenue men, and so to the Revenue men they were left, and in nearly every record it may be seen that the Revenue men got the worst of it.

29

The Fight at Mill House Farm

Mill House Farm was the last on Beelzebub's list, and in the dyke facing the house, but on the other side of the highroad, crouched the King's men, commanded by the bos'n. They were as still as mice, for the Captain had given strict orders on that score; but they need not have put themselves to such pains, for, owing to the extreme vigilance of Sexton Mipps, the smugglers knew exactly where they were and what they were going to do.

Now it is depressing to the most seasoned fighters to have to crouch for hours in a muddy dyke waiting for an outnumbering enemy—for it was common knowledge that if smuggling was carried on upon the Marsh, it was well organised, and relied for its secrecy upon the strength and numbers of its assistants. So the bos'n had no easy task in keeping his men from grumbling; for whatever Captain Collyer's opinions may have been with regard to maintaining the law and his duty, it was pretty evident that his men had no great relish for the task. The bos'n heartily wished that the Captain had not left him responsible, for his absence was having a bad effect upon the men. It is one thing to fight an enemy, but quite another to shoot down your own countrymen; and although every man Jack of them was itching for the French war, they felt no enthusiasm for this smuggling business. The whole of the countryside was with the lawbreakers, and who knows how many of these same King's men had not themselves done a profitable trade with illegal cargoes from France!

Such were the feelings of the King's men as they lay in the dyke opposite Mill House Farm, listening to the noise of ponies' hoofs in the yard, and waiting to fire upon any one who presented himself.

But the order "not to kill, but to fire low' also damped their spirits—for what chance would they have against fellows desperate to keep their necks out of the rope, who would most certainly aim to kill?

The bos'n had great difficulty in preventing one old sea-dog who lay next him in the ditch from voicing his opinion of the proceedings in a loud bass voice; but what he did say he after all had the good grace to whisper, though none too softly.

'What the hell's the sense, Mister Bos'n, of sending good seamen like we be to die like dogs in this blamed ditch? Ain't England got no use for seamen nowadays? 'Tain't the members of Parleyment wot'll serve her when it comes to fighting, though they does talk so very pleasant.'

'They don't talk as much as you do,' was the hushed retort of the bos'n.

'Look ye 'ere, Job Mallett,' went on the other, 'you've been shipmate o' mine for longer than I well remembers, and you be in command here. Well, I ain't a-kickin' against your authority, mind you, but I'm older than you be, and I want to give my views to you, which is also the views of every mother's son in this damned ditch. Why don't we clear out of this, and be done with the folly? We looks to you, Job Mallett—I say we looks to you as our bos'n—and a very good bos'n you be—we looks to you to save us bein' made fools of. We wants to fight the Frenchies, and not our own fellows. The Parleyment's a-makin' a great mistake puttin' down the smugglers. If they only talked nice to 'em they's find a regiment or two o' smugglers very handy to fight them ugly furriners. For my own part, I don't see why the Parleyment don't put down other professions for a bit, and leave the smugglers alone. Why not give lawyers a turn, eh? They could do with a bit o' hexposin'! Dirty swabs! And so could the doctors, wot sell coloured water for doses. But oh, no! It's always the poor smugglers, who be hard-working fellows, and very good fighters too, as we'll soon be called upon to see.'

All this time Job Mallett tried to silence him. But threats, persuasions, and arguments were useless.

'Old Collywobbles thinks the same as wot we does.'

'I'll have you to remember,' whispered the bos'n stiffly, 'that I, bein' in command in this 'ere ditch, don't know as to who you' be alludin' to when you say "Collywobbles." I don't know no one of that name.'

'Oh, ain't you a stickler for duty!' chuckled the sea-dog. 'Still, I respec's you for it, though perhaps you'll permit me to say as how it was you in the fo'c'sle of the *Resistance* as gave the respected Captain Howard Collyer the pleasant pet name of Collwobbles. P'raps that's slipped your memory for the moment?'

'It has,' answered the bos'n.

'Very well, then, but you can take it from, me as how it was. And a very clever name it be, too. But there, you always was one of the clever ones, Job Mallett.'

'I wish I were clever enough to make you shut your fat mouth,' muttered the bos'n.

'Now then, Job Mallett, don't you begin getting to personalities. But there, now—I don't want to quarrel with you. You're always had my greatest respec's, and as we'll probably be stiff 'uns in a few minutes, we won't quarrel, old pal. But I give you my word that I don't like being shot down like a rabbit, and I'm sorry as how it's you as is in command, 'cos if it was any one else I declares I'd get up now and walk home to bed.'

'If Captain Collyer was here, you know you'd do nothing of the sort.'

'Why ain't he here? That's wot I wants to know. Strike me dead, it's easy enough to send out poor old sea-dogs to be shot like bunny rabbits. I could do that. There ain't no pluck in that, as far as I can see.'

You ain't a-settin' a very good example to the younger men, I'm thinkin',' said Job Mallett. 'You, the oldest sea-man here, and a-grumblin' and a-gossipin' like an apple-wife. You ought to think shame on yourself, old man.'

'Oh, well,' growled the sea-dog, 'I won't utter another blarsted word, I won't. But if you does want to know my opinion on these 'ere proceedin's it's—hell!'

'I don't say as how I don't agree with you,' returned Job Mallett, 'but there it is, and we've got to make the best of it. It won't do no good a-grumblin'. We'll make the best of a bad job, and I hopes as I for one will be able to do my duty 'cos I don't relish it no more than you do.'

'Well, strike me blind, dumb, and deaf!' thundered the seaman in a voice of emotion as he clapped Job Mallett on the back, 'if I'd been a snivellin' powder monkey I ought to be downright ashamed of myself. And seem' as how I be the oldest seaman here instead, well, I'm more than downright ashamed. Job Mallett, I thanks you. You set a good example to us all, Mister Bos'n, and I'll stand by you for one. Damn the smugglers, and wait till I get at 'em, that's all!'

'Thank'ee,' said the bos'n; 'but you'll greatly oblige me by keeping quiet, 'cos here they be, if I ain't mistook.'

Indeed, at that instant along the road came the sound of the sharp, quick steps of the pack ponies. At present they were hidden in the mist, which floated thickly about that part of the Marsh, but they could be heard—and not only the ponies, but a voice singing as well. This voice was raised in a wailing monotone, and the words were repeated over and over again. They were intended for the ears of the wretched sailors who were waiting in the ditch for the attack.

'Listen, oh you good King's men, who are waiting to shoot us from the damp ditch. We have got your kind Captain here. A blunderbuss is looking at the back of his head. If you fire on us, good King's men, then the blunderbuss will fire at the good Captain, and then:

'All the King's horses and all the King's men
    Could not put Captain together again!"'

Even if the words were not sufficient to explain the situation
to the sailors, the first figures of the cavalcade were sufficient. A
donkey led by two Jack-o'-lanterns on foot jolted out of the
fog. Upon its back was a man bound and gagged, supported on
either side by two devil-men. That the gagged wretch was the
Captain it needed no words to tell, for his uniform showed by
the lanterns' light, and there, right behind him, sure enough,
was the blunderbuss in question, pointed by a snuffy little devil
called by his colleagues Hellspite, who sat hunched up on a
shoddy little pony. This group halted at a convenient distance
from the sailors in the ditch, and Hellspite again rehearsed his
speech, ending up with:

'All the King's horses and all the King's men
    Could not put Captain together again!'

Now the poor bos'n in command had all his life grown so
used to taking other people's orders that he didn't know what to
do for the best. He liked the Captain, and didn't want to see
him killed, though he knew what he must be suffering in his
ridiculous position. He knew that, had the Captain but got the
use of his speech, he would have shouted, 'Fire, and be damned
to 'em!' But, then, the Captain had not got the use of his speech.
The Scarecrow and Hellspite knew enough of the man to see to
that, and as they had no great desire to be fired at, they had
seen that the gags were efficient. So it was, after all, small wonder that the old grumbling sea-dog next to him, who possessed
a rollicking vein of humour, laughed until he rolled back into the
mud. The rest of the men divided into two classes, some following the example of the bos'n and being struck stiff with
amazement and powerless wrath, others joining the laughing
tar in the muddy ditch, and guffawing over the ridiculous situation of their Captain, for he was not the build of a man to sit
an ass with any dignity.

It was this sudden surprise that made the sailors unprepared for what followed. A large party of horse swept out of the mist behind them, and when they turned to see what fresh thing was amiss, there was a line of terrible cavalry pulling up on their haunches a few yards in their rear. Thus they were cut off on both sides: the devils with flaming faces, on horses of alarming proportions at their back, and in front their Captain waiting for them to shoot—to meet his own death by the little demon's blunderbuss.

'If you fire, you good King's men,
Then the Devil shall blarst your Captain!'

'And you as well, you good King's men!' shrieked and howled the demons at the back, who covered with pistol or blunderbuss every Jack Tar in the ditch.

Then another rider appeared on the scene. He was tall, thin, and of ungainly countenance, and he rode a light-grey thoroughbred. He was the Scarecrow, and all the devils hailed him by that name as he appeared. Behind him came the pack ponies, some sixty or seventy in all, and on each pony was a woolpack that would have meant a human neck to the King's hangman if only Collyer were free to work his will. The Scarecrow drew up in the road, and watched the great procession of ponies pass along toward the coast. When they had all but passed he gave a signal, the doors of the Mill House barn were opened, and ten more heavily-laden ponies trotted out and joined the snake of illegal commerce that was wriggling away to the sea. Then, like some field-marshal upon the field of battle, did the Scarecrow slowly ride over a small bridge and along the front of his demon cavalry. Jerry Jerk heard him give a short order to Beelzebub as he passed, and then saw him gallop away after the pack ponies.

Now came the ordeal for the King's men, for they were kept in that absurd position for a full two hours or longer. Folly to move, folly to fight—there they had to stop: a foolish-looking group of fighting men if you like, but more foolish had they attempted resistance, 'for they were outnumbered in men, in arms, and in wits. Once, indeed, did the bos'n nearly lose his head, and that was when Hellspite lowered his blunderbuss and produced a clay pipe, which he lit. The bos'n saw a chance, spat in his hand, grasped his cutlass, and clambered from the dyke. But instantaneously came the ominous noise of cocking pistols, and the old sea-dog grabbed his leg and pulled him back swearing into the mud. Hellspite chuckled and smoked his pipe, the horseman covered every man in the ditch with cocked weapons, and so another hour passed over the curious group. Suddenly from across the Marsh came the cry of a curlew, repeated seven times. Hellspite put up his pipe and muttered an order to the two devils by the donkey. Then he addressed the sailors.

'Now, good sailors, we will trouble you for your arms. Pass them up to good Job Mallett, and he shall stretch his legs and lay them at my feet.'

But again Job Mallett lost his head. He arose in the ditch and sang out bravely: 'You and the rest of you are damned cowards in silencing the mouth of our Captain. Had he his voice you know what he'd say—"Shoot, and be damned to you"—and well you know it. Why don't you meet us in fair fight, instead of using such devil's tricks?'

''Cos we ain't so bloody minded as the good King's bos'n,' answered Hellspite in a piping voice, which drew forth a great laugh from the devils.

One of the seamen, considering that all eyes were now upon the bos'n, leapt from the ditch and made a rush for Hellspite with his naked cutlass. Five or six pistols cracked behind him, and over he fell, face downwards in the road. Every shot had taken effect—he was dead.

'Oh, do keep your little heads, you silly King's men,' wailed Hellspite— 'for look how we've spoiled that nice little man. He's no use now to fight the French—no use at all. Oh, what a pity, what a pity, what a pity!'

Again came the cry of the curlew seven times.

'Now, then, those weapons!' ordered Hellspite sharply; 'and if they don't come along quick, we'll put this Captain out of service along with his man there.'

There was nothing for it. They were in their power. The smugglers had proved that they were good shots, and that they meant business. There was nothing for it but to hand over their arms to the bos'n, who with a bad grace laid them upon the roadway, whence they were picked up by the Jack-o'-lanterns, who bore them into the barn.

'Now, then, my fine fellows,' said Hellspite, 'we'll plump this 'ere Captain on the road. You will pick him up if you want him, and take him home to bed, for the dawn ain't far off, and as the woolpacks are safe and away we'll bid you good repose.

The Captain was accordingly lifted from the donkey and laid upon the road. The sailors were filed up around him, and conducted ingloriously back to the vicarage barn. Three devils, told off for the purpose, bore away the body of the dead seaman; so that before the dawn lit up the Marsh there was no sign of smugglers anywhere upon her. Jerry Jerk, after disrobing with the others at the coffin shop, was packed off by Beelzebub to bed, where, without disturbing his grandparents, he fell immediately asleep, and dreamed his whole adventure over again.

Just as the dawn was breaking, Mipps was returning from the vicarage barn, where he had deposited a bundle of weapons outside the door, when he saw a yellow-faced man creeping along the field by the churchyard wall. As he watched the figure disappear into a deep dyke, he muttered, 'I wonder if that there thing is real or unreal. I wonder if it did get off that reef in his body. If he did, what the hell's he findin' to live upon; and if he ain't—well, God help one of us in this 'ere place!' And he scurried back to the coffin shop by back ways like a prowling rat.

30

Captain Collyer Entertains
an Attorney from Rye

It was something of a difficult position which Captain Collyer was called upon to face. That he had cut a ridiculous figure no one was more conscious than himself, and being made absurd before his own men made the situation doubly difficult. But Captain Collyer preserved his dignity in a manner that did credit to the British Navy.

When the smugglers had gone, and the bos'n had freed him from his bonds, he stood up in the barn and addressed the sailors.

'My men,' he began, 'we have been badly beaten. Without a blow you were forced to lay down your arms, which I well know must have been a hard thing for you to do. After I had given the bos'n orders of the night's plan, I went out to verify certain suspicions that I had formed about certain folk upon the Marsh. I was congratulating myself on how well I was succeeding, when I found myself a helpless prisoner in the wretches' hands. I had walked blindly into a very clever trap. As you saw for yourselves, my captors made such a complete job of me that I was helpless to speak to you or give you any sign. Under the circumstances, I must thank the bos'n for his behaviour. I appreciate what he did, for he saved my life; although, perhaps, I could almost find it in my heart to wish that he had acted otherwise, for a good seaman's life is now on my hands—brave Will Rudrum, who was shot dead on the road. I also cannot find it in my heart to reprimand Joe Dickenson for his fit of laughter, because nobody saw the humour and disgrace of my position as much as I did myself. But when a man's life is forfeited, all humour slips away, and so it has for me, and for you, I'm sure, who were Will Rudrum's comrades. I am very thankful that my life has been spared for one purpose—to avenge poor Rudrum's death; and if any one should and can avenge him, I hold myself to be that man. For this purpose I intend to take you all into my confidence. Having failed dismally so far, I do not wish to fail again; therefore listen. In the first place, we are not a strong enough body to cope with these Marsh men. I shall therefore demand reinforcements. There are redcoats at Dover; and there are seamen at Rye. To both of these towns I shall send messengers. Also at Rye there is a remarkable old man, a wise man—an attorney-at-law. He will meet me this very day at the Ship Inn, and will undertake all the legal points with regard to the arrests which I shall make as soon as I have gathered up a few more facts. This corner of England is a very hotbed of enemies to the Government. Bos'n, you will serve out an extra allowance of rum at once, for we must drink together.'

The rum was served, and the Captain raised his pannikin.

'To the swift avenging of poor Will Rudrum, to the quick regaining of our dignity, and to the speedy hanging of His Majesty's foes!'

The men drank, and then Joe Dickenson shouted, 'And to our Captain, God bless him, and blast them as does him dirty tricks!'

This toast was drunk greedily, and then the bos'n led three cheers—three cheers which went echoing out of the old barn across the Marsh with a strength that made many a smuggler turn in his bed uneasily.

When they opened the barn door at daybreak to let the Captain go forth, they found there a neat pile of. weapons. His Majesty's pistols and His Majesty's cutlasses were all returned.

'Ay, but there's some honour amongst thieves, sir,' exclaimed the bos'n.

'Devil a bit of it,' cried the Captain. 'The rascals know that we can soon get substitutes, and they've no wish to have such tell-tale things discovered on their premises. There's more good sense than honour in it, I'm thinking, Job Mallett.'

At ten o'clock that morning a coach rolled up to the door of the Ship Inn, and out stepped Antony Whyllie, Esq., attorney-at-law from Rye, a man of sixty-five, but upright and alert as any youngster. He was attired in a bottle-green coat, black satin breeches, silk stockings, silver-buckled shoes, and faultless linen. His grey wig, tied concisely with a black ribbon, completed a true picture of the Law: a man to desire for one's defence, a man to dread for one's accusation.

The Captain received him at the door of the inn, and conducted him to the privacy of his own bedchamber.

There he unburdened his mind to the lawyer, stating all his suspicions, and clearly showing how he had arrived at them. By the end of the morning they thoroughly understood each other, the lawyer returning by coach to Rye, with orders to the Governor of the Castle to prepare accommodation for a large number or prisoners, and to see to it that there were enough chains. But, strange to relate, that lawyer in bottle-green never reached the little town of Rye, for his coach stopped at a certain farmhouse beyond Romney. Here he alighted to make room for another lawyer—a real lawyer, a man of sixty-five, who had left Rye that very morning to consult with a certain Captain Collyer residing at the Ship Inn, Dymchurch. This lawyer had never arrived at Dymchurch. For, at a lonely spot on the road outside Romney, a strong body of men had awaited the arrival of his coach. While two or three of them removed the driver from his box to the farmhouse, where they speedily made him drunk, two or three others had entered the coach, securely gagged and blindfolded the occupant, and conveyed him after his coachman. The coach immediately proceeded to Dymchurch with another driver and another lawyer—a man in a bottle-green coat.

The blindfolded lawyer had been scared out of all knowledge, especially by the sound of a certain man's voice known as the Scarecrow. This terrible ruffian had told the lawyer that if, on returning to Rye, he breathed a word of what had happened, they would most certainly catch him again and do away with him, adding that there was no place more convenient than Romney Marsh for the hiding of a body. So, with the exception of telling his awful experience to his wife, whom he feared nearly as greatly as he feared the Scarecrow, Antony Whyllie, attorney-at-law, held his tongue, being only too thankful that the rascals had let him off so easily. The coachman, who was muddled with drink and with falling off his box at least a dozen times on the way back, never even remembered what had happened or to whose kind offices he was indebted for the privilege of becoming so gloriously drunk. So the affair passed unheeded by the public, and the gentleman in the bottle-green, having changed his clothes, might that very afternoon have been seen going towards the church at Dymchurch. Down into the crypt he went, and there, at a dirty table lighted a candle set in a bottle's neck, he aided two other men to work out certain accounts that were spread before them in a book marked 'Parish Register of Death'. But there were no deaths registered in that book. It was full of figures accounting for cargoes of wool, full of receipts for coffins loaded with spirits.

Sexton Mipps and the gentleman who had worn the bottle-green coat then unlocked an old chest and took out certain money-bags, which they emptied on the table. The third gentleman, whom they addressed as the Scarecrow, helped them to sort the coin, French in one pile, English in another; and then, referring to a list of names in the register, the three managers of the secret bank portioned out their servants' wages. When this was accomplished, the gentleman who had worn the bottle-green coat presented his little account—which was promptly paid in guineas—and left them, saying that he was very sorry that it was the last time that he would draw so many golden Georges from the bank.

'Yes, the bank closes accounts today,' said the Scarecrow, striking his name off the list, 'though perhaps some day we shall open it again—who knows?'

'Let's hope so,' said the gentleman, shaking hands with the Scarecrow and the sexton; 'and let's hope we meet again. Good-bye.' And he was gone, Mipps locking the door behind him.

'It's all right to a penny,' said the Scarecrow.

'Hooray, I calls it,' chuckled Sexton Mipps, rubbing his hands together. 'I'll get this little lot of coinage nailed up in a coffin and sent to Calais, and old What's-his-name wot's just gone up the stairs had arranged with the Calais people to get it transferred to the Bank of Lyons, so you can get at it yourself from Marseilles, can't you?'

'Yes, we're all square now—everything ship-shape. Mother Waggetts I've settled with, and Imogene gets the iron-bound casket. I've seen to it all. But it's time I was off. I've a certain gentleman to see before nightfall.'

'Who's that?' asked Mipps.

'The Squire,' replied the Scarecrow, laughing, as he tied up the money-bags.

'And I have a gentleman to visit, too,' said Mipps.

'Who's that?' asked the Scarecrow.

'Parson Syn—Doctor Syn—the worthy Vicar,' replied Mipps, winking, at which the Scarecrow laughed and went out of the crypt.

Mipps, after locking up the money in the chest, followed leisurely, and as he crossed the churchyard he saw Doctor Syn ringing the front-door bell of the Court House.

'Well,' murmured Mipps to himself, 'I've met one or two of 'em in my time, but he's a blinkin' marvel!'

31

Doctor Syn has a 'Call'

'Do you mean to say that you're going to leave Dymchurch?'
The Squire was positively angry—a thing he had never been
with Doctor Syn in all the years that he had know him. 'You are
undoubtedly pulling my leg. God bless my soul, sir, there's precious few fellows can do that, and precious few that dare to try;
but that's what you're doing, isn't it?'

'I'm afraid not Sir Antony. My dear Squire, my good friend,
I am afraid that for once in my life I am most dreadfully in
earnest.'

'But what don't you like about the place? Is it something I've
done? Do you want your stipend raised? Damme, I'll treble the
blessed thing if it's that. Oh, it's that rascally son of mine that's
been putting you out. It's that Denis scamp, who never took to
his books, and never will. But I'll make him. I'll take my riding
whip to the young whelp if he causes you pain. It is he. He's at
the bottom of it. My soul and body, I'll give the young puppy a
shaking up. He doesn't know a good tutor when he sees one.
The impertinent young popinjay. God bless my soul, why, he's no
more respect for me than a five-barred gate. He's always doing
something to jar me. Why, do you know that the cool-faced
young malefactor announced the other day in the most insolent
manner that he was going to marry a girl from the inn! Yes, I
assure you he did. He announced to me, sir, in the most conde-
scending tones, as if he were conferring an inestimable favour
upon my head, that he thought I ran a very good chance of having that girl Imogene for my daughter-in-law. You know,
Imogene that serves and waits and does dirty jobs at the Ship

Inn. And when I expostulated in fatherly tones, why, bless me if they young spitfire didn't fly into a passion, crying out that it was high time one of the Cobtrees introduced some good looks into the family. Said that to me, mind you—his natural father that brought him into the world. I told him that—used those very words—and what does he do but begin to bow and scrape and praise and thank me for bringing him into the world at the same period as that black-haired tavern wench, just as if his mother and I had timed the thing to a nicety! Why, when I come to think of it, she's the daughter of a common pirate—that rascally, scoundrelly Clegg who was hanged at Rye. Isn't she, now? And she's to be my daughter-in-law! Now, Doctor Syn, in the name of Romney Marsh, 'what the devil—I say, what the devil would you do if you had a son like that to deal with?'

The Squire had to stop for breath, and Doctor Syn, who had been vainly trying to get a word in edgeway; replied, 'Well, sir, I should candidly confess that my son was a lucky dog if he succeeded in getting her—which I should very much doubt. In fact, were I in your place, I should go so far as to bet my wig that he would never win the girl. I'm fond of Denis—devoted to him, in truth—but I'm afraid he'll have a great difficulty in marrying Imogene.'

'I should bet my eyes he will, sir. I need none to tell me that. Difficulty in marrying her? Ay that he will. My son will marry position, sir, money, sir, and if beauty comes along of it, well, then, beauty, sir, and all the better for my son, sir.

'Provided, of course, that the lady is willing,' put in the Vicar.

'Willing? What minx wouldn't be only too willing to marry my son! Old Cobtree's son—and not so old either, sir, eh? And as for a tavern wench, the daughter of a dirty pirate hanged in Rye, why, poop-pooh, my dear Doctor! Laughable!'

'Well, I think differently in this case, Squire,' said the Doctor. 'I should call Denis a lucky dog—I might even stretch a point and, at the risk of being unfrocked, say a damned lucky dog— if he succeeded in marrying that girl Imogene.'

'What?' cried the Squire.

'Of course,' said the Doctor, 'you mustn't go entirely by what I say, because I hold myself very seriously gifted in the judging of attractive women.'

'And so do I, sir. I know she's attractive—a damned fine upstanding young woman—and if she were a poor gentle-woman, I might stretch a point and accept her. Beauty comes last on my list.'

'But Imogene possesses all the other requirements. Rich she is, and very rich, though she doesn't know it; and although her mother was but a dancer, she was descended from an Incan princess. As you said "Pooh-pooh!" to me, sir, why, I'll say "Pooh!" back, sir: pooh to your Kentish ladies of quality—for when Imogene comes into her own, why, damme, she could chuck their fortunes on to every horse in the village steeple-chase!'

'Is she wealthy? That girl at the Ship Inn? Well, perhaps I am wrong in saying that the match is so very uneven. Perhaps I am.'

'Yes,' went on the Vicar, 'there is just the possibility that it might be brought to a successful issue, though, if you'll excuse my saying so, you are tactless at times, Squire.'

'What do you mean?' cried the Squire hotly. 'I am none too sure that I should care for my son to marry an inn girl, though she were the daughter of Crœsus himself!'

'My dear Squire, calm yourself, I beg. As an inn girl I admit Imogene is below Denis as regards position, but as an Incan princess, why, my friend, she is as far superior to the Cobtrees of the Court House as is the reigning house of England.'

The Squire gasped and said nothing.

'And it's for the fortunes of Imogene that I must leave you,' went on the cleric—'that is, leave you for a time, you under-stand. For although I shall bestow upon her certain things of value that I hold as her guardian, the bulk of her fortune has been lying idle; but now that she is growing into womanhood it is high time I fulfilled my duties and looked after her money for her.'

'Then she's your adopted child, is she?' said the Squire, push-ing his wig back and scratching his head.

'Well, I suppose that's how it stands in a sense,' replied the Doctor. 'When that rascal Clegg died he actually paid me a good sum of money to see that his daughter was provided for, and of course I've kept that money for her till she came to years of discretion. He also told me where England's treasure was buried, and that's what I'm off to get.'

'England's treasure? What's that?' asked the amazed Squire.

'Clegg was a partner of England, the notorious pirate. It is said that he killed England in a quarrel, though nothing was proved of it. Anyhow, Clegg was the only man who knew of the hiding-place. At his death he imparted the secret to me, after I had given solemn oath upon the Bible to keep it to myself.'

'God bless my soul!' said the Squire, leaping to his feet; 'and do you mean to say that you've kept the secret all this time, and not fitted out a ship and gone to lift it? Why, there may be millions there.'

'There are,' said Doctor Syn. 'I'm certain of that. That's why I've been at pains to keep the whole matter to myself, not even telling the girl, for it will want careful handling. Once let any one know that I am off to lift Clegg's treasure chests, and every dog in Christendom will be nosing on my tail. Clegg had the same fear of this secret being stolen, and so committed the exact lie of the island to my memory, and to no map; but he did it so uncommon well that I can see point, bays, lagoons, soundings, and tracks just as if I had piloted ships there all my life.'

'Then all this pious talk of wanting to go out as a preacher to the smelly blacks is simply balderdash?'

'Merely a cloak to hide my real designs.'

Good Lord deliver us!' said the Squire, pushing his wig clean off and allowing it to lie unheeded on the floor.

Just then there entered a servant, who announced to the Squire that the girl from the Ship Inn was outside with a note, which she desired to give to him.

'Ask her to be so kind as to step in,' said the Squire, with a touch of deference and awakened interest.

Imogene came into the room. Perfectly at ease, she stood there, until with almost regal grace she accepted the chair that the Squire brought forward. Yes, he thought, the Vicar was right. Her clothes were rough, indeed, but her manner would have sat well on an empress.

'You have brought a note for me, I think—Imogene?' said the Squire at last. He was ridiculously uncertain whether to call her Imogene as usual, or Madam; in fact, in his confusion he was as near as not saying Mistress Cobtree, which would have been awful.

Imogene held out a small sealed packet and looked at the fire, and so taken up was the Squire with looking at her and thinking of the Incan millions, that if Doctor Syn had not shuffled his foot he would have forgotten to open the letter at all. But the moment he had, the girl, the Incan millions, his anger against his son—everything was forgotten. He crunched the letter in his hand, threw his head back, and, looking at the ceiling with the most appalled expression on his face, cried out:

'If there's a God in heaven, come down quick and wring this Captain's neck!'

'What is it?' cried the Vicar.

'Read it out,' yelled the Squire, flinging the crumpled paper ball upon the table. 'If you love me, read it out, and tell me what to do!'

Doctor Syn recovered the note, which had bounced from the table to the floor, and when he had unravelled it and smoothed it straight and flat, he read:

'SHIP INN.

'To SIR ANTONY COBTREE, of the Court House,
        'Leveller of Marsh Scotts.

'Sir,—I beg to inform you, on behalf of the British Admiralty, that the person of Mr. Rash, Dymchurch Schoolmaster, has disappeared. I feel convinced that there is somebody in power who is organising Romney Marsh for his own ends. Somebody is running wool to France, and from the clever organisation to these runs I know that some powerful brain is directing affairs. Your attitude of utter indifference forces me to suspect you. As

Leveller of the Marsh Scotts you are in a safe place to control such a scheme, and so I have taken a strong measure, in attaching the person of your son, Mr. Denis Cobtree. If the body of that unfortunate schoolmaster, dead or alive, is not produced before me within the next twenty-four hours, I shall take steps to force your hand.

(Signed)   'CAPTAIN HOWARD COLLYER,
                                  'Coast Agent and Commissioner.

'P.S.—There is a press gang at work in Rye, who will ship your son to sea in twenty-four hours.'

'Now what am I to do? Press-gang at Rye! Twenty-four hours! What have I got to do with that flabby-faced school-master? Where's he got to? How the devil should I know? P'raps he thinks that I have danced him off somewhere. Never heard of such a thing in my life! But what am I to do? That's what I want to know. What am I to do? My poor Denis! Why, I wouldn't have quarrelled with him if I'd known. Why has that school-master disappeared? By what infernal right, I say, has that insignificant idiot disappeared?'

Doctor Syn then briefly related the bos'n's story of Rash's disappearance, which the Squire listened to impatiently.

'Well, sir,' the latter explained at the conclusion, 'as far as that schoolmaster's concerned, I don't mind if he's roasting on Lucifer's spit, for I dislike the man. But when his disappearance concerns the safety of my son, my God, he's got to put in an appearance, and be quick about it! I'll have him routed out of his infernal hiding-place. I'll rouse the Marsh men, and have him routed out!'

'That's all very well, Squire, but how?'

'How, sir?' echoed the irascible gentleman. 'How? Do you ask me how? Well, I don't know! How? Yes, how?'

'That's the question,' ruefully remarked Doctor Syn.

'Of course it is,' returned the other. 'Well, how would you set about it yourself?'

'I'd beat the Marsh up from border to border.'

'So I will, sir—so I will!'

'And I should get that mulatto and hang him, for he's a sor-
cerer—a witch-man—and I believe that as long as we have such
a Johah's curse amongst us nothing will come right.'

'I'll do that at once. But we've only twenty-four hours'

Imogene stood up and looked at the Squire, and in a steady
voice, as if she were pronouncing a judgment, she said 'It is
enough for me. I will undertake to find your son for you, and the
schoolmaster too.' Without waiting for a reply she swiftly passed
out of the room.

'But what can we do?' stammered the Squire.

'I should find that mulatto and hang him.'

'But I don't care a fig about finding him.'

'You must,' persisted the cleric—'for he is the cause of the
trouble. Find that mulatto, and leave the rest to Imogene. She
has spoken, and you may be sure she'll keep her word. But find
that mulatto!'

32

A Certain Tree Bears Fruit

Jerk was kept busy all day at the Ship Inn, for Imogene had left her post, and Mrs. Waggetts, who appeared to have grave matters of her own to fuss about, left the young pot-boy in command. He was sorry about this, for he was unable to visit his estate upon the Marsh, and he was eager to view his latest purchase, the gallows. But to his great satisfaction he heard it discussed by a farmer and a fisherman who sat drinking at the bar.

'I tell you that there's a gallows erected on the Marsh nigh Littlestone Point,' the fisherman was saying. 'I could see it quite plain at sunrise when we were running up on to the beach.'

'And you say that there was a man a-hangin' from it?' said the farmer.

'Ay, that's what I said, and I thought as how you could tell me what man it was.

'I don't know nothing,' replied the farmer, 'except that the demon riders was out again last night, and if what you says is right, why, they're at their tricks again, I suppose. And the farmer gave the fishermen a knowing wink.

However, this didn't trouble Jerry, for the laugh was all on his side. Not content with an empty scaffold, he had gone out the night before, whilst Doctor Syn and the Captain had been chatting in the sanded parlour, and collected two great sackfuls of dried sticks and sand, which, with the help if a few tightly knotted lengths of twine, he had converted into the semblance of a man, and this same dummy he had hanged from the rusty chain. It had looked splendid swinging there with the mist wrapped round its feet. This, indeed, was playing hangman's games with a vengeance. Impatient as he was to see the fruits of his labour, impatient he had to remain, for he was not released till nightfall, when Mrs. Waggetts entered the bar with Sexton Mipps. Freed at last from duty, he stepped outside, pulling his hat over his eyes and tucking up his collar, for the wind was blowing up for a cold night. He was leaving the yard with a brisk step when he noticed a cloaked figure coming to meet him. It was Imogene.

'Jerry,' she whispered, 'who put up that gallows on your plot of land?'

'It's my gallows,' answered Jerk proudly. 'I paid for it, and Mister Mipps it was wot helped me to set it up.

'It's a real one, Jerry,' the girl replied.

'Yes, that it is—and ain't it fine?'

'But there's a man, a real man, hanging there.'

At this Jerk slapped his knee with enthusiasm, and cried aloud, 'Now, by all the barrels of rum' (this was a great expression of his; he had heard a seaman use it, and had adopted it), 'if I ain't fit to take in Old Harry hisself! For that same corpse what you've see'd a-danglin' from my gallows tree ain't a corpse at all, but sticks, sand, and sacks, what I invented to look like one.'

'Are you sure, Jerry?' said the girl.

'I'm a-goin' out there myself now; so come along and see for yourself.'

'I've been there once this evening, Jerry.'

'Well, come along of me, and you shall give the old Scarecrow what's a-swing on my gallows a good sharp tweak in the ribs.'

So off they set through the churchyard and out over the Marsh.

'Jerry,' whispered the girl presently, 'there's something queer going to happen soon. Perhaps tonight—perhaps tomorrow night. And it's something uncommon queer, too.'

'Now, what makes you think that?' said Jerry, looking up at her.

'I believe, Jerry, that there are certain tides that run from the Channel round Dungeness that wash up the dead sea-men from the deep waters, and all the time that they lie near shore waiting for the ebb to take 'em back to their old wrecked ships in the deep, their spirits come ashore and roam about us. I feel that way tonight. I can smell death in the air.'

'Well, that's a funny notion,' remarked the boy, turning it over in his mind; 'but I dare say you are right. After all, the sea, what does look so tidy on the top, must have lots of ugly secrets underneath, and I don't see why it shouldn't want to wash 'em ashore once in a way. I've often wondered myself about the dead what moves about inside the sea, and I thinks sometimes, when the high tide runs into the great sluice and fills the near dykes, that perhaps it buries things it's sick of in the mud. Perhaps it's a-doin' it now, and that's what's given you them notions.

'Perhaps it is, Jerry.'

Now the mist was so thick that they did not get a far view of Jerk's gallows. Indeed, they had crossed the oneplanked bridge over the dyke and half-climbed Gallows Tree Hill before they viewed it at all. But as soon as they did, Jerry sprang forward, crying, 'Who's been messing about with my bag o' sticks?'

The sacking had been torn, and from the slit appeared a hand. Jerry seized the hand and pulled. The rusty chain squeaked, one of the rotten links gave, and the ghastly fruit of the gallows tree fell upon the young husbandman, who was borne to the ground beneath the falling weight. Imogene with a cry pulled it from him, and Jerk scrambled to his feet. Then they both looked.

The mildewed sacking, wet with the dense mist, had severed in the fall; the threads had rent at a hundred points, and from the fragments of scattered debris the dead face of Rash looked up with eyes that stared from the blood-streaked flesh. Jerk's gallows had borne fruit.

For minutes they stood looking. The cloak had fallen from the girl's shoulders, and the shrieking wind flapped in her rough dress, and tore at her streaming hair. Jerk, with his ambitions fulfilled, found himself most uncomfortably scared. For minutes neither of them spoke. There was too much to say. They could only stare—stare at the huddled horror and listen to the jangle of the broken gibbet chain. Suddenly Imogene remembered something, which brought her back to consciousness.

'Jerry, after seeing that, are you afraid to return to the village alone?'

Jerry had not yet found his voice, so he shook his head.

'Then go to the Court House and report what we've found to the Squire, and tell him that Imogene has gone out to keep the rest of her promise.'

Jerry got her to repeat the sentence again, and he watched her leap the dyke and disappear into the mist. Then from behind the scaffold stepped the Captain.

'You'll do nothing of the kind, pot-boy,' he said, seizing Jerk's arm, and leading him away from the scaffold. 'I've other work for you to do. We're going back to the village to make our experiment.'

As they stumbled across the Marsh, scrambling the dykes that skirted the fields, the wind got up off shore, scattering the mists, and driving them across the sea towards the Beacons of France. Half an hour later, as the Captain and Hangman Jerk approached the vicarage, a small fishing boat, carrying no light but much sail, raced before the screaming wind towards Dungeness; and with a firm hand grasping the tiller and a heart beating high stood Imogene, blinded with lashing spray and her drenched streaming hair, fighting the cruel sea to keep her word.

33

The Captain's Experiment

They entered the vicarage by the back door, and found the bos'n roasting chestnuts in the bars of the kitchen fire. There was another man there with his back to the door, and by his black clothes and scholarly stoop Jerry recognised the Vicar. So quietly had the Captain opened the door, however, that neither of the men roasting chestnuts was aware of their presence. They went on roasting the nuts, when an astonishing thing happened. The Vicar, in trying to take out a hot chestnut from the bar, knocked three of the bos'n's into the red-hot coals, which so enraged the bos'n that he administered with his forearm a resounding thump on the back of the parson's head. Jerry thought this a gross liberty, but the Vicar only laughed; and when he turned round, Jerry saw that it was Morgan Walters dressed in an entire clerical suit, and not Doctor Syn at all.

Morgan Walters looked sheepish and uncomfortable when he beheld the Captain, but the latter declared that he was magnificent; that his black hair, which had been carefully sprinkled by the bos'n with flour to make it grey, ridiculously resembled the real man; and that Morgan Walters was evidently intended by Providence to be a parson. Thus encouraged Walters strutted about the kitchen, and the likeness to Doctor Syn (for he was of the same build, and Doctor Syn had always the sailor's rolling gait) was so ridiculous that Jerk began to rock with laughter.

Now, remember, Walters,' the Captain said, 'there's no danger in this if you do exactly as I told you, but you will have to be spry.'

'If he sticks me, then I deserves to be struck,' replied Morgan Walters. 'I've been Aunt Sally at the country fairs afore now, and never got whacked, not once. I always could bob down on time in those days, and I didn't have no bos'n's whistle to help me.'

Thus began the Captain's experiment; and in spite of its tragic purpose, a humourous game it was.

The bos'n, whistle in mouth, was hidden in the little front garden; the Captain and Jerk crouched in a corner of the room of which the window had no view; whilst Morgan Walters, in all points resembling Doctor Syn, sat reading in the ingle seat by the fire—sat reading a book with his back to the window, from which the shutters had been thrown open and the broken casement set ajar. It was a strange occasion; the Captain crouching down in the corner holding on to young Jerk with a warning hand, and the knowledge of the bos'n hidden in the garden, and the firelight aided by one candle upon the table throwing the two wavering shadows of the pseudo-parson upon the whitewashed wall. Jerk could hardly persuade himself that it was not the Doctor, and he could hardly forbear letting out a laugh as the crafty seaman kept turning the pages of the theological book. But he had ample time to control himself before anything happened, for a whole hour he had to wait, an hour which seemed a lifetime. Then the happenings were swift and terrible.

A shrill whistle sounded from the garden. Down went Morgan Walter's head; and with a thud which broke the surrounding wall plaster into a thousand powdery cracks, a great harpoon trembled in the wall, exactly one foot above the settle.

'Gone,' shouted the bos'n from the garden, and he immediately tumbled up through the window, closing the shutters behind him.

'Well, sir,' said Morgan Walters, 'it wasn't the ducking I minded when it came to it, but the waiting wasn't pleasant.'

'You did well, my man,' said the Captain. 'And now, potboy, after that little experiment, I'll know how to proceed, how to prescribe like an apothecary. So as it's Sunday tomorrow, which ain't far off now, we'll get back to the Ship Inn, bos'n, and you can light us there, whilst Morgan Walters can change his clothes and get back and to sleep.'

So they left him there, the bos'n stepping before the Captain and Jerk with a lantern to the door of the 'Ship'. Just as they reached the door, a horseman galloped up from the Hythe Road, and, saluting, asked if any could direct him to Captain Collyer. As soon as the Captain had made himself known, Jerk saw the rider hand the Captain a blue paper, which the latter put carefully into his pocket. Then he led the rider and the bos'n into the sanded parlour, and gave them beer, and Jerk went home to bed and slept sound.

But back in the vicarage, just as Morgan Walters was about to divest himself of his ecclesiastical robes, Mr. Mipps entered with a loaded blunderbuss, and requested him to turn round, hold his hands above his head, and precede him to the coffin shop at the farther end of the village.

Doctor Syn slept at the Court House, for he did not intend to go to the vicarage any more at night. He had a dread of that sitting-room of his. The horrible whirring of a certain weapon boring a hole through the shutter was still squeaking in his ears, and he could yet see a terribly eye magnified by the bottle glass of the casement looking in at him from the darkness. No, he had had enough of that room, he told himself, and so he welcomed the Squire's invitation to pass the night in the Court House. Complaining of tiredness, he went to his room; but the Squire sat up late wondering how Imogene was faring, and whether or not she would succeed in rescuing his son, and how in the world she was setting about it.

About two o'clock in the morning he detected a smell of burning. He went upstairs. The smell seemed to be corning from the room assigned to Doctor Syn, but there was only the firelight showing under the door, so, thinking that the Doctor was asleep, he put his eye to the keyhole. But the Doctor was not asleep. He was dressed in shirt and breeches, and the sleeves of the shirt were turned up. He was standing by the fireplace with a red-hot poker in his hand, looking at a seared mark upon his forearm.

'What the devil's he burning his arm for?' thought the Squire.

Doctor Syn then began to whistle under his breath; to whistle that old tune the words of which the Squire knew so well—*'Here's to the feet that have walked the plank.'* The Squire remembered certain words of the Captain—*'Clegg's one tattoo.' 'The picture of a man walking the plank, executed badly upon his forearm.'* Good God! Was it possible? No! Ridiculous! An uncanny feeling came over the Squire, and he went downstairs quietly, without knocking at the Doctor's door, as he had intended—went down-stairs to the fire in the library, relit his pipe, and began to think about Doctor Syn.

So when Sunday morning broke, two more strange things had happened. Morgan Walters, for one thing, had disappeared, parson's clothes and all; and Doctor Syn, on going to the vicarage, discovered a new ugly gash in the plaster of the wall, and felt indeed thankful that he had passed the night at the Court House.

The villagers heard it announced at morning service that, in order to undertake a great mission to the heathen, Doctor Syn was leaving Dymchurch that very night; leaving after evensong by fishing lugger, which was timed to pick up a certain Spanish trader bound for Jamaica, and sailing upon the next day for the port of Rye. So all that Sunday afternoon, with much sorrow in their hearts at the thought of losing their faithful shepherd and good friend, they prepared great beacons along the coast sea-wall as far as Littlestone, in order to light and cheer their Vicar on his lonely journey.

34

Adventures in Watchbell Street

Imogene had got safely to Rye through the deuce of a bad sea. It was Sunday morning, and by the time that the church bells were ringing for service, she had safely beached her boat with the help of two fishermen who knew her well. With these old salts she breakfasted. A rude meal it was, served in a hut upon the shingle; but fish, bread, and hot broth were things that she liked, and she was hungry. She was sorely in need of sleep, and the old fellows tried to persuade her to rest; but time pressed, and she had much to do.

Before leaving Dymchurch, Mrs. Waggetts had provided her with a case of pistols and a sealed packet. This packet she now examined. It contained two papers. It was fortunate indeed that Doctor Syn had in his charity taught her to read. One of the papers was a letter of instructions, telling her the easiest way of setting about the rescue of the Squire's son; and she knew the advice to be sound, for the signature bore the great name of the Scarecrow. What's in a name? More than Master Shakespeare gave credit for; because, as the name of Robespierre had carried terror and power in France, and as the name of Napoleon was changed to Bony for the frightening of children by English nurses, so the title of the Scarecrow worked magic on Romney Marsh; for it meant that the power of the smugglers was behind it; and it would be used to force obedience to the Scarecrow's behests. Imogene knew that her papers were of power, credentials that would get her a hearing, and the rest must be left to her own wits and courage, and to chance. She read the letter of instructions till she had thoroughly mastered its

contents, and then burned it on the bucket of live coal outside
the hut. The other letter she kept, for she had great need of that.
It was addressed to one Antony Whyllie, attorney-at-law, of
Watchbell Street in Rye.

'We find that we have further need of your help. The son of
our Squire is in the hands of the Rye press-gang. We have
accordingly dispatched to you one of our messengers, a young
girl upon whom no suspicion will fall. You must see to it that
you and the girl succeed in rescuing the young man. If the girl
returns without him, it will be the worse for you both; it will also
be the last of you both. We would have done well, perhaps, to
send you more help in this difficult venture, but this we cannot
do, the girl being the only one of our servants available.
However, you will find her a young woman of great resource and
of high courage, and those qualities, added to your own well-
known ability and cunning in getting out of difficult comers,
should enable you to carry out our wishes for our own conve-
nience, and for the saving of your life, which, we presume,
affords you some interest.

(Signed) 'SCARECROW.'

With this useful letter tucked away in her breast, in company
with one of Mrs. Waggett's pistols, Imogene, after bidding
farewell to the two fishermen, struck out from the beach across
the mile or so of flat country that lies in front of the little town
of Rye. Her heart beat high as she looked up at the great bat-
tlements and the quaint little houses that clustered in all shapes
around them, higher and higher until they reached the church
tower, the highest point of all.

She did not enter the town by the north gate, but skirted the
wall and ascended the long irregular stepway that rises from
the river wharf. It is a ladder of stone that climbs zig-zag the surface of rock till you find yourself at the top of the wall, and
standing upon the cobbled roadway of Watchbell Street, a thor-
oughfare made green with moss and rank grasses, and rendered
vastly attractive by the picturesque houses that flank its little

pavements. To one of these houses Imogene made her way; a little white house, with a quaint little white front door. She pulled the brass chain, and in response to the bell, a serving-maid announced that Mr. Whyllie was not at home, having gone to church with his wife. So perforce she had wait a little until the master and mistress, having been released from a long sermon, and thoroughly ready for their Sunday dinner, wended their stately way homewards. A quaint old lady was the wife of the starchy old lawyer. She was dressed in highly flowered brocades, with a curious bonnet under which her round little face shone out with much animation. A clever little face it was, with a queer little pursed-up mouth, and a tiny little nose with an upward tilt, and her eyes were lively. Imogene saw them coming, and gave them a profound curtsy as they drew near to the front door.

'Lord love you, Mr. Whyllie,' the old lady exclaimed, 'and what's the pretty wench bobbing at us for?'

'It may be that she would speak to you, my dear,' replied the lawyer.

'Then why doesn't she, sir?' answered the little lady, raising her glasses and quizzing Imogene from head to foot. 'A handsome face she has, Mr. Whyllie. A handsome face, indeed, refined yet rough, but then again rough yet refined, take it how you will. But, Lord love you again, Mr. Whyllie, she has positively the most obnoxious clothes you could wish for to meet, and no shoes. Neither has she stockings, but shapely legs, sir, good legs indeed, though you need not embarrass the child by quizzing them, Mr. Whyllie.'

Mr. Whyllie looked away awkwardly, and, raising his hat, inquired whether Imogene wished to speak to them.

'I have come to speak to you, sir, on most grave business.'

'To do with one of my cases, I suppose,' he answered, by way of explanation to his wife, for he had no wish that she should suspect him of having any dealings with such a handsome wench.

'Which case?' snapped the suspicious little wife.

'Well, really now, I cannot say off-hand,' faltered the lawyer. 'Probably the Appledore Land claims; but I wouldn't swear to it, for it could equally be something to do with the Canver squabble. In fact, more likely to be, quite likely to be. Probably is— probably is. It might so very well be that, mightn't it, my love?'

'Yes and it might *not* he that,' returned his wife with scorn. 'Why don't you ask the girl if you want to know, instead of standing there like the town idiot. Being a lawyer, I naturally suppose you have a tongue in your head.'

'I have, my dear,' exclaimed the lawyer desperately, 'but hang it, ma'am, you will not let me wag it.'

'You blasphemous horror!' screamed the lady, sweeping past him into the house, for the serving-maid was holding the front door open for them.

It was, by the way, a good thing for Antony Whyllie that his house was situated in a quiet corner of Watchbell Street—a very good thing, for these sudden squalls would repeatedly burst from his wife, regardless altogether of publicity.

With a sigh the attorney begged Imogene to follow him, and led the way into a little breakfast-room whose latticed windows looked out upon the street. It was a panelled room, but the panels were enamelled with white paint, which gave to the place a most cheerful aspect. Upon each panel hung a mahogany-framed silhouette portrait of some worthy relative, and neatly over each panel, was hung a brass spoon or brazen chestnut roaster, each one polished like gold, and affording a bright contrast to the black portraits below. There was in one corner of the room an embrasure filled with shelves, the shelves in their turn being filled with china. A round mahogany table, mahogany chairs, and a mantelpiece with shallow carvings made up the rest of the furniture of this altogether delightful little room. Thither Imogene followed Mr. Whyllie, who placed a chair for her and shut the door. He then sat down by the fire and awaited her pleasure to address him. Imogene handed him the paper which had been prepared for her, and as he began to read she drew the silver pistol from her blouse, and held it ready beneath a fold of her dress. That the lawyer was greatly startled was only too plain, for as he read the letter he turned terribly pallid in the face.

'God bless me, but it's monstrous,' he said, starting up with his eyes still on the paper. 'Not content with holding up my coach, comandeering my horses, and making me look extremely ridiculous, they now force me, a lawyer, an honest lawyer, to break these very laws I have sworn to defend. It's monstrous-utterly monstrous. What am I to do? What can I do? My wife must know of this. My wife must read this letter,' and accordingly he took a step to wards the door.

But Imogene was too quick for him. With her back against it, and the pistol levelled at his head, the lawyer was entirely nonplussed.

'If you please, sir,' she said. 'I have orders that you were not to leave the room—indeed, that you were not to leave my sight—until I was quite satisfied that you would carry out the Scarecrow's orders.'

'Rubbish!' exclaimed the lawyer.

'Yes, indeed, sir,' replied the girl; and then added, in a frightened voice, 'If you disobey the Scarecrow it is just as well that I should shoot you here, for all the chance you will have to get away. Besides, if you do not help my by obeying the letter, you will not only be killing yourself, but me too.'

The lawyer looked blankly at Imogene, and then retreating from the unpleasant proximity of the pistol, sank into his armchair.

'Put it down, girl. Put that pistol down, for heaven's sake, for how can I think whilst I am being made a target of?'

Imogene lowered the weapon.

'I really don't know what to say,' went on the wretched old man. 'I am entirely fogged out of all vision. Muddled, muddled—entirely muddled. I wish you would let my wife come in. I do wish you would. Whatever her faults may be, she is really most excellent at thinking out difficulties of this kind. In fact, I must confess that she does all my thinking for me. Women sometimes, you know, have most excellent brains—quick brains. They have, you know. Really they have. Quick tongues, too. My wife has. Oh, yes, really, you know, she's got both, and the tongue part of her is developed to a most astonishing degree.

But, give her her due—give her her due, so's her brain, so's her brain. A most clever brain—most clever. Very quick; exceptionally alert. As clever as a man, really she is. In fact, she's absolutely cleverer than most. She's cleverer than me—oh, yes, she is. I confess it. I'm not conceited. Why, she does all my work for me. Writes all my speeches for me. Really, you know, I am utterly useless without her. She guides me—absolutely guides me. Why, alone I'm helpless. How on earth do you suppose that I can get a young man out of the hands of the Rye press-gang? They're the most desperate of ruffians—the most desperate set of good-for-noughts that you could possibly wish to meet.'

The handle of the door turned suddenly, but Imogene's foot was not easily shifted.

'There's something in the way of the door, you clumsy clod-hopper,' called the voice of Mrs. Whyllie from outside.

'I know there is, my love,' faltered the husband. Then to Imogene, 'Oh, please, let her come in. She will be quiet, I'm sure.' Then in a louder tone, 'You will be quiet, won't you, my love?'

'Antony,' called the voice of the spouse, 'are you addressing yourself to that handsome girl? Are you calling her your love?' Then in a tone of doom, 'Wait till I get in.'

'Oh dear! oh dear! she's misunderstanding me again. Don't let her come in now, for heaven's sake!'

But Imogene had already opened the door, and in had burst the little lady. Without heeding Imogene, she rushed across the room, and administered with her mittened band a very resounding box upon her husband's ear.

'Now, perhaps you will behave yourself like a respectable married man, like an old fogey that you are, like everything, in fact, that you ought to be but aren't, and never will he. Will you behave yourself now, you terrible old man?'

'Certainly, my love,' meekly replied the lawyer; 'but do look at this young lady.'

'Sakes alive!' she exclaimed, when she did look at Imogene, 'for if she hasn't got a pistol in her hand you're no fool, Antony.'

'She has got a pistol in her hand, my love, and I'll not only be a fool but a dead fool if you don't find some way out of the difficulty.'

'And what is the difficulty, pray?' she asked, looking from her terrified husband to the extraordinary girl. 'Oh, keep that pistol down, will you, my dear, for there is no immediate danger of my eating you. Just because I keep this fool of a husband of mine in his place you mustn't think me a virago.'

'I am afraid it is me that you will be thinking a virago,' answered the girl. 'But indeed I cannot help myself. This horrid situation has been forced upon me.'

But the old lady cut in again with, 'I beseech you both to cease making theatrical idiots of yourselves, and tell me calmly and clearly what all this to-do is about. Now, Antony, speak up and tell me all about it. Come along, sir. Make haste, and tell me, if you have any ideas left in that silly head of yours. No doubt you've been getting yourself into another pretty mess. Isn't it enough for you that you go out, sir, a-driving, and get robbed or your coach and cattle? I should have thought that had been quite enough to keep you out of mischief for a day or two. But no. Here you are again—in trouble again. No doubt you have quite forgotten the little lecture I read to you upon that occasion.'

'No, my dear, I cannot forget it, I assure you. It is still very vivid to me, I promise you.'

'Oh, yes, you have forgotten it,' went on the irrepressible lady. 'You must have. Now tell me, what on earth have you been doing to make this handsome girl behave in such a ridiculous fashion?'

With one hand still rubbing his boxed ear, and with the other holding out to his wife the terrible letter, the lawyer explained, as coherently as possibly, the whole situation. He told the facts in a timid voice, for he was greatly troubled a to how his wife would take it. But her manner was the most shocking surprise to him, for it was so entirely different from anything he might have expected. When she heard about the press-gang, she clapped her little mittens together, and, laughing aloud, urged her husband to go on with the tale, which she found the most refreshing she had heard for a month of Sundays. At the conclusion she gave way to the most extraordinary capers of excitement, literally tripping round and round the round table, exclaiming that nothing could have been more fortunate, for, 'La, sir,' she cried, 'this little affair is truly a godsend to me.'

'In whatever way?' asked the amazed lawyer.

'Why, you disproportionate dullard? Who is head of the press-gang, eh? Answer me that, now, and you've got it.'

'Captain Tuffton, isn't it, my love?' said the lawyer

'Captain Tuffton, of course, it is,' cried his wife. 'Captain Tuffton, of a truth. That insufferable coxcomb, that atrociously obnoxious, scented profligate, on whom I shall now be able to pay off old scores.

'Old scores, my love? Old scores?'

'La, sir, have you utterly forgotten how he snubbed me at Lady River's card-party, and again at his lordship's water-picnic? Has that slipped your memory too? How he got that painted besom of a Parisian actress to imitate me to my face? Lord love you, Mr. Whyllie, I have long sworn to get even with that young idiot. Why, it was only this morning that I was pulling out a thousand schemes all through church for his undoing, and here comes a direct answer to my prayers. Why, Mr. Whyllie, here is not only a chance to humble him to the dust, but a most admirable occasion for his disgrace as well.'

'I am truly glad to hear you say so,' was the husband's comment. 'But I'm hanged if I can see how you are to set about it.'

'Through the help of this girl here, stupid, and by the bewitching charms of your handsome niece from India, who has returned to England with her large fortune derived from the British East India Company.'

The lawyer stared at his wife blankly; then genuine concern for that lady's health got the better of his amazement. 'Can I fetch you your salts, or anything, my love? Your pounce box or your vinaigrette?—for I declare that you are wandering in your mind, my dear. I never had a niece in all my life, my love;

and as for the British East India Company—well, I have heard of it, of course, but little else indeed—very little else.'

'Well, for today you will have to know a good deal about it,' said Mrs. Whyllie, 'so you had better step into the library and read up its history. And as to your niece, your favourite niece, you will please do me the favour of remembering that you possess her too, sir. Now then, Mistress,' addressing Imogene, 'as soon as this husband of mine has taken himself off, I'll tell you your part of this affair.'

Taking the hint, the lawyer beat a retreat to the library, gladly leaving the difficult business in the hands of his wife.

'Now, girl,' she went on, when they were alone, 'I suppose I shouldn't be very far wrong if I surmised that you are head over ears in love with this young man that the press-gang have taken, eh?'

'Yes, I love him,' said the girl quietly.

'Ah,' sighed the lady, 'that's all right; and I suppose I'm also not far out if I suppose that you would do a good deal to save him from being shipped off to the wars, eh?'

'I will do anything to save him from that,' said the girl.

'Good,' replied the old lady. 'Then come upstairs with me.'

Out of the room and across the little hall they went, and so up the broad white staircase to the sweetest little bedroom imaginable, with a small four-posted bed with chintz frills and hangings, and a dressing-table set with bright silver ornaments.

'Now, this room is for you, my dear—for my handsome niece from India, you understand? I must ask you to change your clothes and get into some pretty frock or other; and I must have you to know, my dear, that I have been married twice, and by my first marriage I must tell you that I had a daughter, a really beautiful daughter. This was years ago, of course, but she was just about your age, as I remember her. By the way, what is your age, my dear?'

'About sixteen, or I might be seventeen, perhaps,' said Imogene.

'Ah, well, my daughter was just nineteen when she died,' went on the old lady. 'She was all I had in the world, for her father had died when she was quite a child. Yes, she was all that I had to love for fifteen years, and when she was taken I was so desperately lonely that in a weak moment I married that foolish Mr. Whyllie, who is really very kind-hearted and quite a good man, but oh, how dull! Indeed, my dear, he would never have been in the position he is now if I hadn't pushed him there. You see he hasn't much brain. But, on the whole, I am glad that I married him, because he had given me such a lot to do helping him make other people believe that he isn't a born fool. I really must not talk such a lot, for we have a deal to do, my dear. But I must explain this. I spent a good deal of money upon pretty frocks for my daughter, and oh, how sweet she used to look in them! Well worth the money it was to see her look so pretty. Now every one of these dresses I have kept, and kept carefully, too. If the sweet child came back to me now, she would find all her things as well cared for, as clean and as fresh as when she left me; for this was her room (this house belongs to me, my dear, not to that fool downstairs), and in these chests and in that tall-boy there I have kept everything that reminds me of my darling. See.' And, taking a key from a casket upon the chimney-piece, she unlocked the tall oak cupboard, displaying a sight to make a girl's mouth water. The daintiest dresses were there, and in the brass-bound coffer at the end of the bed, the most costly laces and fine linen, and all kept sweet and pure in a strong scent of lavender. From these sacred treasures the old lady made selections, and by the time the gong had sounded for the three o'clock dinner, instead of the handsome fisher-girl, there sat before the mirror, having the finishing touches put to her hair, a beautiful young girl in a gown of country splendour, jewels at her neck, and a diamond brooch of great beauty pinned in her bosom.

While she had been dressing her the old lady had, with great tact, got all Imogene's history out of her, at least as much of it as she knew. Just before they stepped from the room, as she surveyed her *protégée* with admiration, she held up her little quaint face, and requested Imogene to kiss her—which you may be sure she did.

'And now, my dear, we will go down to dinner, and while we are eating I will tell you exactly what we are to do. And I declare,' she added with enthusiasm, 'if that Squire's son, whom I regard as a fortunate young fellow, does not marry you, well, I'll horsewhip him myself—ay, both him and his father—and adopt you as my own daughter. What a relief it would be to have you in the house to look at, for you know you are vastly prettier than my foolish Mr. Whyllie.'

Had Imogene been in reality the old lady's daughter, returned to her from the other side of the veil, she could not have been shown more love and attention. Even Mr. Whyllie had a happy time of it, for the little old lady, his wife, was in the best of tempers. Indeed, at the conclusion of the meal, the lawyer found himself pushed into a comfortable chair, with a small table at his side, upon which stood a fine old bottle of port; and, much to his astonishment, there was his wife, having filled a churchwarden pipe with tobacco, and rammed it home into the bowl with her own delicate fingers, holding a lighted taper spill all ready for him. So he also began to bless the coming of his niece from India, regretted that she had not been invented sooner, and only wished that she was going to remain in the house to the end of the proverbial chapter.

Then Mrs. Whyllie, over a dish of tea with Imogene, unfolded her plan of campaign for the rescue of young Denis.

35

A Military Lady-Killer
Prepares for Battle

That insufferable coxcomb Captain Tuffton was in the act of sprinkling his lace handkerchief with the scent that old Mrs. Whyllie found so obnoxious, when his valet entered the room with a note. The insufferable one went on with his sprinkling, and languidly inquired whom the note was from.

'I really cannot say, sir,' returned the valet.

'Cannot say?' repeated the dandy, lifting his pencilled eyebrows into the higher regions of astonishment. 'Indeed, my good Transome—and you call yourself a valet? It is not a bill, I trust, strayed in upon the Sabbath out of cunning—for I have not seen a bill these many years now, and the sight, I feel convinced, might upset my stomach.'

'I think, sir, that there is no valet in Europe so quick to smell out a bill or so nimble at tearing them up as your humble servant.' Transome could be tremendous upon occasion, and he certainly was when he added, 'And under your livery, sir, I venture to suggest that my practice of bill-nosing has been unlimited.'

'Now come, my good Transome, you disrespectful dog, I'll not have you chiding me—upon my soul I won't—for I have a most infernal head on me this forenoon. I generally do get an infernal bad head on me o' Sundays. All a-buzz, I declare, and it's all those demned exasperating church bells. I never met anything so persistent in my life. They go on, they go on, and there's no stopping them. If ever I have to oblige Parliament by sleeping in it, I shall endeavour to keep awake to vote for the abolishment of church bells.'

'And you might, sir, at the same time do away with bills. It would be most convenient, sir.'

'Well, I suppose it would. If I ever do get in—which I think extremely unlikely, as I most heartily thank my Maker, knowing how unutterably bored I should become—but if ever I do get in, I will most certainly abolish bills and bells; and it there should be any other little thing that you think might sensibly be abolished, why, you must jog my memory, Transome. And jog it hard, won't you, my dear fellow, for you know what a memory I have—demned bad, upon my soul it is!'

'Ah, sir,' sighed the valet, 'you will become a great orator—a very great orator.'

'I might, my dear fellow—I really might—although I am positive I shan't, because, you see, I know that I shall go to sleep. I shan't be able to help myself.'

'You must really make an effort, sir, to keep awake for the sake of your country, sir—for you will make as great a statesman as you are a soldier. You cannot help it, sir. Talent such as yours, genius such as yours, is like murder, sir—it will out.'

'No, I am a lazy good-for-nought—upon my soul I am—and a statesman I shall never become; for even if I do get pushed into a seat, what shall I lay on my sleeping in it all the time? A pack o' dogs, sixteen fighting cocks, and a nag? Will you take me?'

'Against what, sir?'

'Against nothing, you disrespectful dog. Upon my honour, against nothing but my sleeping. What are you flashing that silver tray about for? It catches the light in a most exasperating manner, and causes the most acute suffering to my wretched eyesight. Have you no feeling at all, my good Transome, or have you lost it as well as your respect? I declare that my poor wretched head is executing positive manoeuvres this morning. Musket drill and cavalry charges are going on inside it the whole time. Oh dear, oh dear! How I wish you would open that demned note, instead of flourishing it about again! You surely don't expect me to open it, do you?'

Accordingly the valet opened the letter, and announced to his master it was a lady's handwriting.

'Then you had better give it to me,' drawled the Captain with a resigned air; 'for if you pry into the contents of the poor thing's soul, it will be all over the town in an hour or so, and another woman's reputation will have disappeared. Why, Lord love us,' he added, as he glanced at the note in question, 'if it isn't from that she-dragon herself—that most terribly and alarming Mrs. What's-her-name—Mrs.—Mrs. oh, what the devil is her name, eh?'

The valet suggested humbly that the lady in question would most probably have signed her name at the end of the letter.

'Oh yes, of course. What a downright sane fellow you are, to be sure! Now, with all my brains, I should never have thought of that. Ah, I remember who the woman is now, without looking. She's the wife of that idiotic lawyer fellow who always fastens up his fat stomach in a white waistcoat a cut or two too small. But I'm demned if I can remember even his name, so we are not much nearer to it, are we, now?'

Again the valet repeated the brilliant suggestion of looking to the end of the letter; and his master, having graciously accepted his suggestion, announced that the mystery was solved at last, and that the name was nothing more nor less than Whyllie.

'And I wonder what the devil she can want with me, Transome?'

The valet again made the acute suggestion that, if he would take the pains to read the letter, he would in all likelihood discover. So, with a very bored air, the perfumed soldier read the note right through, and threw it down upon the dressing-table with a great smile of self-complacency.

'She desires me to wait upon her this afternoon, my good fellow. She wishes positively to let bygones be bygones, and desires that I will bury all past differences by partaking of an hour's hospitality at her house. She also states that she has a wealthy niece but just returned from India, and she desires that this same niece may have the privilege of meeting the cream of the Rye bachelors. My dear fellow, what a truly terribly age we do live in! I have never heard of such 'daring and unblushing match-making. Well, I suppose it is a thing that we must expect in a God-forsaken little hole like this, where the available bachelors are few indeed, and possess not the smallest knowledge of how to decently deport themselves.'

'Besides, sir,' the valet ventured to remark, 'the red cloth of the military has a great attraction for match-makers. It is always so very respectable, and it carries a most remarkable tone with it, to be sure, sir.'

'Well, I think I will go, at all events,' went on the gentleman, 'and throw my eye over the niece. Though I really cannot expect much in the beauty line, for she will probably be forty if she's a day, judging by the ancient aunt. However, it may not be bad sport. Have you ever practised the art of exciting elderly spinsters? If not, do, my dear fellow, for it has its humours—and really, now, humour is about all that is left to us nowadays. Hurry up, my good fellow. No, you dolt, I am not on duty. What do I want my sword for? Swords get most infernally between your legs at the wrong moment. They are positively useless lumber. I cannot think why they are not abolished. Ugly, clanking things, always in the wrong place, and tripping one up when least on one's guard. I'll take my cane. No, no, you positive Judas, the one with the scarlet tassel, of course. And my perfume box; no, no, that's a snuff box. I hate snuff. You know that I always endeavour to leave it behind whenever possible, for it has a habit of getting up my nose and bringing on the most acute attacks of sneezing. Now, my hat and —no, perhaps not the cloak. A cloak, my good fellow, has a most annoying habit of hiding the curve of the waist. And I really do think that even my most bitter detractors must own that my waist is entirely and absolutely right. Now, how are we, eh? Has the most captious valet in the world got anything to remedy, anything to suggest? I think we can do little else with the cravat?'

'It would be passed by Mr. Brummel himself.'

'Then we are ready, are we? *Au revoir*, therefore, my inestimable friend. Keep you courage up, and don't forge my name
to a bill in my absence.' With which piece of raillery Captain
Tuffton swaggered out of the room, swinging the red-tasselled
cane, and humming in well-modulated tenor a Spanish love
song. Literally tripping into Watch-bell Street, he approached
the little white front door behind which were waiting three good
people. He rang the bell languidly, little thinking it a tocsin of
battle and of sudden death.

36

Scylla or Charybdis

 Captain Tuffton could certainly not complain of his reception, for the lawyer was positively nervous in his en-deavours to please; while Mrs. Whyllie, in her anxiety to let bygones be bygones, seemed to bask in the sunshine of his glory. As for Imogene, she had the speedy satisfaction of knowing that her appearance had caused havoc in the heart of the lady-killer.

'And so you are back from India,' he said to the beautiful niece.

'So it appears, sir,' answered Imogene, with a smile.

'Ah, yes. Of course, it is only too obvious,' answered the soldier, 'for here you are, aren't you, now? It's a beastly place out there, isn't it? I never could abide elephants or snakes!'

'La, sir, then you must not venture there, for they abound most vastly,' answered Imogene.

Mrs. Whyllie by this time was tittering behind her fan, and old Whyllie looked greatly troubled at the whole proceedings.

'A devilish climate, too, for the complexion, isn't it?'— stroking his smooth, weak chin.

'La, sir, indeed, if you say that, I take it as a poor compliment to myself.

'Do not mistake me, I beg,' urged the officer, 'for in your case the Indian sun has been most gentle. He has kissed you with a light hand—er—a light mouth, indeed. Lucky sun, lucky sun!'

'You are being gentle with my complexion, sir, but I perceive you to be a most accomplished courtier and turner of compliments.'

Madam, I speak from my heart, I assure you.

'Who ever heard of Captain Tuffton possessing one!' tittered Mrs. Whyllie.

'You wrong me, madam, I assure you,' he declared with conviction. 'My heart is too large for my scarlet tunic. It was an empty shell this morning, I confess, but the beauty of your accomplished niece, which it has been drinking in with rapture, has filled that poor receptacle, and made it swell and stretch with deep emotion.'

'La, sir, how prettily you use the English tongue! How the Indians would adore you, sir!'

'Pooh, pooh, indeed,' said Mrs. Whyllie, with a great show of decorum; 'you must not take for gospel what the Captain says. He is a very prince of dandies; indeed, he is second only to the Regent and Mr. Brummel in all matters of deportment. I never trust dandies myself.'

'Oh, madam, pray, pray, make me the exception.'

'No, Captain, for you are not only a dandy, but a soldier; and soldiers are another class I distrust.'

'Ah, madam,' lisped the officer, 'you are cruelty itself.'

'I cannot help it, my dear sir. Soldiers are not to be trusted, and well you know it. They walk about with gay apparel, appearing the most gentle of creatures; but we know how dangerous they are, with their minds full of most terrible conquests planned against poor women, and their pockets stuffed to the bursting-point with explosives and weapons.

'La, madam, you are mistaken, upon my soul. Take my case now, as an example. I came here, I confess it, with thoughts of conquest in my mind; but I am conquered, I am vanquished. I am beaten most demnably myself. The eyes of your niece have sown my very foundations with salt.'

'Indeed, sir, that's bitter,' exclaimed Imogene, blushing.

'And as to the belief that soldiers—officers, that is—are loaded with explosives and weapons, why, pish! madam, it is a fallacy,

I assure you. We leave explosives to the sergeants, and our weapons to our orderlies. It is not only most dangerous to carry fire-arms on one's person, but it is most damaging to the set of one's clothes.'

'And you mean to say, sir, that you, a Captain, walk abroad in your uniform, unarmed?'

'And with the place infested with French spies!' added Imogene, shuddering.

'Why yes, madam, I assure you it is so. When I walk abroad, I rely entirely for my personal safety upon my tasselled cane, and I venture to suggest that I could put up a very pretty fight with it.'

'But it would not be of much service against pistols, would it, Captain?' said Mrs. Whyllie.

'Perhaps not, madam; but who would want to put a pistol to my head?'

'You must have many enemies surely, Captain,' suggested the old lady, 'for are you not in command of the press-gang?'

'Yes, and a poor job it is for an officer,' said the soldier. 'I take no interest in the sea at all, and the authorities are endeavouring to transfer me to the marine service!'

'The press-gang does most cruel work, too, I hear,' went on the old lady.

'Well, that cannot be helped, madam. War with France is a certain thing, and if our navy is not able to smash Napoleon on the sea—well, we shall not be able to sing "Rule, Britannia!" any more. And if young men won't join the navy—well, we have to make 'em, and that's what the press-gang's for. If you cannot get a thing done for love, you know, you must get it done by force. Do you follow me?'

'Perfectly, my dear Captain,' said Mrs. Whyllie. 'That little maxim of yours is admirable, I declare, and we shall put it to most instant practice.'

Thereupon the old lady got up from her chair and pointed a pistol at the Captain's head. 'And it's most fortunate, I vow, that your tasselled cane is reposing safely in the hall.'

'What does this mean, madam?' spluttered the Captain. "Are you joking?'

'My dear niece,' said the old lady, 'this admirable Captain really asks us if we are joking!'

The Captain turned his terrified eyes to Imogene, only to discover that she also held a pistol at his head.

'What is the cause of this terrible behaviour?' he stammered.

'You are going to pay your debts, my dear Captain,' said the old lady—'to pay your debts in full. You have owed me apologies for a long time which you have taken no pains to tender to me. You made me a laughing-stock in public. Well, I am now going to return the compliment, and Heaven shield you from the scorn of your brother officers, the anger of your superiors, and the greedy wits of the neighbourhood! I say, Heaven shield—for I shan't! Antony, my dear, get the paper out of the drawer in the desk there.'

Old Mr. Whyllie moved behind the Captain and went to the desk. The Captain moved towards Mrs. Whyllie.

'Stay where you are,' she ordered. 'If you move again, I shall fire.'

'A likely tale!' he spluttered. 'You wouldn't dare!'

'I can easily contradict you on that score,' quickly remarked the old lady, and she pulled the trigger. The Captain fell back upon the sofa, his pale face blackened with powder, his eyes blinded with smoke, and a sharp, pricking sensation in his left shoulder.

'My God,' he cried, 'you've hit me!'

'And shall do so again of you give me any more trouble,' said the old lady. 'Only,' she added, 'next time I aim to kill,' and she took up another pistol from the mantelpiece. 'You see, sir, were were quite prepared for you.'

Then the lawyer set a table before him, with pen and ink, and requested him to sign a certain paper that he had already drawn up. This paper was addressed to the petty officer in charge of the press-gang, and commanded that the young man of the name of Denis Cobtree should be driven immediately in a hired coach to the house of Antony Whyllie, attorney-at-law,

Watchbell Street, who would give them further commands. To this paper Captain Tuffton signed his name—indeed, he could do nothing else—and a servant was set off to the castle to deliver it.

In half an hour or so the noise of a coach was heard rattling over the cobblestones, and Antony Whyllie left the room to see if Denis were safe. In the meantime the Captain had signed another paper, declaring Denis free to return over the Sussex border into Kent; and this paper having been shown to the petty officer, and a guinea piece having been put into his dirty hand by the lawyer himself, the sea-dog saluted respectfully, and swung off down Watchbell Street whistling a tune. The lawyer explained the situation hurriedly to Denis, and then went in to take Imogene's place as guard over the wretched man. But the Captain was suffering acute spasms in his left shoulder, and this being his first experience of bullet wounds, he was nearly unconscious at the horror of it. So Mrs. Whyllie was able for a moment to lower the pistol in order to kiss Imogene, and, having recommended her to Denis's care, bade them urge the coach quickly out of Rye and into Kent.

'Shall I change my clothes first, or send them back to you?' asked Imogene.

'Neither, my love,' answered the old lady, again levelling the pistol at Captain Tuffton's head; 'for, when we have packed this ridiculous soldier back to his place in an hour or so, I am going to see to it that Mr. Whyllie draws up legal forms for adopting you as our daughter. This is, providing, of course, you raise no objection. I shall do myself the honour of calling upon Sir Antony Cobtree himself within the week.'

With this she dismissed the young people to the coach; and when the driver had received a handsome fee from the lawyer, and had been promised a further one if he made good pace to Dymchurch, he touched up the horses, and the cumbersome coach clattered through the great gate of Rye, and so out on the smooth highroad, where the long whip cracked and the wheels began to spin. For a whole hour the wretched Captain stayed a prisoner in the white house, until he besought the old lady to let him go home and have the surgeon to dress his wound. So at last she consented; and another coach having been hired, he was lifted into it, and in a few moments reached his rooms, where the most captious valet in the world pulled from his shoulder a steel pin. With the exception of this deep pin-prick there was no mark of a wound—as, indeed, why should there have been—for Mrs. Whyllie had only fired a blank charge and the old lawyer, according to careful instructions, had got behind the Captain and dug in the pin at the crucial moment!

While the valet administered brandy as a restorative, a boy and a girl sat hand in hand in a great old coach, which swayed and jolted as it dashed along the Romney Road towards Dymchurch. Useless, indeed, to follow that coach from Rye, for the necks of the four horses were stretched to a tight gallop, the harness pulling near the breaking-point, the wheels tearing round the axles, and the busy driver's long whip cracking like pistol shots above the pounding thunder of the flying hoofs.

37

Holding the Pulpit

Never was there such a congregation as upon that night in the dim old church. The news that Doctor Syn was to leave immediately after the service brought everybody to bid him farewell, and Mipps had great difficulty in packing them all into the pews. In fact, full half an hour before the vestry prayer the pews were choked, and late comers began to perch themselves upon the high oak backs. Benches were even arranged across the aisles, and boys climbed up on to the window ledges; in fact, every available place in the church capable or not capable of supporting a human being was utilised. Jerry Jerk perched himself without ceremony upon the font cover, much to the indignation of the sexton, who, in his capacity of verger, tried to signal him off. But Jerk, knowing well that Mipps could not get at him over the benches that crowded the aisles, remained where he was. Right under the pulpit, immediately opposite to the Squire's pew, sat Captain Collyer, and, two pews behind that, some half-dozen sailors fumbled with hymn-books under the large eye of the bos'n. Once Captain Collyer turned round to see if his men were there, and Jerk noticed the corner of a blue paper bulging from his pocket.

Doctor Syn conducted the service from the top box of the three-decker pulpit, with Mipps below him carefully following the printing in the great Prayer Book with a dirty thumb running backwards and forwards. Now Doctor Syn, although appearing to the congregation to be wrapped up heart and soul in the farewell service, had found occasion to notice two things—that blue paper in the Captain's pocket, and the swinging lanterns of men outside the church. He alone could see them, for from the great height of the three-decker he had a good view through the window, and the flashes from the lanterns had revealed one important thing—the red coats of soldiers. The church was surrounded with soldiers. Every door was barred and every window watched; and upon the face of Captain Collyer appeared a look of triumph.

But none of these things hindered the service, which continued with great spirit. The sea salts in the choir bellowed the hymns louder than usual, although there was no schoolmaster to start them off on the fiddle. The hymn before the sermon was just finishing. Doctor Syn closed the great Bible upon the red cushion, and placed it upon the shelf below. The 'Amen' was reached, and the congregation clattered back into their seats. Then the Vicar leant over the pulpit side and addressed his flock for the last time.

'My friends,' he began, 'this is surely no occasion for a theological discourse. I am leaving you tonight—leaving you suddenly, because partings are such cruel things that I would not linger over them; and although I have for some months contemplated this sad step, I have been at pains to keep it to myself, lest you should misunderstand my motive, and look upon my leaving as a desertion. As I announced this morning, I am going on a mission to the far-off lands, a mission to our poor, ignorant black brethren. There are so few who can give up all to this work. Most of my colleagues are bound to their benefices by the ties of home. Being a single old fellow, with no relatives dependent upon my income, I am able to volunteer my services for this great task, well knowing that my place here can be filled by a better man than myself. This it is that makes me willing to tear myself away from the bonds of affection that tie me to Dymchurch, though I well know that those bonds can never be loosed from my heart; and I trust that, whatever my failings

may have been, you will sometimes think of one who has loved
you all. Upon an occasion of this sort perhaps it is expected
that I should sum up the poor results of my work amongst you.
This I cannot bring myself to do. What I have done, you have all
seen and know, little and worthless though it be. As your parson,
I have tried to do my duty, and, I fear, have in great measure
failed. Let me therefore leave that branch of my work to rest in
silence, and speak of something else, which will be of vital interest to you all. There was much poverty and wretchedness when
I first came amongst you. This, I believe, had been greatly alle-
viated, and the man who brought that about was not your Vicar,
as you all so fondly imagine. No; that has been the work of
another man—a man of whom I would speak: for whom I
would appeal to your generosity. For you all know that one
man has risked his life and reputation in organising a great
scheme of benefit to the Marsh men. You all know of what
scheme I am speaking; but few, if any, guess to what man you are
indebted. There was a man hanged at Rye whose name was
Clegg.'

'Clegg was never hanged at Rye!'

The great Bible skimmed over the side of the pulpit and struck
the Captain's hand before he could utter another word, and a
flint-locked pistol clattered over the front of his pew and fell
upon the stone floor. So suddenly had this happened that the
congregation merely heard the interruption and the rapid rush
of the Bible through the air, and lo! there was Doctor Syn holding the pulpit with a long, brass-bound pistol in each hand. And
there was also Mr. Mipps, the sexton, leaning over his desk and
pointing a great blunderbuss at the Captain's head.

'I must beg of you, sir, not to take the words out of my
mouth.'

The Doctor spoke in just the same tones as the rest of the
sermon, and continued as if nothing had happened, with two
pistols grinning over the red-cushioned desk

'There was a man hanged at Rye. His name was Clegg—so it
has always been believed. But the real Clegg was never hanged
at Rye. Clegg had the laugh of the authorities all his life, and cer-

tainly he had the laugh of them at his hanging, for he was never hanged at all, although he was present to see the affair conducted properly. Oh yes, he was present to read the prayers over the man whom he had got to take his place. You see, my dear brethren, it was all so ridiculously simple. The man condemned for the Rye tavern murder was one of Clegg's own men, and, most fortunately for Clegg, the rascal had a daughter that he loved—that everybody loved. This girl would have no guardian had the murderer betrayed his captain, and this is how the captain saved his life. The murderer confessed to the parson that he was Clegg, and so got a public hanging, and a funeral of which a lord might well have been proud. So you see he got well paid for taking Clegg's adventures upon his shoulders. He received the curses of the military and the admiration of the country-side as he marched with the redcoats to the scaffold; and the joke of it all was that the solemn-eyed parson, who was exhorting, my dear brethren, the poor fellow to repentance till his body jangled in the chains, was hardly able to keep back his laughter. The idea of Clegg, the notorious pirate, being a country parson had, of course, not occurred to any one. Funny it certainly was, although there were only two to enjoy the joke—myself and my friend on the gallows. Funny the end was then—funnier the end will be now; for our good friend, Captain Collyer, having come down here to discover the ringleader of the wool-running business, brought with him a man, a murderous rascal who was marooned many years ago. I marooned that man for sedition and mutiny. He was a Cuban priest, and was a dangerous practicer of black magic; and as I didn't choose to have such Satan's tricks aboard my God-fearing vessel, I left him on the reef. How the man got off the reef I know not; for it was a thing impossible for a mortal. But get off he did, and it must have been by some hell's trick that he managed it. To get him caught, I forced Rash, our former esteemed schoolmaster, whom you all admire for his good work, to commit murder upon Sennacherib Pepper, who was seeing more upon the Marsh than was altogether healthy for him; but when my faithful Rash began thinking of King's evidence, I had to see that he was removed by the Marsh witches. I like you to know all this, because I am something of a vain fellow, and I never can abide people having the laugh of me. And so, my dear friend, Captain Collyer, oblige me, like a good-natured and sensible fellow, by handing over that blue paper that is sticking out of your pocket with my death written thereon.'

'No. I'll be damned...'

'If you don't, there will be such a nasty mess for Mr. Mipps to clear up in that pew.'

A man stepped from the choir, snatched the blue paper from the Captain, and handed to to Doctor Syn.

'Thank you, my man,' said the parson, taking it. 'And now for my farewell. You are all of you in this church in imminent peril. The place is surrounded by redcoats who are in danger of being badly hurt when the fight comes. Every one in this church is in danger if I am caught by the redcoats, and obliged to turn King's evidence to save my life. I should be very loath to do such a dirty thing—so you had better persuade our friend the Captain to let me go quietly.'

Doctor Syn deliberately thrust both his pistols beneath his black gown. At the same moment the Captain sprang at the pulpit, but was knocked over with a violent blow from the brass candlestick that Doctor Syn had snatched from the socket. The sailors clambered out of their pews, but were met with a volley of hymn-books and hassocks from the salts in the choir. One or two pistols flashed, and in a second the entire church was a writhing, fighting mass of men. The women screamed, and were trodden down as the red-coats entered the west door and forced their way over the up-turned benches in the aisles. Above the congregation flew a medley of missiles—hassocks, books, hats, sticks, anything that could be grabbed, went flying through the air; and Syn leapt the pulpit and fell upon the writhing mass that was fighting below.

It took the redcoats a quarter of an hour to restore order in the church; and then Mr. Mipps and Doctor Syn had disappeared.

But although Collyer was very badly cut and bruised, he was confident; for the church had been surrounded, so he knew that the miscreants couldn't escape. Presently a cry from the vestry rang out—'Help!' It was Mipps's voice. Collyer rushed the door, followed by some of his men. The remaining redcoats, who had been watching the church, were ordered inside to help in the arrest. These men cried out that they had seen the Doctor in the vestry from the window, and they were one and all eager to be in at the death.

Within the vestry stood Sexton Mipps with a blunderbuss at the head of Doctor Syn, who was crouched in terror at the old oak table.

'There he is. Seize him—the devil!—the murderer! Seize him.'

'So you've turned King's evidence after all, have you, Mr. Sexton?'

'But Mipps only cried again, 'There he is. Ain't none of you a-goin' to take him?'

Captain Collyer obeyed the sexton, and cried, 'Clegg, I arrest you in the name of the King!' and, coming forward, he laid his hand upon the Doctor's shoulder. But the Doctor did not move. The Captain shook him, but he did not move. Then the Captain put his hand upon the white hair, and the Captain's hand was covered with something white.

'My God,' he cried, 'he's nailed to the table. It's not Syn—it's Morgan Walters. Where's that damned sexton?'

But the sexton had disappeared, and Clegg had gone, and there, with three nail—one through the neck, and one through each arm—driven right into the table, lay the theatrical figure of Morgan Walters, in all points resembling Doctor Syn.

38

The Dead Man's Throttle

Then the redcoats had a bad time, for a great fight was put up by the Dymchurch men. Doctor Syn's popularity had gone up, too, at a bound. He had gauged his audience to a nicety; and had he declared himself to be the Prince Regent, he couldn't have bettered his position. For around Cleggs's name a million romances had been spun, but none so romantic, so daring, so altogether impertinent as this last announcement that he was the preacher Syn. That the greatest pirate hung should have unhanged himself upon the pulpit of a three-decker was indeed a colossal piece of impudence, and calculated to appeal to the innermost hearts of the Dymchurch folk, who at this period of history knew more about wool-running, demon riders, and Calais customs than anything else. Add to this the admiration that they had always borne towards Clegg, only surpassed by their dread of him; and couple this with Doctor Syn's popularity and the Scarecrow's ingenuity, not forgetting the remark in the sermon about King's evidence—and the Cleric's escape was assured. For Doctor Syn could give evidence to hang them all; and although they thought he was sportsman enough to hold his tongue if it came to a crisis, they didn't like to risk it—for Clegg had proved himself true enough to his friends, but utterly ruthless towards his foes. For all these reasons they put up a fight, and a sharp fight it was.

There was a rumour that Doctor Syn and Sexton Mipps had taken cover in one of the smugglers' retreats at the Ship Inn; and although Mrs. Waggetts innocently protested against it, the order was given to ransack the place from cellars to attics. But it was none so easy to ransack such a rambling old house, defended as it was by desperate ruffians fighting for the secrets of their livelihood; for since Doctor Syn had hidden the wool-running scheme under his black gown, money had flowed freely amongst the Dymchurch men. But the blood of the redcoats was up, for three of their number had been shot dead, and several had been badly wounded so when they eventually got possession of the inn, they showed Mrs. Waggetts' property no mercy.

Meantime a lugger was trying to catch the breeze, and get out of the great bay to the open sea. But the wind had failed; so certain men aboard had out the oars and pulled away with a will. Then some fool lit one of the piled beacons on the shore. Others followed suit, and the flames shot up all along the wall to Littlestone. The King's men managed to launch the Preventer's cutter, and set to chasing the lugger. The fellows, routed out of the Ship Inn, crowded to the wall to hinder the launching; but Collyer was in command, and bravely kept his men's heads for them.

The cutter was not long in swinging alongside the lugger, and Collyer clambered aboard with three or four of his men armed with pistols and cutlasses. The crew of the lugger had stopped rowing when they saw that they had no chance of escape; and as soon as the Captain hailed them, they surrendered sullenly.

The men at the oars were ordered into the cutter, and then the Captain turned to the cabin. Outside the door sat Sexton Mipps, with his blunderbuss lying across his knees. But he appeared quite calm, and was enjoying his short pipe.

'Good-evening, Captain,' he said. 'Coming out fishing with us, are you?'

'Lay that blunderbuss of yours on the deck,' answered the Captain, 'and step aboard the cutter after your pals.'

'I should like to know what you be,' said Mr. Mipps, 'to order a respectable parish sexton about?'

'You won't make it easier for yourself, my man, by lagging back,' said the Captain. 'I know quite enough about you to send you to the gibbet.'

'May I ask what?' replied the sexton, puffing away at his pipe.

'I've been having a look at that coffin shop of yours, and I've seen enough there to get you a free rope from the Government; so get along, and make the best of a bad job.'

Mipps pulled desperately at his short pipe, and sent over his lap a heavy cloud of tobacco smoke. Under cover of this, his fingers were stealing towards the trigger of the blunderbuss. He was calculating his chances, for there were three pistols pointing at him from the King's men. If he was shot, he meant to take the Captain with him.

'There's one chance of saving your dirty carcass,' went on the Captain, not noticing those crafty fingers moving.

'What's that?' said the sexton, behind the blue curtain of tobacco smoke.

'There's one man I'd sooner hang than you, and that's Clegg. Tell me where Doctor Syn is, and I'll give you twenty-four hours to make yourself scarce.'

'Thank you kindly,' went on the sexton. 'But I hain't no wish to make myself scarce. I'm quite happy where I am—and if you've a fancy to make yourself scarce, I'll be happier still.'

Just then there was a noise below of singing, and something splashed into the sea. The Captain looked over the side and saw a black bottle. It was not a dark night, and he could see it floating away towards the shore, where the beacons were alight.

'He's in that cabin,' the Captain shouted. 'He threw that rum bottle out of the stern hole.'

'If he is there,' replied the sexton, 'I wouldn't advise you nor any other of my friends to go in, for it'll be the worse for you if you do. Hark, he's in song tonight, and when Clegg's in song, you can take it from me that he's in a devil of a mood.'

From the cabin came that horrible song:

> 'Here's to the feet wot have walked the plank—
>   Yo-ho! for the dead man's throttle.'

And then the words were uttered in a drunken voice—the voice of a drunkard in terror.

'It's the drink. There's nobody there—there's nobody in this cabin, I say. It's a shadow, nothing but a shadow. He couldn't have got here. It's a shadow risen from hell to mock me, I say. He couldn't have got off that reef. There was nothing for him to live upon, but the filthy body of the yellow cook—and would even the foulest man eat food not fit for sharks? There was nothing else. I can hear the surf now breaking into the lagoon. There, listen. There, hark at him cursing. It's no use, tell him. The crew's afraid of me—they're only muttering; they daren't speak again, for I've settled with Pete, the yellow cook—broke his spine in with a capstan bar. There goes Pete's body over the side into the clear water. Ugh! what a horrible splash it makes. The water don't seem to hide him much. There's his ugly yellow face still. Why don't the water hide him? It hides lots of other ugly things, damn it. The breeze, thank God. We are slipping away—faster, faster. The reef is sinking into the deep sea. The marooned scoundrel, the damned mulatto, can't throw a harpoon from there, he can't. He's dead already. Cram on the canvas, every inch. Get up aloft. Won't take my orders, eh? Get up! get up! I'll learn you who Clegg is. Ah! look there! There's something following the ship. What a horrible face it has. My God, it's yellow. Horrible! It's coming out of the sea. It's creeping over the stern, along the deck. It's coming to the Round House. Lock the door. No! No! It's here inside the Round House. You've locked it in with me, you fools. You cowards, it's following me round. It isn't him. It isn't him. It's a shadow. A damned silly shadow. Where's the rum? Mipps, you damned little pirate, where have you hid the rum?—

'Here's to the corpses afloat in the tank,
      And the dead man's teeth in the bottle.'

The song turned into a scream of agony. There was the noise of a soul-sickening thud, and something leaped through the cabin door, tumbling Mr. Mipps all over in a heap. The three pis-

tols of the King's men flashed; another scream tore the air, and
a tall figure sprang high into the night and disappeared into the
sea.

'It's Clegg. It's Syn,' shouted one of the King's men.

'And we've shot that damned little sexton too,' shouted
another; for Mr. Mipps lay flat on his face with fingers outstretched upon the deck.

Collyer rushed into the cabin, whilst the men reloaded a pistol in case the head of Doctor Syn should rise from the sea.

'Bring a light,' shouted the Captain.

The cabin was small, but larger than might have been expected from the size of the craft. When a lantern had been passed
through, it showed a little room whose walls were the sides of
the boat. On one side was a heavy flap table, fixed into the ribs
of the vessel with rusty iron sockets. Upon this table, flat down
on his face—indeed, in the very position that Morgan Walters
had appeared upon the vestry table—was Doctor Syn.

'My God!' cried the Captain. 'Look at the face!'

The dead face pressed against the table was indeed a face of
horror, for driven through the neck was Clegg's harpoon.

'It's Doctor Syn! It's Clegg!' ejaculated the three seamen who
had entered the cabin. 'Then, in God's name, what did we shoot
out there?'

'The mulatto,' said the Captain. 'He has been here before us.'

'Then we shot the mulatto, sir!' exclaimed one of the men.

'You shot the sexton,' cut in the Captain. 'But for the mulatto—well, it's my honest opinion that—but there, that sort of
thing is beyond a sailor.'

'Here, you' (to one of the sailors), 'just get a piece of sail-
cloth from the deck, and we'll stitch this body up; and you two
help me get this harpoon from his neck. There's a ballast shot in
our boat that'll do for his feet—for I'm not going to take this
body ashore. It might cause a fresh outcry amongst the people.
Besides, now that old Clegg's log is entered, I've no desire to
hang him in chains. If ever a man deserved to be buried at sea,
Clegg did, for, rascal though he was, he was a wonderful seaman; so a seaman's grave he shall have, or I'm no sailor.'

Suddenly a cry arose from the man who had gone from the cabin in search of the sail-cloth.

'What is it?' called the Captain.

'My God!' cried the sailor, dashing back into the cabin—'the sexton, the sexton!'

'What of him?' demanded the Captain.

'He's not dead—he's not dead,' yelled the man.

'All right, all right,' said the Captain. 'Will he live to hang?'

'But he ain't there at all, sir!' shouted the sailor.

'Not there?' cried the Captain.

'No, sir; he's gone, and there's no signs of him anywheres.'

So they had not even shot the sexton, for as soon as the Captain came out of the cabin door he saw that the body had gone true enough. Mipps, who had not been touched by the three bullets, had bided an opportunity, and let himself quietly over the side away from the cutter, and struck out through the water with a stronger stroke than any one would have thought from such an ancient man.

They searched for him and for the mulatto's body to no avail; and the horrible corpse of Doctor Syn was buried that night at sea by the Captain's orders, sewn up in a sail with a shot at his feet. So his song came back to him for an epitaph—for a pound of gunshot was tied to his feet, and a ragged bit of sail *was* his winding-sheet.

39

Dymchurch-under-the-Wall

The next week came war with France, and every available man was pressed for the service. Collyer was recalled from Dymchurch with all his men, and he was one of the first to fall under Nelson's command. His death was the saving of many necks in Dymchurch—for he had found out about everything. The demon riders and their steeds he could have marked down by day; and he had discovered how they transformed themselves, for in Mipp's coffin shop he had come across a recipe for the preparation of the sand phosphorus with which the sexton used to daub the riders and horses. With the Death of Doctor Syn came the death of the wool-running. Sir Antony discovered in the vicarage much money stored away; and a sea-chest full of valuables, which Clegg had evidently amassed in the Southern Seas. A bar of gold and a wonderful ruby were sufficient in themselves to create a comfortable fortune; and as Doctor Syn had left a will leaving everything to Imogene, Sir Antony stretched a point and kept the matters to himself—for he was afraid that the wealth would drift to the Crown by law.

However, as Leveller of the Marsh Scotts, he found that it was easy enough to hush affairs up, for the French war was in everybody's mind. So eventually Denis married the daughter of the Incan princess, and the adopted daughter of Mrs. Whyllie of Rye. Though Sir Antony could never really prove her origin, he would never admit even to himself that most probably Doctor Syn had been romancing. The secret of England's treasure died with Clegg; but whether that was only a lying excuse of the scoundrel to get away from Dymchurch, remained under the wall. Although Doctor Syn was succeeded by more righteous vicars, none were so popular as he had been; and the few Dymchurch men who survived the French war would miss the long extempore prayers on a Sunday, and the dry-as-dust sermons, preached by a man who was a man before he became either a parson or a scoundrel.

Dymchurch is very quiet again, and the wild adventures of the days recorded in this book were forgotten after Trafalgar; but the Doctor was never forgotten by those who knew him, and it would bring tears to their eyes did anyone chance to sing his quaint old capstan song:

'Here's to the feet wot have walked the plank—
    Yo-ho! for the dead man's throttle.
And here's to the corpses afloat in the tank,
    And the dead man's teeth in the bottle.

For a pound of gunshot tied to his feet,
    And a ragged bit of sail for a winding-sheet;
Then the signal goes with a bang and a flash,
    And overboard you go with a horrible splash.

And all that isn't swallowed by the sharks outside,
    Stands up again upon its feet upon the running tide;
And it keeps a-blowin' gently, and a-lookin' with surprise
    At each little crab a-scramblin' from the sockets of it
    eyes.'

40

Echoes

Off the Malay Peninsula lies the island of Penang. Upon the mountain outside the little town, and overlooking the sea, stands an ancient Chinese monastery. Every evening when the dusk hour falls, and when English sextons go to ring the Evensong, an odd little man throws sacred crackers into the red-hot stomach of the Chinese God of Plenty. After this office is performed he repairs to the great pool, where the sacred turtle live, to enjoy an evening pipe of opium. And there, as the turtle crawl upon the flat slab rocks that fringe the pool, he delights his colleagues, the yellow priests, with horrific tales of demons and ghosts that inhabit the old parts of Britain.

All the priests in that far-off temple know of Romney Marsh by reputation, and they would never go to England for fear of it. If a traveller from Kent ever reached that place in his journey through the world, he would think it strange and homely to hear the yellow priests discussing tales of Romney Marsh; but he would understand, if he could recognise in the odd little man, dressed in the dirty blue robe of the yellow race, the Dymchurch sexton, Mr. Mipps.

What's he doing there? How did he get there? And how long will he stop there? Who knows!

Perhaps the ancient fellow has still unfulfilled ambitions, and dangerous, profitable enterprises tucked away under that Chinese sleeve. But it is pretty certain that Dymchurch-under-the-Wall will see him no more.